The Faelin Chronicles

BOOK ONE

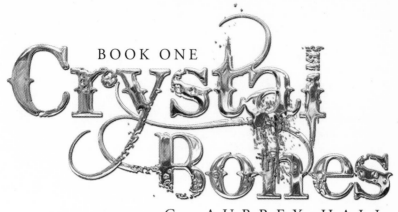

Crystal & Bones

C. AUBREY HALL

MARSHALL CAVENDISH

Website: www.marshallcavendish.us/kids

This book is a work of fiction. Names, characters, places, and incidents are products of the author's imagination and are used fictitiously. Any resemblance to actual events or locales or persons, living or dead, is entirely coincidental.

Other Marshall Cavendish Offices:
Marshall Cavendish International (Asia) Private Limited, 1 New Industrial Road, Singapore 536196 • Marshall Cavendish International (Thailand) Co Ltd. 253 Asoke, 12th Flr, Sukhumvit 21 Road, Klongtoey Nua, Wattana, Bangkok 10110, Thailand • Marshall Cavendish (Malaysia) Sdn Bhd, Times Subang, Lot 46, Subang Hi-Tech Industrial Park, Batu Tiga, 40000 Shah Alam, Selangor Darul Ehsan, Malaysia

Marshall Cavendish is a trademark of Times Publishing Limited

Library of Congress Cataloging-in-Publication Data
Hall, C. Aubrey.
Crystal bones / by C. Aubrey Hall.
p. cm. — (The Faelin chronicles ; bk. 1)
Summary: Suddenly and violently orphaned, Diello and his sister Cynthe learn secrets about their heritage when their parents' goblin enemies come searching for a powerful sword that has been kept hidden for many years.
ISBN 978-0-7614-5828-9
[1. Orphans—Fiction. 2. Fantasy.] I. Title.
PZ7.H141137Cr 2011
[Fic]—dc22
2010015435

Book design by Alex Ferrari/ferraridesign.com
Editor: Robin Benjamin
Printed in China (E)
First edition
10 9 8 7 6 5 4 3 2 1
Ⅲⅽ Marshall Cavendish

ACKNOWLEDGMENTS

I owe several people gratitude for helping to bring this book to publication. First of all, I must thank my agent, Al Zuckerman, for his patient guidance. Margery Cuyler of Marshall Cavendish gave this project the green light. Senior Editor Robin Benjamin worked indefatigably to make this story shine its best. All the art, editorial, production, and marketing staff at Marshall Cavendish have been splendid. And last, but not least, my friends Karen, Rosemary, and Lucy supplied encouragement and a sounding board at all those sticky points where I threatened to tear out my hair. My deepest appreciation goes to you all.

chapter one

Shortly before the dawn of Diello's thirteenth birthday, a summer storm burst over his parents' farmstead. In the darkness, thunder boomed hard enough to rattle the rafters and shake the boy awake. His small room was tucked upstairs, directly beneath the roof. When the downpour started, it sounded like a thousand drums, all beating at once.

He lay wide eyed in his bed and listened to the howling wind claw at the roof thatching, trying to tear its way inside. *No*, he thought. *Not again.*

"Lwyneth!" came a sobbing cry. "Lwyneth, come forth!"

That was his mother's name. What was out there? Why was it calling her? Resisting the temptation to pull his blanket over his head, he sat upright and snapped his fingers, flicking fire to light his bedside candle. Its feeble glow did little to hold back the shadows. Diello drew a steadying breath, forcing himself to listen.

Rain drummed harder, but it couldn't drown the shriek of the wind. "Lwyneth! Lwyneth!"

A forceful smack against his window shutters made him

jump. His candle went out as if snuffed by an invisible hand. Hearing the thumping against his shutters, Diello knew it was only a tree branch, but he could not slow his thudding heart. While he wasn't usually afraid of storms, he feared whatever was out there. *Why did it come here?* he wondered. *What does it want with Mamee?*

Lightning struck something nearby with a sizzling bang that nearly deafened him, and the whole world seemed to be on fire before the intense white light faded. Springing from his bed, Diello threw open his shutters. A huge tree at the edge of the clearing was shining an eerie yellow-white from base to canopy. As he stared at it in wonder, its massive trunk suddenly split with a shower of sparks, revealing the glowing heart of the tree. In the next moment the leafy top burst into flames.

It was not—thankfully—the hollow chesternut tree he liked best, but he and his twin sister had climbed this tree and played invasion with armies of twig and clay among its gnarled roots.

Groaning, the trunk continued to split down to its base. Its burning canopy slowly tilted and crashed to the ground. As the downpour put out the fire, Diello could smell smoke, seared wood, and a pungent, metallic odor.

"Lwyneth!" cried the wind.

Diello jumped back, slamming his shutters and fumbling to bolt them. He stood there, shivering and damp. *It isn't real*, he told himself firmly. *It's only a dream.*

As he lied to himself, he felt a queer sensation running along his arms and legs. His arms rose into the air, and his legs twitched. For an instant he felt as light and insubstantial as paleweed fuzz, light enough to float above the floor, and maybe even be sucked out through the shuttered window by the wind.

He dived back into bed, where he sat with his knees drawn up, clamping his arms tightly around them. Still, his bones went on tingling and itching. He felt the strangest urge to run outside and answer whatever was calling his mother.

"Lwyneth!" called the voice within the wailing wind. "Come forth!"

This was the third night in a row Diello had been jerked from slumber to listen to a voice that could not be real.

"Lwyneth!" howled the wind. "Pay heed!"

A loud slam from downstairs made Diello spring out of bed again. Leaving his room, he crossed the landing at the top of the stairs to his twin's door. Although he pressed his palm flat against the boards, he didn't touch the latch. Cynthe had recently made it clear that he couldn't enter her room for any reason, unless she invited him in. It was silly, but after Cynthe had pinned him to the ground a few weeks ago and made him eat dirt for having trespassed, he dared do no more now than scratch at her door.

"Cynthe," he whispered urgently.

She gave no response. Unlike Diello, she was a heavy sleeper. He did not call out louder, lest he wake everyone. Around him, the cottage stood dark and silent. No one else seemed to have heard the cry.

Outside, thunder rolled across the skies. Diello crept downstairs to the hearth room. He fumbled his way through the shadows and flashes of light to peer in the kitchen, then the room beyond. There, Mamee's loom rose taller than his head, its framework draped with the cloth she was presently weaving. He told himself that he was being foolish, that Mamee had better sense than to wander outside and answer the wind's call, yet here he was, prowling anxiously through the house.

If it knew my name, it might call me, too, he thought and shivered.

A shutter was loose in the workroom, banging back and forth. Mindful of the rain blowing in, rain that could damage the delicate cloth on the loom, Diello wrestled the shutter closed and latched it.

As he made his way back through the cottage, the front door swung open just as a flash of lightning lit a figure standing there.

Diello choked back a yelp—for it was no ghoul coming in but only his father, burly and broad shouldered, smelling of damp soil, rain, and wood shavings.

His father closed the door gently. "What are you looking for?"

Diello swallowed hard. He never lied to Pa, but he didn't want to confess his night fears. Pa was human and didn't always have patience for what he called "fanciful notions."

"Well, boy? I asked you a question."

"I—I heard something."

Pa moved toward him in the shadows. "Lightning struck the old walner tree, the one your mother wouldn't let me cut last year to make a new table." His voice was low and soft.

Diello kept his voice quiet as well, relieved that he didn't have to explain. "You can have the wood now."

"No. Lightning-struck wood's worthless for making

things. Can't saw it straight. Can't drive a nail into it. I should have brought it down last winter, the way I planned."

Diello said nothing. No matter how his father grumbled, they all obeyed Mamee's wishes. That was the way of their family.

"It was so loud," Diello whispered. "Did—did the strike wake Mamee up?"

"No. She slumbers still, unless you woke her by blundering downstairs."

Diello shook his head. Even with the rain drumming hard on the cottage, he was less afraid now. There was something solid and comforting about Pa's presence, despite his withered hand and arm. To be near him was like standing under sturdy shelter. Yawning, Diello rubbed his eyes.

Abruptly the rain stopped. The wind died down and the thunder rolled faintly in the distance. One of the cows lowed. Diello sensed there would be no more calls to his mother this night. He lifted his head in relief.

"It's nearly dawn, anyway, time to be up and doing," Pa said. Then before Diello could squeak his dismay, Pa reached out and gripped his shoulder. "Aye, son. I know it's your birthday today. Go back to bed for a bit. I'll see to the milking for you this time."

"Thanks, Pa!" Grinning, Diello started upstairs.

The door to his parents' room opened. Mamee appeared, her Fae skin casting a faint glow of silvery light. "Stephel?" she asked. "Is something wrong?"

"Lightning brought down the old walner tree, that's all," Pa said. He pointed at Diello, who was frozen on the step, staring at his mother and feeling the temptation to blurt out questions that would get him into trouble. "Do as I bade you, boy."

"Yes, Pa." Diello headed up the stairs.

"Diello?" Mamee called. "Wait. Something *has* happened. What is it?"

He turned back to her. Mamee's skin glowed even brighter, illuminating her features. When their eyes met, hers widened.

She knows, he thought. Fresh fear squeezed his heart. *I didn't dream it.*

"Diello?" she asked. "Was it only the storm that disturbed you?"

"Well—"

"Stephel," she said nervously, "did you check the cistern?"

"I did," Pa said. "All's well, Lwyneth. As for you, Diello, off to bed with you."

Diello obeyed. He wasn't ready yet to ask Mamee why the wind was calling to her. Not because Pa was standing there, listening to every word. But because Diello feared she might tell him the truth.

It seemed Diello had barely shut his eyes when a touch on his shoulder awakened him. The shutters stood open, and sunlight flooded his room. His father's dark-bearded face, serious and searching, was looking down at him. Diello had the feeling that Pa had been sitting beside him for a while, studying him.

That wasn't like Pa at all, but then, being human, Pa wasn't always predictable.

Diello sat up on one elbow, pushing his curly hair out of

his eyes. "Did I sleep too late?" he asked in confusion.

"Late enough. It's bidding to be a hot day. Your mother says you haven't been sleeping well." Pa frowned at him. "You look tired, right enough. What's keeping you awake nights?"

Diello avoided his father's gaze by staring at the thin, green-striped blanket lying across the foot of his bed. Mamee had woven it for him. "Things I can't explain," he said awkwardly. "Strange sounds and—"

"You're growing up. It's natural for a boy to turn restless."

Diello glanced at his father in frustration. Pa didn't like hearing about the ways of Fae, and he insisted that Diello and Cynthe behave as humanlike as they could. Sighing, Diello said, "Bad dreams, Pa. They make it hard to sleep."

"Then you need more work to do. A tired boy is a boy that sleeps well."

Diello opened his mouth to protest, met his father's eye, and swallowed his objections. "Yes, Pa."

"Well, then. With that settled, your mother can stop worrying."

Diello plunged into something he'd wanted to ask for weeks. "Next year I'll be old enough to join the auxiliaries. How can I train to make myself stronger? Taller?"

"Those scuts? Those blundering louts too weak kneed or simpleminded to make it to the rank of Shieldsman?"

"I meant the Faelin auxiliaries. Not the Antrasin ones."

"Hardly better. No son of mine will sign on for such a position."

"But, Pa!"

"Do you know how many leagues a day those poor devils are forced to cover, quick-marching behind the horses and eating their dust? They're fed the worst food in the king's army and bedded on hard ground with not even a blanket to cover them. They're expendable, the first to die on the field of battle. No glory, no chance to rise in rank, no future. An auxiliary indeed. Whatever put such a daft-fool notion in your head?"

"I can't be a Shieldsman," Diello said resentfully. "I can't even touch a sword."

"Ah, but not all swords are made of tempered steel. And hilts can be wrapped in—" Clearing his throat, Pa broke off. "Well, no need to go into such details. You weren't born for that kind of life."

Diello knew the future Pa had mapped out for him. Farming. When all he yearned to do was be a Shieldsman and see the world. *I'll find a way somehow*, he vowed to himself.

"A blessed birthday, son." Pa pressed a small package into his hand.

"My new whistle!" Diello pulled the wrapping away, only to stare, confused, at the wooden object. "A tinderbox?"

"Something practical this year, now you've turned thirteen."

Diello looked at the collection of twelve whistles on his shelf. Carved from varying woods and each tuned to a different bird call, they were by turns plain or whimsical, depending on Pa's mood when he'd made them. Diello loved them, loved going into the woods and blowing them to see if the birds would answer. Pa had given him one on every birthday of his life, and this year Diello had been hoping for a warbler. He'd dropped plenty of hints in recent weeks, but Pa kept saying that warblers were difficult to get right and not to fuss about it. Diello had never dreamed that Pa would stop making whistles for him.

"You're not a child anymore," Pa was saying. "Time to put your toys and fanciful dreaming away. My father gave me a tinderbox when I turned thirteen and could be trusted to use it right and not burn down the barn with foolery. It's a tradition in our family, you might say."

Diello stared at him, struggling to hide his disappointment. *The tradition*, he thought sadly, *was the whistles.*

"Yes, Pa. Thank you."

"Look inside it. That's a good piece of steel. I waxed it so it won't make you itch when it's in your pocket. If you don't like the flint, you can find a better one for yourself."

Diello opened the box and fingered the contents. "It's good flint, Pa. It will do fine."

"I know your mother taught you to make fire with a snap of your fingers, but magic doesn't always work, does it? A tinderbox is sure."

Diello sighed again. Flicking fire was the simplest, most basic kind of magic in the world, something anyone except a human could do. Leave it to Pa to distrust even that. Why couldn't his father see how magic made their lives better, how it protected the farm and put a gloss on the cattle and grew lush vegetables in the garden? Pa was always pointing out the flaws and weaknesses in magic, always trying to get Diello to do things the human way. The *boring* way.

Diello yearned to tell his father that he didn't care about some stupid old tinderbox. And he'd train himself for the auxiliaries no matter what Pa said about them.

"Right then. Time to get on with chores." Pa ruffled Diello's dark gold hair, letting his good hand—thick and work callused—linger a moment on his son's head. Pa's dark eyes softened. "It's good that you're growing old enough to have questions, son. I know you think I cut you short just now, but whether it's about training up your strength or certain issues that may trouble you, I'm the one to ask. Your mother's mighty wise in the ways of her lore, but there are things a man should ask a man."

Diello's chest swelled with pride. He felt as though Pa had opened a door to a place where only the two of them belonged. "I will, Pa."

"Good. Now, your mother's busy setting up some kind of Fae birthday nonsense for the two of you. I can't see how it does you any good, but you know how she is."

Diello knew it would be wonderful, no matter what his father said. "Yes, Pa."

The aroma of frying ham and hot bread wafted up through the cottage. His mouth watering, Diello reached for his clothes—clean ones, neatly folded on the stool by his bed. Mamee must have placed them there while he was still asleep. He began thinking about the market-day fair held today—as if the whole world knew it was his and Cynthe's birthday and wanted to celebrate.

Pa paused by the doorway. "The milking and feeding are done. But mind you don't take long eating. I want you out weeding new field today, and the sun will get hot fast."

"New field! But Cynthe and I were going to—"

"The field won't wait." Pa's look was kind, but there was no yielding in his voice. "We needed the rain, but it hit too hard. Mind that you lift the seedlings off the mud and straighten all that haven't been snapped off. As for the weeds, they'll be sprouting fast now that the ground's had a good soaking."

Not this morning, Diello thought gloomily. *Even weeds don't grow that fast.*

"Don't sulk. You're old enough now to know the farm comes first."

Diello knew better than to argue. No one worked harder than Pa. He loved this land—a gift from a long-dead king—which now had been in his family for generations. Most of the neighboring farmsteads belonged to the baron, but Pa answered to no one and proudly wore a silver deed seal around his neck to prove it. Trouble was, Pa expected his son to love the farm exactly as he did. Diello cared for the land and the woods—they were *home*—but he just wasn't cut out to be a farmer. *Why can't I be a warrior, too, like Pa used to be? Why can't I be born to it, just because I'm half Fae?*

Besides, he'd never had to work on his birthday before.

Diello felt a sudden hard stab of hatred for the farm and its endless, dreary round of chores. Shocked by his feelings, he looked up swiftly, hoping Pa didn't notice. "I understand, Pa," he whispered. "The farm comes first."

"You're a good boy, Diello. Now get along. I'm going to rouse your sister."

By the light of day, the hearth room was a cozy space

filled with sturdy furnishings passed down through Pa's family. The long, well-worn table was already set with two plates of shimmery, rainbow-hued Fae glass, a steaming platter loaded with ham and stacks of bread fried in egg batter, and a jug of sweet brown syrup. Two cups held fresh, buttery milk with flecks of mysterious Fae spice floating in it.

It was time! Mamee had long promised that they could taste *agligar*—renowned for its magical powers and very costly—on their thirteenth birthday. For the last week, the tiny package had rested on the kitchen shelf, sending both Diello and Cynthe into a fever of anticipation.

Mamee had told them that the *agligar* would allow them to experience—just slightly—what it was like to be entirely Fae.

Diello reached for his cup and drank half its contents in three swift gulps.

The top of his head seemed to explode with colors. Giddy and laughing, he jumped up and turned a partial cartwheel, balancing effortlessly upside down on his hands. His body felt lighter than air. The urge to lift his palms off the floorboards and just float away was so strong that he tried it. For a short moment he felt himself suspended in midair and then he crashed to the floor. That was funny, too. Chuckling, he scrambled upright. The world was blurred and ablaze with colors so intense they hurt his eyes.

A fresh wave of dizziness made him stagger, and he dropped back onto his stool with a howl of glee.

"Stop!" Cynthe called out, rushing down the stairs. She looked tall and slim, wearing a boy's tunic and leggings, with a pair of split-leather moccasins laced to her knees. Her hunting bow and a new leather quiver were slung across her shoulders, and her waist-length blonde hair was braided so tightly that her ears stuck out from her head.

"If that's *agligar*," she said—using what Diello called her *bossy voice*, even though she was his elder by only a few moments—"you're supposed to sip it, not get drunk on it."

Diello was glad he'd swallowed it too fast. He loved the effect. His disappointment with Pa didn't matter anymore. When Cynthe strode up to him, he saw three of her. He could see her as she'd looked at their little sister Amalina's age, as she looked this morning, and as a grown woman clad in a long gown of silver cloth like hammered metal.

Stunned, he realized that he was seeing a foretelling. Was this *Sight*? He didn't want a magical Gift like that! In the next blink, three Cynthes became one sulky sister, who whisked his cup from his hand and slammed it down on the table out of reach.

"Why didn't you wait for Mamee's ceremony?" she asked. "If you manifest your Gift before I do, I'll—"

He flung his arms wide and lifted himself off his stool. "What, like flying?"

Cynthe's eyes narrowed, then as he plopped back onto his stool, laughing, she threw a piece of bread at him. Diello lunged, deftly catching the food with a snap of his teeth. A delightful burst of flavors filled his mouth. Butter, cream, and grain had never tasted better, yet unexpectedly they were mixed with the pungent flavors of rain-dewed leaves, freshly plowed soil, and something oddly reminiscent of that fuzzy moth that had once flown into his mouth by accident.

His lips puckered. He wasn't sure whether to swallow or spit it out, but then he decided he liked the combined tastes and grinned as he reached for one of the laden plates.

"You've never tasted a breakfast like this one," he said. "Eat, before it gets cold."

"Stop feeding your face and wait for Mamee. You're as rude as a goblin this morning."

He kept munching, and stuck out his tongue to show her his food.

Cynthe went to peer inside the kitchen. "Where is she? Mamee?"

There was no answer. At the back of the cottage came a thump and then the rhythmic clacking and thudding of Mamee's loom. He and Cynthe exchanged a surprised look, and Diello's giddy mood burst. Pa was already trying to spoil this birthday. Now it looked like Mamee was, too. It seemed that he and Cynthe were being punished for growing older.

Cynthe's coppery, green-flecked eyes—exactly the same color as his own—appeared bewildered. "Why is she weaving? For weeks, she's been telling us how special turning thirteen is. She promised that we'd do magic today—real magic, not the stupid Faelin kind."

Diello snapped his fingers, lighting all the lanterns and candles in the room. Even the logs on the hearth caught fire. "The *agligar* really works," he said. "Usually I can only light one candle at a time."

"If you're lucky," Cynthe muttered. She clapped her hands together, and all the flames went out with quick pops.

"Drink your milk and see how you feel," Diello urged her. "The colors are amazing!"

"I'm not interested in flicking fire or seeing colors,"

Cynthe said. "Mamee said the *agligar* would make our Gifts manifest today. That's what I care about."

"Actually," Diello said thickly around another mouthful of food, "she said it *might* do that. Try it!"

"We should wait for her and do this properly instead of fooling about!"

Diello shrugged and kept eating. His head was clearing, and the blaze of intense colors was wearing off, but the world remained bright and rich with detail.

"So is it happening to you?" Cynthe asked, picking up her cup and sniffing the contents. "Do you feel anything?"

"The food tastes better."

"Is that *all*?"

He put down his fork. "What do you want me to say?" he asked, no longer joking. "Maybe the *agligar* is slow to take full effect. Or maybe I'm not going to have much of a Gift."

Cynthe's gaze dropped, but not before he glimpsed a flash of pity in her eyes.

"Anyway," he went on, "maybe Mamee didn't put the complete potion together since we can't celebrate our birthday like we intended. What's the point?"

Cynthe placed her bow and quiver on the table and sat heavily on the bench. "Why did Pa have to spoil this? He knows how much we've been looking forward to—"

"Stop blaming Pa," Diello said, glancing over his shoulder to be sure neither of his parents was in earshot. "You know better than that."

"I want my Gift," Cynthe said stubbornly. "I want to know what it *is*. I'm tired of waiting."

Diello pushed her milk toward her. "Then drink. And don't be a coward. Drink it down fast. Dare you."

Cynthe immediately tipped back her head and gulped it down. When she lowered her cup, she had a white ring of foamy milk on her upper lip and her eyes looked dazed.

She didn't speak. She didn't move. She didn't even blink.

"Uh, Cynthe?"

She dropped her cup and fell off the bench with a thud.

Horrified, Diello ran around the table, kneeling beside her just as she began to convulse with laughter. He was furious at the trick, but as she went on shrieking, holding her sides and writhing about, his lips twitched and then he was laughing, too. He helped her to her feet and watched while she giggled her way through her breakfast.

"Are you seeing two of me?" he asked.

"Don't be daft. One of you is bad enough." She lifted her arms above her head and frowned with concentration, then lowered them with a grimace. "No."

"No, what?"

"No, I don't feel like I can fly." She stopped eating and propped her jaw in her hands, staring into the distance. "I really, really, really wanted to fly."

"Faelin can't. No Faelin ever has."

"I *know*. Diello, this is horrid. We've never done chores on our birthday before. I thought Mamee would at least sing to us like she usually does." Cynthe shook her head. "Why is she listening to Pa? Did he convince her we're too old to celebrate birthdays?"

"Stop whining. If we work together, we could be finished by mid-afternoon. We'll go swimming."

"Swimming! We were going to the fair!"

"Well, we can't," he said flatly. "They've seen to that." He was thinking of Aona, the tailor's pretty daughter. She was twelve, with black hair so long she could sit on it and eyes like a fawn's. He'd hoped to see her today.

"When will market day ever land on our birthday again?" Cynthe asked.

"We'll make the best of what we've got. How about a climb to Egil's Point?"

She made a face, but nodded. "It's better than nothing, I suppose."

And then Diello noticed her skin starting to glow faintly and pinpoints of silver sparkling in her pale hair. "Cynthe! You're changing!"

"What is it?" she asked eagerly. "What do you see?"

"What do you *feel*?"

"Light," she said in amazement. "I feel light, like I weigh nothing."

When she held up her hands, Diello could see through her flesh, like she was made of glass. Frightened, he glanced away.

"I feel like I could run all day through the woods and never tire," she said. "Like I could climb Egil's Point and all the trees in the forest and still have the energy to dance." Whirling around, she reached across the table and gripped his forearm. "We have to go to the fair now. We *have* to!"

He felt his own surge of recklessness and pulled free. "You know we can't run off and disobey Pa."

"I don't care what Pa said! We shouldn't waste this. It would be throwing away Mamee's gift, and I don't want to!"

Diello could almost hear the sounds of the fair in his mind. "We could work awhile and then sneak off," he said slowly. "Pa will be angry, maybe enough to take the strap to us."

"Worth it," Cynthe said.

He drew a deep breath, feeling his heart quicken. "All right then. Get outside before Mamee senses what you're thinking. Work hard at your chores until I give you the signal. Agreed?"

Cynthe spat in her palm and held it out.

"To the fair."

Diello spat in his palm, and they shook hard on the pact.

"To the fair," he echoed.

chapter two

Weeding. A backbreaking, thankless job. Pausing to wipe the sweat from his face with one grubby hand, Diello stared at the long row of seedlings in disgust. He was halfway down the third row, with still a dozen to go. Sunlight burned into his shoulders and back. As Pa had predicted, the morning was already hot, with no breeze to cool him.

Usually Pa retreated into his barn workshop and didn't emerge until midday. This morning, however, almost as if he sensed the twins were up to something, Pa kept popping outside to mend things or putter around.

Go away, Diello mouthed at Pa's back, watching him disappear into the barn once more. *Stay in there and don't come out.*

At this rate, they would never get the chance to slip away.

A sudden racket caught Diello's attention, and he saw a whole flock of noisy black rooks alighting on the cottage roof. Six rooks on the ridgepole meant bad luck, but here were a dozen or more. It was the worst possible omen. *The sign of death.* He shuddered.

"Diello!"

Cynthe stood at the far edge of the field, waving her long arms. "Diello, come at once! Mamee wants us."

He glanced toward the barn for help, but Pa wasn't in sight. Diello dropped his wooden weeding stick and ran across the field rows to her.

"What's wrong?" he asked. "Is Amalina hurt? Did she catch her fingers in the loom? Has she fallen in the well?"

Cynthe's eyes were bright. "Are you daft? No! Mamee has an errand for us."

"But the rooks—"

"What rooks?"

He looked at the roof, but the birds had vanished. Diello rubbed his forehead. "But I saw them. The Death Flock."

Cynthe rolled her eyes. "Death Flock, my big toe. Do you think something like that could come in past the *cloigwylie?*"

The *cloigwylie* was a protection spell of sorts; well, less an actual spell than a barrier, rather like the wattle-and-daub fences used by the villagers around their cottages. Only, instead of willow sticks and mud, the *cloigwylie* was fashioned by Mamee from tall stakes of safety woven with magical threads of protection and light. Invisible to most— Diello could see it only if he squinted at an angle on a moonless night—it encircled the farmstead just at the edge of the woods and across the creek. Its purpose was to keep out vermin and warn his parents of larger creatures trying to break in. Humans could walk through it, of course, although they might feel uneasy and not know why. Trogs and other magical beasts of the woods avoided it. Today, thanks to the lingering effect of the *agligar*, he could see it shimmering like the faintest of rainbows along the boundary of new field.

Diello scowled at his sister. "The *cloigwylie* wouldn't keep out the Death Flock," he said. "It's not—"

"There are no rooks."

"I saw them," he insisted.

"Well, they aren't here now. Stay and pull weeds if you like. I'll do the errand myself."

Cynthe headed for the cottage in a ground-eating stride. This year, she'd grown taller and leggier than Diello, and she loved to show off by making him sprint to catch up with her.

"What kind of errand?" he asked, panting as he trotted along.

"Can't you guess?"

The market-day fair? In general the family kept to itself, seldom visiting the village or socializing even with other Faelin families. But where else would Mamee send them today? He didn't care, as long as he escaped the field.

"Race you," he said, spurting past his twin.

Cynthe caught up right away, passing him just as they reached the tidy yard. But then she slowed down to skirt a large water puddle while Diello splashed right through the middle of it, scattering outraged ducks in all directions. He reached the cottage step first and paused on the stone threshold, bracing his arms and legs wide to block Cynthe from entering.

She kicked him in the back of one knee, making him stagger off balance, and shoved her way inside.

"Children," Mamee said, emerging from the workroom with a bulky package in her arms, "can't you ever enter the house like civilized folk?"

Her musical, lilting voice sounded mild, but Diello straightened his mud-streaked tunic and raked a hand through his unruly curls. He saw his muddy tracks on the floor. "Sorry, Mamee."

At his shoulder, Cynthe hesitated before she echoed, "Sorry, Mamee."

"I despair of you," Mamee said, but she smiled. She crossed the hearth room to lay down the package on the long table. A vase filled with flowers grew more vivid in Mamee's presence. "Come here to me."

Diello thought she was the most beautiful person in the world. By day, her skin did not glow so obviously. Still, she was like no one else. When she was very happy, she sometimes let her glamour appear, turning into a glittering creature of silvery sparkles, her skin like snow, her lashes like tiny crystals. But most of the time, she suppressed her true appearance to look like a farmwife in a homespun gown and apron of spotless sacking. Even then, Diello admired the coppery highlights in her hair, hair that was a color indescribable, neither white, nor blonde, nor any other shade to be found in Antrasia. It curled back from her brow and fell in ordered waves behind the pointed tips of her delicate ears. Her eyes, large and luminous, were the hue of tree bark—dark gray mixed with light gray and a tint of green.

He saw now, by the dancing light in her gaze, that she had something special planned for him and Cynthe after all. She loved giving surprises. He felt ashamed for having doubted her, and stupid for imagining some bad omen.

"It is a fine accomplishment to bring children to their thirteenth birthday," Mamee said. "Among the Fae you would be considered grown today, and we would rejoice. I am very proud indeed."

Pa had already called Diello a man. Mamee's praise was even better. The pointed tips of Diello's ears grew hot with pleasure.

Beside him, Cynthe straightened her shoulders. "Grown," she said, smiling. "Oh yes, Mamee. We are!"

"Well, not as yet, my dear halflings. Your human blood keeps you younger."

"If we were among the Fae," Diello said, craving more, "how would they celebrate our turning thirteen?"

"Everyone would come, dressed in all the colors of the sky and sea. There would be games to play—a sprite hunt, air juggling, Ring Around the Lake—yes, and dancing, such dancing, until everyone's satin shoes fell in tatters off their feet. There would be a huge feast spread beneath a canopy of lace so fine that it would ripple in the breeze like laughter. And, of course, there would be a special cake for you. A cake filled with nuts off a takia tree and spices of mystery—"

"Better than *agligar*?" Cynthe asked.

"Much better. There would be pieces of fruit baked in the center of the cake. Fruit carved into tiny faces, likenesses of your favorite people or perhaps people you were destined to meet. Most important of all, you would sail to the Isle of Woe and be taken into the Cave of Mysteries to walk three times around the Silver—" Mamee's voice faltered. "You would walk through the Mysteries and thereby discover your Gift," she finished.

Diello hated it when she glossed over something she didn't want to tell them. "Mamee—"

"I was so sure I'd wake up this morning and finally know what my Gift's going to be," Cynthe interrupted, "but it didn't happen. There was only Pa, and my new quiver. Even the *agligar* didn't help."

Diello said nothing. Had he really seen the Death Flock or just imagined it? The Gift of Sight—if this was it—was unsettling, and unlikely to help him become a valiant warrior when he grew up.

Mamee smoothed back Cynthe's hair, pushing stray tendrils behind her ears, where only the slightest of points showed at the tip. "You must be patient. One day you'll know, but when or where I cannot tell you. There will be no rites, no Mysteries to help you, but never doubt that your discovery *will* come in time."

"But I've waited forever. Diello just saw a vision this morning, and I—"

"Visions?" Mamee asked. "Diello, have you the Sight?"

"I don't know. Maybe."

"What have you seen?"

He wouldn't meet Mamee's gaze. He didn't want to tell her about the Death Flock, or the voice he heard in the wind at night.

"Diello?"

"When I drank the *agligar*, I could see Cynthe's bones," he said. "I saw her as she was, is, and will be." His voice rose angrily. "I don't want to be a fortune-teller!"

Mamee's laugh was gentle. "Sight will make you wise. Do not fear it. Seize with courage whatever it shows you."

"It's not fair that he has his Gift first," Cynthe muttered. "I'm the oldest twin. Shouldn't I manifest before he does?"

"It doesn't work that way, my dear."

"You keep telling me to be patient, but Faelin are crip-
ples when it comes to magic. We have *nothing* compared to
real—"

"Hush!" Diello said fiercely, seeing the haunted pain in
their mother's eyes. "Don't talk that way."

Cynthe's face turned bright pink as she realized what
she'd said. For their father was crippled with his withered
hand and arm, unable to wield the old sword that now
hung rusting on a peg in the barn, and much hindered
when managing the plow or the harvesting scythe. Even
their mother was disabled in a way, for she was unable to
fly or work the kind of serious magic that the Fae usually
performed effortlessly. The twins did not know why,
although after years of puzzled speculation they'd worked
out that something awful had once happened to their
mother, something to do with whatever had injured Pa so
dreadfully.

"I'm s-sorry," Cynthe stammered in a rush. "Dearest
Mamee, you know I didn't mean—"

"I know." Mamee gave her a wistful smile. "You are not
like most Faelin, my daughter. Never forget that. And you,
my dear son, will have more than Sight one day. Despite
your visions, you are no prophet, nor are you destined for
that path."

Relief swept Diello, making him almost light headed.
"Will I—"

A gust of wind swirled out of nowhere, blowing in
through the open door. It sent Mamee's skirts billowing and
her long hair streaming back from her shoulders. She ran
outside, lifting her hand as though to catch the breeze.

"Oh, Clevn!" she called, gazing at the sky. "Is that you? Am I forgiven at last?"

The wind died down abruptly. Mamee went on standing there with the chickens pecking about her skirts, still holding up her hands with a look of such intense yearning that it hurt Diello to see it. Mamee had her moods, but he'd never seen her quite like this before.

Diello gestured for his sister to remain where she was and approached their mother alone. "Mamee," he said softly, touching her shoulder. "What is it?"

"Hush," she whispered, still gazing at the sky. "Do you hear . . ."

He listened, hearing only the poultry and Amalina singing to herself somewhere behind the cottage. "Hear what?" he asked.

"Nothing," Mamee said sadly, lowering her arms. Her face had grown white and pinched. "Nothing at all. My family used to send me messages on the wind. I thought perhaps . . ." Her voice trailed away, her eyes darkening with grief. Suddenly they blazed into his. "What do *you* hear, when the Talking Wind comes?" she demanded.

He flinched. Before he knew it, he was saying, "It calls your name. Over and over."

"When? Just now?"

He shook his head. "Last night."

"In the storm."

It wasn't a question, but he answered anyway. "Yes."

"Does it say anything else? A warning, perhaps?"

"Yes. Sort of."

That bleak, pinched look returned to her face. "Then it's

not Clevn, although he often conjures storms when he sends messages. Someone is using a clever disguise, trying to make me think . . . but no, nothing has changed except that the search draws closer. As long as I do not answer, we are safe."

"But who is Clevn?" he asked. "What search? What calls you?"

"The past. Nothing important. And you will forget that name. It belongs to no one who could ever matter to you."

Diello hated being lied to. He was not like Amalina, too little to be told things. Hearing worry in Mamee's voice, maybe fear, he longed to help her. "Is there some—"

"I tell you it's nothing that concerns you."

The finality of her tone silenced him. Instinct whispered that it *did* concern him, but it had always been Mamee's way to keep secrets.

She gathered him close in her arms, pressing her cheek to the top of his head. "Oh, my son," she whispered, "what good are crystal bones to you, living lost in this wilderness as you do? You could have been of such value to the Council. What legacy have I left you? What have I done?"

"Is that how all the Fae send messages to each other?" Diello asked. "On the wind?"

It was the wrong thing to ask. She released him, moving away. "Enough of that," Mamee said. "I don't know what is wrong with me today. We must do as your father does and not look back or suffer regrets. When you make a decision, my halfling, stick with it."

"But—"

"Come along." She kissed Diello on the forehead, the cool touch of her lips sending prickles of icy magic tingling through him. She was putting a seal of *cloigwylie* protection on him, the way she used to when they were little.

Diello wriggled impatiently. Amalina wore the protection all the time to keep her from falling in the creek, but he had outgrown it. Mamee also put a seal on Cynthe, who rolled her eyes.

"I am sending you to the castle today," Mamee announced. "Instead of serenading you at your breakfast, I've finished weaving Lord Malques's banquet cloth." She smiled at their astonished faces. "I'm entrusting you to take it to his lordship's steward and to bring home the payment."

Cynthe clapped her hands. Diello's heart started hammering. Last year, he'd gone with his father to the castle, which stood just beyond the village of Wodesley. Diello had been left outside the massive gates, unable to see much while Pa conducted his business. But this time Diello would be inside! The idea of going on their own, of collecting money on their mother's behalf the way Pa usually did . . . Diello glowed at Mamee's trust in him.

"Mind you are not cheated," Mamee said. "The steward is a rude man, but pay no heed to that. Hold Master Timmons to the agreed price of three pieces of Antrasin gold. Do not accept Faelin script."

Diello nodded.

"Be very careful, both of you, as you pass Wodesley. I know the fair will tempt you, but avoid it. That is my command."

Diello frowned, and Cynthe stared at the floor.

"I am not harsh. You're no longer young enough to pass as Antrasins. My blood is starting to show in you, especially *you*, Cynthe, with your height and natural glamour. You draw too many looks. The fair is not safe. There are too many strangers."

It was the same old refrain of *caution, caution,* and more *caution.* "Yes, Mamee," Diello said, managing not to sigh. Both his parents worried too much about being around Antrasins. On his rare visits to Wodesley with Pa, Diello had seldom heard a rude remark. Pa was respected in the village. Diello saw no reason why today should be different.

Cynthe grabbed his quarterstaff from behind the door and tossed it to him. "Let's go!" she cried.

Diello tucked the quarterstaff under his arm and picked up the package. Handing their lunch packets to Cynthe, Mamee followed them outside, still giving them warnings.

"Once you have that gold in your pockets, come straight home by the road and don't cut through the woods. Gold attracts trogs, you know."

"We will," Diello said, barely listening. "Come on, Cynthe!"

They ran outside into the hot sunshine, laughing in excitement.

Little Amalina, smeared with mud and clutching a handful of feathers, blocked their path. "Del!" she called.

Diello halted by her, crouching down for her to entwine chubby arms around his neck. At three years old, she looked entirely human, with curls as bright as sunshine and enormous blue eyes. She smelled of summer grass and mud pies.

"Hello, Amie," he said, kissing her to make her giggle. "Have you been plucking the poor ducks again? Don't make them bald or they can't swim."

She kissed his cheek and threw the feathers on the ground. "Love you, Del."

He hugged her tight.

"You can play with the sprout later," Cynthe said. "Hurry up!"

As he stood, Diello glimpsed his father emerging from the barn, carrying a pail. Lifting his withered arm, Pa shouted something, but Diello pretended not to hear. He didn't want to be delayed, or worse. *Let Mamee explain*, he thought. She understood birthdays and how special they should be, even if Pa did not.

"Let's go," he said urgently.

And he and Cynthe ran.

chapter three

the village of Wodesley—normally quiet and sleepy—
rang with noise and bustled with activity. Throngs of
people pushed and crowded everywhere, filling the village
green and swelling the narrow lanes between shops and
houses. From common pilgrims on foot to wealthy travelers
riding in the luxury of a cart, all sorts of folk had been drawn
by the festivities.

Shoulder to shoulder, the twins stood concealed behind
a tall stack of wooden casks, craning their necks.

"Did you ever see the like?" Cynthe asked. "Look at
that!"

Diello was too busy gawking to answer. *So this is a fair.*
He was never going to find Aona in this crowd.

The noise struck him the most. Used to the farm and its
surrounding woods, he'd never before heard such uproar. Pie
sellers crying their wares, the blacksmith's hammer banging
away on an anvil, music from strolling troubadours, shrill
whistles from tumbling acrobats, the babble and laughter of
the crowd—it all created a confusing yet thrilling din.

Everything, it seemed, was for sale. Past the smithy—

swarming with customers wanting their horses shod and their broken hardware repaired—Diello could see tinkers mending cooking pots beneath a spreading walner tree. Withered old women dangled bright ribbons and bottles of potions in front of giggling girls. A basketweaver stacked her wares precariously on her head like a very tall hat. A man wearing a coat made from an infinite variety of scraps and colors offered doves to buyers. Watching the birds fluttering white and frantic inside a wicker cage, Diello wished he could set them free.

"Mamee should have made cloth and blankets to sell here today," he murmured.

"She'd never come to something like this," Cynthe replied. "The whole shire must be here."

"Half of it, at least," Diello said. His sister was right. Their mother acted so confident at home, almost regal and imperious at times. But let a stranger approach their door, and she vanished into her workroom. She refused to go near the village even on its quietest day. Pa said she was shy, but Diello felt there was more to it than that. It often seemed as if his parents were hiding from something . . . or someone. He thought of her words this morning.

"I'm starving," Cynthe said. "And I smell meat pies."

Diello could smell them, too. His stomach started growling. Their lunch of cheese and apple had worn off already. Besides, nothing could compare to a delicious meat pie.

But when Cynthe stepped out from their hiding place, Diello clutched her tunic. "Don't! Remember Mamee's warning. We dare not go closer."

Cynthe slapped his hand away. "Don't be such a fraidy. I tell you my stomach is flapping against my spine."

"You haven't any money. And neither have I, so don't bother asking."

Cynthe held up a coin. "Here's the penny I carry for luck."

"You shouldn't spend that. A penny spent is a penny gone."

"Don't quote Pa at me. We'll buy a pie and share it, or four buns. Come on!"

"Cynthe, wait!"

She plunged right into the thick of the crowd.

Groaning, Diello went after her. The bulky package under his arm hampered him, and he lost her. Hemmed in on all sides, half-trampled, jolted, and pushed about, he pressed forward, eventually finding his sister among the onlookers watching mummers enact a play.

Tall and straight in her hunting clothes, her bow slung over one shoulder, Cynthe looked like no other girl. Exactly as Mamee had warned. People were staring at her, elbowing each other and murmuring. Cynthe seemed unaware of this as she munched on a bun and watched the performance.

"Are they not a wonder?" she asked Diello, laughing at the mummers' antics.

"Cynthe—"

"Take this." She pushed the half-eaten bun into his hand.

"Couldn't you have saved me more of the buns?" Diello asked, staring at the gnawed piece she'd given him.

"More? I got only two for the price. They aren't even good. Eat the rest of mine and here's yours."

It was outrageous to spend a whole penny for two meager buns, but he'd make the best of it. Prying his sister away from the mummers, Diello led her back through the crowd. As he walked, he chewed the tough bun, which had the consistency of leather and much the same taste.

A blaring trumpet made him jump. Cynthe pushed him out of the way just as the crowd parted. Shieldsmen came first, their chain mail and breastplates polished, hauberks a vivid crimson, cloaks blue. They rode enormous war steeds in armored saddlecloths. Even at a processional walk, the mighty beasts' iron-shod hooves—the size of chapel collection plates—thudded loudly, striking sparks off the cobbles. Next came two pennant bearers garbed in blue-and-crimson livery. Both held tall white poles; the shire's banner streamed proudly from one, and the baron's crest flew from the other.

It isn't possible, Diello told himself. They couldn't be so lucky, not even on their birthday. Especially this birthday.

But they were. A cheer rose through the crowd, and then Lord Malques was riding by. Diello was somewhat disappointed to see he was clad not in armor, but in a tunic of rich, deep blue and an ornate gold chain studded with jewels that flashed in the sun. His brown hair, streaked gray at the temples, flowed to his shoulders in the style favored by nobility. Although he didn't smile, he lifted his gloved hand to wave at the cheering crowd. Beside him rode his lady wife, sitting sidesaddle on a dainty mare adorned with mane ribbons of pink. Unlike her stern-faced husband, she smiled and laughed merrily.

As the procession ended, the crowd flooded back into the street. Diello and Cynthe grinned at each other.

"We saw the baron," Cynthe said with glee. "We saw her ladyship!"

"Did you see his sword?" Diello asked. "And his spurs? Silver!"

"And the size of the sapphires in his chain! Did you see his ring? Wait until we tell Pa and Mamee—" She broke off. "We can't tell them, can we? We aren't supposed to be here."

"But we are supposed to go to the castle," Diello said, still caught up in the glory and the colors. To have seen their armor and their weapons up close, close enough to touch a horse's flank or even catch the baron's stirrup if he'd dared— why, that was almost like grabbing some tiny bit of their valor for himself. All his yearnings rose in his heart. Someday, he promised himself, he would be grown and stalwart enough to bear arms for the shire, just as Pa had . . . long ago. The Faelin auxiliaries couldn't be as bad as Pa had said. Diello swallowed. "We'll tell them that Lord Malques is in residence. They needn't know where we saw him."

Cynthe uttered a short laugh. "And you think you'll fool Mamee with some half-baked falsehood? Better we don't talk of this at all."

"But if we—"

A youth wearing a serf's ragged hood bumped into Diello, almost knocking him over. "Move aside, Faelin piglet!" the serf said in a gruff, accented voice.

Diello felt a sudden clamminess crawling through his body, like he'd eaten too much sweet pie and was about to be sick. At the same time, the serf's face became a transparent mask through which Diello could see brown-mottled features, including a needle-sharp nose and small, mean eyes. Gasping, Diello jerked to one side, half-lifting his quarter-staff as the goblin hurried on.

"Look, here's a troubadour!" Cynthe said, her voice sounding distant and odd through the buzzing in Diello's ears. "Let's pause a moment and hear his song . . . Diello? Is something wrong?"

He felt made of wood, unmovable. "Sure," he said faintly. "I'll be glad to."

"What?"

He swept his gaze around the crowd, looking for other boys about his size or smaller, and saw several now that were masked by magic, all of them secretly possessing beady, close-set eyes and harsh goblin faces.

Goblins, he knew, were the mortal enemies of all folk with Fae blood. Goblins ate Faelin children for breakfast and carved spoons from their bones. What, in the name of the Ancient Harmonies, were they doing sneaking about Wodesley?

Cynthe gripped his sleeve. "You've gone greenish. Are you sick? Diello, answer me!"

His knees buckled. Cynthe threw her arm around him, supporting some of his weight, and pushed him against a building. Propped against the wall and very grateful for its support, Diello was trembling.

"Is it Sight?" Cynthe asked, rubbing his shoulder. "A real vision?"

Now his teeth were chattering, despite the heat. He couldn't speak.

"Give me the package," Cynthe said, taking it from him. "Bend low if you think you're going to faint."

"I w-won't."

"Stop holding your breath. That makes it worse."

He gritted his teeth and drew in several deep breaths. His head was clearing now. He stopped shivering, and the nausea went away, but he still felt icy cold inside and peculiar, as if his body had been hollowed out. They needed to get away from here. There was going to be trouble, and they mustn't be caught in it. He wanted to run, but his stupid legs were too weak to hold him.

Why couldn't I have been born lame or hunched, he raged, *anything besides crystal bones?* Whatever magic was in use near Diello resonated through his body. It usually meant his limbs tingled for a while, making him restless and edgy. Mamee had explained to him that his presence could amplify someone's magic, making it stronger and more effective, which is why she liked to have him near when she worked the gentle wisps of spells she could still do. Yet he'd never felt sick before, not even when the wind spoke at night and visions of the Death Flock spooked him. If drinking *agligar* was going to do this to him, he vowed he'd never swallow it again.

Or maybe it wasn't the spice's fault. Maybe his reaction had to do with the goblins. Diello could feel something evil and rotten all around him. All his life he'd dreamed of having adventures, and now, in his first brush with dark magic, he nearly fainted. It was mortifying to turn all limp and stupid like this. How could he ever hope to go to battle someday?

"Are you thirsty?" Cynthe asked. "Let's draw some water from the well. I'll help you."

Diello pulled himself together. Glancing around to make sure they weren't overheard, he whispered, "There are goblins here."

Cynthe blinked at him. She opened her mouth, then pursed it tightly. Scanning the crowd with her keen eyes, she said, "I don't see any."

"They're dressed like ordinary Antrasins and under disguising spells."

"So this is what Sight can do," she said. "I wish I had it, but not if it makes you sick."

"It's not Sight," he said. "I mean, I think I can see through their disguise because of Sight, but it's their magic that's making me . . . It's rotten, horrid."

She squeezed his hand. "It must be an awfully powerful spell."

Diello was glad she understood and didn't just think he was a coward. "We should get out of here."

She didn't argue, which meant she must be as scared as he was. They moved cautiously away from the building.

The noise and excitement of the fair now seemed sinister. The crowd was oblivious to the danger creeping through it. Goblin raids were common enough in some of the shires, but not here. The creatures usually attacked at dusk. These were bold indeed, Diello thought, if they were planning to raid the village today. Yet what better time, with coins clinking from hand to hand?

Although his first impulse was to run around, shouting

warnings, Diello didn't think any of the fairgoers were likely to pay heed. Even more, he didn't want the goblins to know that he could see through their disguises. In this crowd, it would be easy for a goblin to pounce and silence him and Cynthe—forever. The best thing would be to notify the castle warden, or even the nearest Shieldsman.

Feeling stronger now, Diello took the package back from Cynthe and led her through the crush. He tried not to flinch whenever he brushed against one of the goblins. But the more of them he saw, the more afraid he grew.

Cynthe stuck close to him. "They all look human to me. Are you sure?"

"Very sure," he answered grimly, sidestepping a green-skinned goblin with warts and orange eyes.

"How many are there?" she asked.

"I've seen twenty. Maybe more."

"Would they dare raid with this many folk about?"

"I don't know." He pushed her to one side to avoid a taller goblin with teeth like spikes. "This way!"

They were crossing the village square. A trio of burly Shieldsmen was flirting with a group of giggling maidens. Even without their armor and weapons, the men looked brawny and tough enough to handle any problem.

Cynthe flipped her braid over her shoulder. "I'll tell them!" She skipped up to one of the men and plucked at his elbow. "Sir!" she called. "Sir, there are—"

He shook her off so roughly that she staggered, and then he spat on her. "Keep away, you Faelin maggot!"

Diello joined her, his fists up, but the Shieldsmen walked away, laughing with the girls. Cynthe's face was white as she cleaned the spittle off her tunic.

At that moment, Diello would have given his left arm to undo what had just happened. "Cynthe—"

"Let's cut through that way and get out of the square," Cynthe said. She wouldn't look at him as she hurried off.

Turning to follow her, Diello bumped into a crooked-shouldered man nearly as tall as Pa, who was wearing a cloak and hood. Growling something, the man pushed Diello out of his path. That's when Diello found himself gazing into a horrible scaly face of greenish-gold. *Not a man at all.* The creature was too tall to be a goblin, yet with hair like tree roots, a cruel slash of mouth, and ruddy, deep-set eyes that pierced Diello like gimlets, he could be nothing else.

"Gor-goblin," Diello breathed aloud before he could stop himself.

The creature's red eyes snapped his way. Hissing slightly, the gor-goblin bared long fangs and leaned closer, peering down at Diello as if to memorize his face. The hot, sour breath of a predator touched Diello's throat.

All the while, Diello wanted to run, yet his legs were frozen. He knew that of all goblin kind, a gor-goblin was the meanest and most dangerous.

Through the fogging panic in his brain, he wondered, *What is a gor-goblin doing here?*

Hissing again, the gor-goblin gripped the front of Diello's tunic with a gnarled, black-clawed hand, only to flinch as the *cloigwylie* flashed between them. Releasing Diello, the gor-goblin flexed his hand in pain. Diello glimpsed a band of gold around the creature's wrist, etched with symbols he didn't recognize.

He smirked at the creature with newfound confidence, but then the gor-goblin grabbed him again. This time, as the protection spell flashed between them, the gor-goblin slapped Diello's forehead. The *cloigwylie* was shattered, and Mamee's magic dropped away.

"What are you staring at, little Faelin morsel?" The gor-goblin's whisper was harsh and guttural, like iron grating on stone. "What do you see?"

The creature leaned even closer, his gaze holding Diello's the way a snake might mesmerize a mouse. The gor-goblin's pupils were black squares, drawing him in. Desperately, Diello forced himself to stare instead at the creature's long, crooked nose.

His head began to hum strangely, and something icy and horrid touched his mind.

As Diello flinched, the gor-goblin hissed in surprise and withdrew from his thoughts.

The gor-goblin started shaking him. "You are her spawn! You are—"

"Let my brother go!" Cynthe stamped on the gor-goblin's foot.

Yelping, the creature reeled back. Diello wrenched free, hearing the rip of his tunic. The gor-goblin's talons slashed, but Diello eluded them, and he and Cynthe fled.

"He's following us!" Cynthe yelled.

Glancing back, Diello saw the gor-goblin coming fast, cloak flying behind him like flapping wings. Changing direction, Diello pushed between two merchants chatting and ducked down an alley. Cynthe followed nimbly.

"Thief!" one of the merchants yelled. "Stop, thief!"

Cynthe gave Diello a shove. "Don't look back," she panted. "Faster!"

He saw a man ahead of them moving to block their path. "Here now, young 'uns," the fellow called out, gesturing for them to stop. "Happen you've stolen that parcel under your arm?"

The injustice of the accusation made Diello furious, but with the gor-goblin closing in on them, there was no time to protest. Diello spun to one side and ducked through a narrow space between two houses. It was just wide enough for him to fit through.

Breathing fast and loud, Cynthe crowded at his heels, her hands pushing at his shoulders. "Go, go, go!"

Behind them, Diello heard an angry shout and then a furious shriek from the gor-goblin. Diello tried to look back, but Cynthe thumped his head.

"He can't get through here," she whispered. "Go faster!"

So Diello kept running, skinning his elbow on the stone wall and ignoring the brief flare of pain. It was dank and dark in here. The space grew so tight he had to slow down and squirm his way through. He felt like a thread being pushed through the eye of a spindle on Mamee's loom.

At the other end of the alley, he found the way blocked entirely by a precarious stack of rubbish—mostly stones and broken pieces of timber—all piled in a rat's nest that reached nearly head high.

"Now what?" he whispered.

Cynthe dug her fingers into his shoulder in a silent warning to be quiet. Diello stilled his breathing and listened with all his might. What if the gor-goblin had run around the row of houses and was waiting for them just past this pile of rubbish? If they climbed over, they might find themselves right in the clutches of the monster.

His hands were clasping Mamee's package so hard his knuckles ached. Gor-goblins were said to eat hearts. His own was pounding hard inside his chest. Without Mamee's protection, he felt exposed.

"Go on," Cynthe breathed in his ear.

"What if he's waiting for us?"

"What if he's not? If we retreat, those merchants will say we stole the banquet cloth. If a goblin can make them think he's human, he can make them believe we're thieves."

"I'd rather explain than be eaten."

She reached past him to pull at one of the boards. It knocked some of the stones down, and they clacked together as they hit the ground. Diello jumped back to avoid getting his toes smashed.

"Quiet!" he whispered.

"Hurry," she insisted, reaching for another board. "If we're quick, we'll be out before he gets to this end."

Diello gave in. He helped her pull at the timbers and then clambered atop the unsteady mass while it wobbled. His weight sent another portion of it tumbling down, but he jumped forward like a cat and scrambled over the top before more of it could collapse. Dust rose everywhere, and he went shooting out into the lane and landed in an untidy heap. As he sat there, a little stunned in the hot sunlight, the package containing Mamee's banquet cloth sailed out and hit him in the head.

"Hey!" he said.

Cynthe waved frantically, then her bow came flying at Diello. He caught it before it could whack him in the face. A moment later, she joined him, crawling crablike over the shifting pile. Covered in dirt, she gave herself a cursory brushing off and surveyed the lane.

"Let's go," Diello said, pointing west.

They ran, not slowing down until they reached the end of the lane and could see the crowd again. Cynthe edged forward, peering around the corner. Diello followed suit, just in time to see the gor-goblin pushing through the laughing throng, searching in all directions, still wrapped in a spell that made him appear a normal Antrasin man. He kept stopping people and asking questions.

Hunting us.

Diello jerked back, and Cynthe did the same.

"What does he want?" Diello asked.

"Us, you fool."

He shot her an exasperated look. "I mean, why? Why doesn't he give up?"

"We'll worry about that later." Cynthe pointed back the way they'd just come. "Hurry!"

"No. We'll spend all day running up and down this lane while he keeps us cornered." Diello took a step toward the crowd, only to be grabbed by his sleeve.

"Where are your wits?" Cynthe demanded. "We can't go that way. He's bound to see us."

Diello didn't argue. He just hoisted Mamee's package higher in his arms and darted into the crowd, ignoring Cynthe's angry shout.

She followed, as he knew she would.

Together they twisted and darted and dodged, and dodged and darted and twisted, between people and vendor stalls and tents. Cynthe watched alertly, her dirty face drawn with fright.

Diello had never felt so scared, but he knew there was only one place in the village where they could hide safely and throw the gor-goblin off their scent.

chapter four

the blacksmith's fire was blazing in its iron forge. The rhythmic tattoo of a hammer beating upon its anvil rang through the air. A sweaty man with muscular shoulders was nailing a shoe to a white horse's hind foot while the blacksmith shaped another shoe with swift strikes on the red-hot iron.

Cynthe skidded to a halt, tugging the back of Diello's tunic to make him stop. "Not here," she said in horror. "Is this what you're trying to do? No! We can't!"

He met her frantic eyes. "We must."

"But—"

"We *must*."

Taking her hand, Diello led her past the forge, past the steaming wooden bucket of water, past the stack of iron rods and flat pieces of metal. With every step, he felt his determination fading. If there was one thing that the Fae abhorred, it was iron. At home, all their door hinges were thick leather straps that sagged and wore out often but were replaced without complaint. Pa built every piece of furniture with wooden pegs instead of nails. Even the cooking pots were made of copper and bronze because

Mamee could not go near anything made of iron without growing ill. Being only half Fae, Diello and Cynthe could stand it slightly better. But taking refuge at the smithy was one of the hardest things Diello had ever done. He forced himself to ignore the iron's effect, keeping a grip on his sister, who was jerking back.

Diello had never seen so much iron gathered in one place. On the few occasions he'd come into Wodesley with Pa, if his father had any business with the blacksmith, Diello had kept his distance. Today, it appeared the blacksmith had stockpiled twice as much metal as usual. Diello led Cynthe to the rear of the smithy. There, they crouched behind a haphazard pile of iron scraps, bent wheels, and broken tools.

By now, he felt sick to his stomach and clammy with sweat.

Cynthe squirmed and grimaced and muttered, rubbing her arms and wriggling until he gripped her shoulder hard.

"Keep still," he hissed.

"I can't stand this," she gasped.

"Be strong, Cynthe."

She looked miserable, her head sunk low and her fists clenched. Diello's skin prickled and itched, like falling into a bed of stinging nettles, but he dared not move, not even to scratch. He knew the gor-goblin would find the metal even more repulsive than they did. The creature wouldn't be able to catch their scent so close to the iron. *Be still, be still, be still*, Diello told himself.

Time crawled by. It was unbearable. He was going mad from it, and still he waited.

He listened to the idle voices at the front of the smithy until a gruff, familiar voice called out, interrupting the gossip, asking if anyone had seen two children carrying a large parcel. There was silence, while Diello's heart squeezed into a small, hard knot. Then the chatter resumed, indifferent to the question that no one answered. The blacksmith's skilled hammer struck with a loud ring, and he didn't hear the gor-goblin's voice again.

Be still, be still, be still, he repeated, shutting his eyes. If he'd guessed wrong, if the gor-goblin did come sniffing back here, the creature would find them. This was the biggest gamble of Diello's life.

Oh, Guardian, he prayed, daring to beseech the supreme Fae deity, *have pity on us and keep us safe, for the sake of the Fae blood that runs in our veins. Protect us from this beast. Give us strength to hide as long as necessary.*

Mamee had taught him that it was permissible to pray to the Guardian occasionally, provided he showed sufficient respect and humility.

Apparently he'd been humble enough, for the Guardian didn't smite him, and Diello found that if he focused on his breathing and clenched his fists very tight, he could keep on waiting.

Two more horses were shod out front. *Long enough,* Diello decided. He stood up on shaky legs and looked carefully about, afraid to take a step.

"Have we lost him?" Cynthe whispered. Her eyes were still shut, and she was crouched in a ball. "Say, yes, Diello. By the mercy of the Guardian, say, yes."

"Yes."

She shot to her feet, craning her neck like a hare looking for bushberries. Her face was bone white, and her eyes had sunk deeper in their sockets. They crept away from the smithy, their balance so clumsy they had to support each other.

Leaving the lanes and the village square behind them, they took refuge beneath a wide old tree out on the common and sank to the ground. It was cool there in the shade, and soon Diello felt better. The soft rustling of the leaves overhead and the gentle flow of water in the nearby creek soothed him. He found his gaze drawn to the bridge just beyond them.

Go home, whispered a voice in his head.

The urge to run home was so strong it made him dizzy.

He rubbed his temples, where his head ached.

"Let's deliver the cloth and be done with it," Cynthe said.

"We'd better get home."

"Not until we deliver the cloth."

Diello scowled at the package lying at his feet. He was sick of carrying it around. "We'll take King's Road and then cut home while that thing is still hunting for us in the village."

"We're going to the castle," Cynthe insisted. "As Mamee told us to do."

"It's too risky now."

"And if we don't deliver the cloth, what do we tell Mamee? Do we lie? How do we explain bringing it home without the money? Do you really want to explain everything that's happened today?"

Diello wanted to throw the cloth in the creek and let the water carry it away. His feelings shocked him. He wasn't a quitter. He tried to remind himself that Mamee had worked hard to finish the cloth so they could bring it today. He mustn't let her down.

"I just—I don't—" His words grew so tangled he stopped trying to speak. He rubbed his temple again.

"The iron has addled your wits," Cynthe said with sympathy. "If we're headed toward the castle, the goblin won't follow us. He surely isn't that stupid."

"Not stupid," Diello muttered. "Dangerous. Gor-goblins are the worst of all the breeds."

Cynthe rolled her eyes. "If he tries again to track us down, I'll put an arrow in him. That will teach him to bother us."

Diello couldn't bring himself to smile at her bravado. He was growing more afraid with every passing moment. He didn't understand why. He wasn't usually so timid. The urge to run came over him again, stronger than ever. He kept thinking about those awful eyes glaring into his and that raspy voice calling him "little morsel."

"We're going home," he said softly. "Now, while we have the chance."

"Use your head," Cynthe said. "Once Mamee knows how we disobeyed her, she'll never let us go anywhere again."

Diello wanted to go home so badly he could taste it, like thirst parching his throat. It was as if worry and fear were being forced on him. His headache throbbed once more, one brief spike of pain, increasing his anxiety.

No! He was no coward. He squashed the urge the way he would a fly, and the panic dropped from him. It was the gor-goblin putting fear in his mind. Without his *cloigwylie*, he was vulnerable now, unlike Cynthe, but he wasn't going to let that creature twist his thoughts and coerce him to do something against his will.

"You aren't really that scared?" Cynthe asked, puzzled. "Are you?"

Diello was embarrassed by what the gor-goblin had done to him and determined to show Cynthe that he wasn't spooked.

He set his hand on the bronze knife at his belt.

"The castle it is."

chapter five

hurrying to the castle, Diello kept looking over his
shoulder. He didn't like the way the woods grew right
to the edge of the road on both sides. It seemed the perfect
place for an ambush. Meanwhile, Cynthe strode along, keeping to the center of the dusty road like she owned it. Once
they had to jump aside for a horse and rider, and a second
time to make way for a heavily laden cart. Diello maintained
a sharp watch, but none of the other people they passed were
goblins in disguise. Even so, he couldn't loosen his tight grip
on his quarterstaff.

A moat surrounded the castle, the brackish water covered in clumps of stinking green slime. A wooden bridge
led across to wide double gates, standing open. But not in
welcome. Armed sentries checked everyone that came or
went, and Diello noted more men positioned on the gray
stone walls. Lord Malques's banner was flying from the front
watchtower, showing him to be in residence.

Everyone looked to be in a hurry or very hard at work.
No one was smiling and making merry here.

Diello expected Cynthe to march up to the gate sentry
and explain their business, but she grew suddenly mute and

rooted herself in the road, squeezing the package in her arms and looking mulish.

"You talk to him," she muttered.

Diello wanted to jeer at her—for who was acting scared now?—but swallowed the impulse. After the Shieldsman had spat on her in the village, he didn't blame her for not wanting to talk to anyone here.

Wondering if he would get the same treatment, Diello approached the sentry. "We've come to see the steward, please," he said, making himself speak up clearly and courteously as Pa had taught him. He looked the sentry in the eye and didn't fidget. "We've brought a banquet cloth from the weaver Lwyneth."

The sentry wasn't interested. "Be off. Your kind can't come peddling here."

"We aren't peddling!" Diello said indignantly. "It's commissioned. We're delivering it."

"So you say, but as to the truth of your prattle, I know not." The sentry made a shooing motion.

Diello stood his ground. "Ask the steward if you don't believe us."

The man grinned, showing the gaps of missing teeth. "Hark at you!" he said in false admiration. "Standing up to me like someone important and demanding I bother Master Timmons on a day like this, when he's so busy he don't remember his own name. Get on!"

"Ask him," Diello insisted. "Or I reckon you can explain to his lordship why there's no cloth spread for his banquet tonight."

The sentry scowled but looked unsure. He beckoned to

a chubby boy wearing blue-and-crimson livery, then pointed at Diello. "You follow this here page, and no wandering off. As soon as you make your delivery, come straight back out. If you're caught begging or peddling, it'll be the boot for you both!"

Diello and Cynthe followed the page silently. Inside the walls, and past the outer ward, it was like entering another village. The Audience hall was a tall, three-story structure built of dark stone. Other buildings crowded next to it, buildings to house the Shieldsmen, buildings for storage, buildings for horses and dogs. People were everywhere—nearly all of them wearing blue-and-crimson livery. Rushing to keep up with the page, Diello tried to take in all he could.

Over by the cookhouse, two shirtless, sweating boys knelt in front of a large oven. They were cramming the blazing firebox with short lengths of wood while a man in a baker's apron yelled directions at them. More servants waited there, holding wooden paddles covered with strips of dough ready to go in the oven, while others were flipping fresh-baked loaves into baskets. The aroma made Diello's mouth water.

At the stables, horses were being groomed until their hides shone clean and glossy. Squires were oiling weapons and saddles while dogs scrounged everywhere, getting in people's way. Most of the year, the baron lived elsewhere in the shire; his holdings were said to be extensive. It was easy to think of the steward as the owner of all this wealth and bounty, for he ruled this manor in the baron's absence, gave the orders, and collected the harvest tithe and taxes.

Just thinking about talking to him made Diello nervous.

"Wait here while I inform Master Timmons," the page said, halting by a narrow wooden door. "Don't wander about."

There was no shade to protect them from the beating sun. Light and heat reflected off the stone walls. Diello sighed, feeling thirsty, and crouched on his haunches with the package resting on his knees.

Cynthe remained standing with her bow ready in her hand. She watched the activity at the stables for a while, then cocked her blonde head to one side and squinted down at her brother. "So do we tell them about the goblins or not?"

"Mamee's business first," Diello said. "Then I'll mention the goblins."

Cynthe shrugged. "Or let the humans take care of themselves."

Watching a stableboy pouring a bucket of water over a cream-colored palfrey, Diello felt thirstier than ever. The horse snorted and flicked its tail. "They could at least offer us hospitality."

Cynthe barked a scornful laugh, but said nothing.

The door opened, and the steward came out. Until now, Diello had seen him only from a distance. Onner Timmons was a portly man, with a way of looking down his beaky nose that made him seem taller than he actually was. The silver toque at his throat proclaimed him to be a servant, but he served only Lord Malques. His eyes were like black beetles, shifting about in search of dung.

"Where is the cloth?" he asked in a shrill, impatient tone. "Why wasn't it delivered a week past? I have a thousand tasks to see to today, and no time to be pestered by a pair of filthy Faelin beggars."

Cynthe stiffened, clenching her bow. Diello stepped forward. He knew that the best way to handle this transaction was to remain polite, no matter what. "Good day, sir," he said, bowing and pulling away the wrapping. "Here is his lordship's new banquet cloth, woven by Lwyneth."

"Careful with those dirty fingers!" The steward took the cloth from him and shook out its folds.

The material gleamed white in the sunlight, displaying an intricate pattern in the weave for which their mother was renowned. Diello smiled with pride.

"Hmm, yes, this is Lwyneth's work. Very fine," the steward murmured, bundling it up rather carelessly. "Tell the woman that his lordship thanks her, although it should have been sent sooner."

As the steward spoke, he started to step through the door. Diello gripped the wood, refusing to let it close.

"First, her payment, if you please, sir."

"It will be sent in a few days."

"No, sir," Diello said. "You will pay now."

"Now? Impossible!"

"Then we'll take the cloth home, and his lordship can have it when paid for." Diello took the cloth out of the steward's hands.

A red tide surged into the steward's plump face. "You insolent puppy! How dare you imply that his lordship will cheat the woman!"

"Her name is Lwyneth!" Cynthe said hotly, pushing forward. "She's not a serf. And my brother didn't mean that Lord Malques would cheat our mother. He meant *you*!"

A terrible silence fell over them. Diello would've liked to throttle his sister. Of all the stupid things to say . . .

The steward was staring at Cynthe as though she were a bad smell.

Diello edged between the man and his sister. The trouble with Cynthe was that she kept assuming that Mamee had been a fine, highborn lady before she came to Antrasia to be with Pa. It was obvious that Mamee hadn't grown up on an ordinary farm, but that didn't mean Cynthe could give herself airs or think herself equal in status to people like the steward, let alone the baron. His sister had to accept the truth some-time, and she was getting too old to pretend otherwise. They were Faelin, like it or not, which made them lower than an Antrasin serf. Hadn't she been spat on enough for one day?

"Sir," Diello said, "we are to collect payment now, as was agreed between our mother and his lordship."

"The agreement was between her and *me*," Onner Tim-mons snapped. "Lord Malques wouldn't recognize Lwyneth if she walked through his hall. But very well." He held out a handful of paper to Diello. "Here."

Diello stared at him and didn't move.

Onner Timmons shook the paper. "Are you deaf, boy? Here is your payment. Hand over the cloth and be quick about it."

"No," Diello said.

"Now see here—"

"No."

The steward's astonished glare made Diello's nerves almost fail him. But Mamee's instructions had been clear. He must do this properly.

Diello's mouth and throat felt as dry as dust. "Lwyneth is always paid in good Antrasin gold, not script. You must have forgotten that, sir."

"Faelin script is good enough for the likes of you." The steward reached for the banquet cloth, but Diello backed up, giving it to Cynthe, who clutched it defiantly.

"You're trying to cheat us," Diello said. "Three gold pieces is the agreed price."

"Consider the script a down payment. The rest will be paid later, in gold."

Diello held the man's gaze steadily and said nothing.

Onner Timmons's face turned redder. A tracery of veins pulsed across his forehead. "Lwyneth will have to wait for her payment until it is convenient. I haven't the gold on hand today. Perhaps she will learn to do her work more promptly in future."

"No, sir. You're trying to haggle down the price for a commissioned piece."

The steward's black eyes grew even colder. "You have insulted me enough, boy. Stephel was a fool to send you here. A fool! If he can't train his Faelin brats to behave better, he'll see no more favor from the castle. And so you may tell him. As for your Faelin mother—"

"Our mother isn't Faelin," Cynthe declared before Diello could stop her. "She's Fae. Full-blooded Fae, from—"

"He doesn't care about that," Diello broke in. Cynthe should know better. Pa had told them over and over never to speak of Mamee's past, never to tell anyone where she came from.

Clearly unimpressed, the steward said, "Then your mother should have stayed where she belonged, among her own sly kind, instead of producing horrid half-breeds like you. Now take the script and go."

"Three gold pieces!" Diello shouted, stung past all caution. "Now!"

Across the inner ward, people paused in their work to watch. Glowering, the steward added two thick coins to the wad of paper. He flung the money at Diello's feet. The coins rang out loudly on the paving stones while the script floated down like dead leaves. "That is all! Do you understand? *All!* Now go, before I order the servants to set the dogs on you!"

His face burning, Diello stared at the money on the ground. One of the coins was a large gold piece. The other was silver. As for the paper, he knew it had scant value. Most Antrasin merchants in the village wouldn't accept Faelin script. His family couldn't survive on it.

Diello didn't pick up the money. "It's not enough."

"It's all you get," Onner Timmons said. "And I shan't send any additional payment, either. Tell your Fae mother *that*. It will be a long while before I give her another commission, if ever!"

He whisked the cloth from Cynthe's hands and shot through the door, slamming it behind him.

The twins stared at each other. Cynthe was wide eyed and indignant. Diello's whole body felt on fire. In the distance, the workers were still watching them. Someone snickered, and Diello found it difficult to breathe. He wanted to walk away and leave the money in the dirt. Instead, although his back was so stiff he thought it might snap, he forced himself to stoop for it.

Cynthe gripped his wrist. "Don't you dare pick it up," she said, her voice shaking. "Don't you dare touch it!"

The plump page walked up to them, with a square-jawed sergeant at his heels. "You can't loiter here," the page said. "I heard the steward tell you to go."

"Aye," growled the sergeant. "Move along, piglets. Your business here is done. And if you don't want that shiny gold piece, my mates and I will be pleased to spend it for you."

Diello bit his lip hard before he slowly gathered the money. The coins were already warm from the sunlight. The paper felt brittle, as if it might crumble to dust.

"No," Cynthe murmured.

The sergeant shoved Diello. "Move on, I said. No dawdling here."

Across the castle bridge, with the moat stinking and swarming with midges, Diello stopped in the road and looked down at his fist. The edges of the coins were cutting into his palm.

"Throw it away," Cynthe said. She looked wild with anger. "Throw it in the moat!"

Maybe, he thought, *if I'd groveled more . . . maybe if I'd begged . . .* but then he felt that knot inside and knew he couldn't have done it.

As for throwing the money in the moat . . . he thought of the seedlings struggling in new field and the too-wet spring that had drowned the other crops. The winter months would bring a lean larder this year. Pa was always talking about responsibility. That meant doing what was necessary, even if the shame of it hurt.

Diello tucked the money inside Cynthe's belt pouch since he hadn't worn his own.

"I won't carry the money!" she yelled.

"Is your injured pride worth more than eating this winter?" he asked harshly. "Can't you grow up?"

Their stares met, neither of them giving ground.

"We'll take it home," Diello said. "Pa can decide whether to keep it."

"*Pa.*" Her eyes shone with tears she wouldn't let fall. "You're just like him. You never understand *anything.*"

"I'm nothing like Pa," he muttered. "He wouldn't have lost his temper. He wouldn't have been cheated."

"You cheated yourself when you picked it up."

Diello knew he could argue with her all the way home and it wouldn't make any difference. She wouldn't back down. But he wasn't going to back down, either. Not this time. Cynthe let her feelings rule, and he was tired of being the only one to think things through.

"There's no more to say," he told her. "Let's go home."

chapter six

the twins trudged along, both stiff lipped and fuming.
Diello hated holding grudges and soon began shooting his sister sideways glances, hoping to see her temper
improving. But Cynthe's face remained sullen. It was like
having Onner Timmons walk with them, his cheapness and
bigotry clinging like the stink of pig. Pa always said that
harsh words couldn't hurt unless you let them. *That's what
I'm doing now*, Diello thought. *Letting the steward hurt me.
And hurt Cynthe, too.*

He sighed, breaking the silence. "Cynthe, you might as
well stop sulking."

"I'll sulk if I want to."

At least she was talking.

"You know I had to take the money," he said.

"Liar. No one made you pick it up. And if you're feeling
sorry for yourself now, it's exactly what you deserve."

Diello's mouth snapped shut, his pride like a huge
sticker ball in his throat. It was bad enough going home
cheated. He wasn't going to apologize to her, no matter
how long she held a grudge. In fact, she owed *him* an
apology.

"I feel like someone's watching us," Cynthe said suddenly. "I have an itch right between my shoulder blades."

Diello looked around. Woods with dense undergrowth bordered both sides of the road. He saw nothing wrong, but then he realized the birds had stopped singing. Other than their footsteps, the place was eerily quiet. And they hadn't met any other travelers since they'd left King's Road.

In his anger, he'd forgotten about the gor-goblin. Pa had taught them that if they ever got into trouble venturing outside the farmstead, it would be because they'd neglected to stay alert and careful.

No matter how exasperating she could be, Cynthe was never wrong when it came to woodscraft. And now that he was concentrating, he could sense a lurking presence nearby, one that sent a faint chill up the back of his neck. It would be a good time to use Sight and know exactly what was around them, but he couldn't seem to control his Gift.

"We're getting close to the cut," he said, looking ahead to where the trail forked. "Do you think there's trouble waiting from Cutthroat Gully?"

Cynthe shook her head. "The bandits aren't going to bother us. They'll be lying in wait for richer targets on King's Road."

"Then do you think it's the—"

"Maybe. We're being followed."

She'd quickened her pace, and he lengthened his stride to keep up. "I don't think we can outrun a goblin on an open road," he panted.

Her gaze was moving here and there. Her hand slid casually along her bow to its carved grip. "We'll have to hide in the woods."

"Mamee said to avoid the woods on the way home."

"The woods are safer than this trail," she said.

"But—"

"We're safer in the trees. I know where to go."

"And if we meet a trog—"

"Better we worry about goblins right now than some old trog lurking in the brush," Cynthe said. "Besides, I can outrun a trog any day, can't you?"

"Uh, sure," he lied.

The memory of the gor-goblin's red eyes filled his mind. He could almost feel the creature's hot breath on his throat. *Stop it!* He wasn't going to be called a coward again today.

"Say when," he murmured.

Cynthe looked around. "Now," she whispered and melted into the forest.

Diello plunged after her, anxious that she not get too far ahead. She was an excellent tracker and could always find her way home no matter how far she ranged, but this area was unfamiliar to him and he had no intention of ending this day by getting lost.

Or eaten.

Only a faint waving of bushes gave him any indication of where she'd gone. He broke into a run, his nerves stretching thin and tight. All the while he was listening for the sound of pursuit. He glanced back often but saw nothing.

A branch slapped him in the face, stinging his cheek, and after that he stopped looking behind him. Ahead, he caught a brief glimpse of a green tunic and golden hair, and then Cynthe was swallowed up in the undergrowth once more.

They were moving ever deeper into the forest. Cynthe doubled back so he could see her and gestured. He nodded silently and followed her into a shallow ravine. He grabbed sapling trunks to keep from losing his balance and tumbling all the way to the bottom. He slid and jumped, his clothing snagging on brambles and his hair full of twigs. Half-rotted leaves flew up around him. When he caught up breathlessly beside his twin, she punched his arm.

"Quiet!" she breathed and crawled under a low, rocky outcropping.

He squeezed in beside her, hot and sweaty, his heart pounding so hard that he could barely hear. A stream trickled along the bottom of the ravine, and there was a stand of bright green cielberry trees growing in a thicket nearby. As a hiding place, it was clever, for the running water, piles of moldy leaves, and exposed limestone would all help mask their scent. Diello would have preferred a cave to crawl into, completely out of sight, but as long as they kept still they were unlikely to be seen by anything on the trail overhead.

They waited, breathing quietly and saying nothing for what seemed like a very long time. As the afternoon slid by, Diello worried about having to make their way home in the dark. He was still very thirsty and listening to the chuckling stream made it worse. The low overhang of stone and the dense growth of trees smothered him, but he dared not move.

At last Cynthe touched his sleeve. "I think it's safe to go on," she whispered.

He nodded in relief, but even then he didn't spring out into the open. He eased himself upright beneath the branches and looked around carefully. He didn't see anything lurking or hear anything except birdsong and the occasional rustle of insects among the fallen leaves.

The sound of normal forest noises was more reassuring than anything.

"How odd," Cynthe said, rubbing her forehead. "My protection is gone. It must have worn off early. Let's go."

She started climbing up the sloping hill. Diello paused by the stream to cup his hands in the cold, clear water.

Something heavy and large hit him in the back, knocking him flat. He pitched into the stream, banging his forehead on a stone with such force the world grew black and wobbly. But the icy water kept him from losing consciousness, and he tilted his face to avoid drowning. He couldn't figure out what was happening. He felt like a boulder had fallen on him.

That was stupid, of course, because the rock would still be on top of him, and it wasn't. Instead, he heard the crashing of something running through the fallen leaves and a weird "huh, huh, huh" sound.

Then Cynthe screamed.

Diello pushed himself up, slinging his wet hair out of his eyes as he turned around. He saw his sister rolling down the steep slope in a tangle of arms and legs. A creature covered in shaggy gray fur reared up on its hind legs and roared, releasing a hot musky stench. It roared again, then loped after her.

Diello saw that the trog was a big one, fully twice his size, and old enough to sport a long mane of coarse white bristles across its neck and shoulders. At this size and maturity, the creatures were almost impossible to kill because their thick hides and bony bodies resisted most weapons. Once they released their musk, they focused intently on their prey and could not be drawn off.

But they weren't long-distance runners. All the twins needed was a head start and they could outrun it. Diello had to give Cynthe a chance to get away.

He gathered up a handful of stones, feeling a fresh wave of dizziness as he bent over. Angrily, he struggled to hold himself together. This was no time to go weak.

Catching up with Cynthe, the trog pounced. Screaming, she whacked at it with her bow, fending off a swipe of its claws. Her attack was ferocious enough to drive it back for a moment. Struggling to her feet, she dodged its lunge, keeping a sapling between her and the monster until the trog snapped the trunk of the young tree and sprang at her.

Cynthe dodged again, struggling all the while to pull an arrow from her quiver. Diello could see that her efforts were futile. The trog was too close. She had no time to draw and aim.

Yelling, Diello threw a stone at the beast. His first throw missed; his second hit it in the head.

But rather than turning toward him, it lunged at Cynthe, who was trying to climb the rocks. It grabbed her ankle and dragged her down.

With another yell, Diello rushed at the trog from behind, bringing his quarterstaff down across its furry back with all his might. Had Diello been a grown man, he might have been able to snap the trog's spine with such a blow. Still, he got its attention.

Bellowing, the trog turned and knocked him sprawling with a swipe of its forearm. Diello hit the ground, but rolled to his feet as Pa had taught him. He was just in time, for the trog sprang at him faster than he expected, grunting and snuffling. Diello jumped aside, swinging his quarterstaff. This time he hit the trog across its blunt snout, wood cracking against bone. With blood trickling from its nostrils, the creature howled and staggered, then it came at him again.

Thanks to his father's rigorous training—for Pa said even farmers should know how to fight—Diello was adept with a quarterstaff, good with skilled blows, and nimble on his feet. But though he jabbed at the trog's small, stupid eyes, feinted, and slammed his staff another time across its injured snout, he couldn't bring it down. He couldn't even stun it. The trog seemed to be made out of rock and, despite its awkward build and size, it was too quick for him.

Back and forth Diello danced, trying to keep his footing on the uneven ground. He whacked or shouted at the trog each time its attention shifted back to Cynthe.

The gold, Diello realized in despair as he began to tire. *She has the gold piece, and that's why it won't leave her alone.* Trogs were gold hoarders. They sometimes even scratched raw ore from streambeds. No one knew why they were drawn to it. *Break into a trog's den*, the old saying went, *and come out rich.*

"Back it against the rocks!" Cynthe shouted. "Hold it there!"

Panting, Diello shook sweat from his eyes and glanced at his sister. She'd regained her feet and was fitting an arrow to her bowstring. She wouldn't run away. He admired her cool courage, but wished she'd hurry and kill this beast.

The trog swiped at Diello, taking advantage of his momentary distraction, and ripped the shoulder of his tunic. Diello dodged, scared nearly out of his wits by the close call, but gamely tried his best to maneuver the trog into position for Cynthe to have clear aim. Taking an awful chance, he jumped in close enough to land a blow on the trog's midsection. The hit would have felled a man, but the trog barely staggered. Its paw slammed into Diello, knocking him off his feet. He landed hard, his head thudding against a tree root, and the world buzzed and blurred around him.

Suddenly his limbs were too slow and heavy to move. His head ached ferociously, and no matter how often he blinked, he couldn't quite focus his eyes.

The trog could have torn him open right then, but it turned to face Cynthe, standing up on its hind legs and roaring again.

"Now!" Diello shouted.

Cynthe's arrow hit the trog in the face, but missed its eyes and bounced harmlessly off the creature's jutting brow. Diello held back a groan. To his knowledge, a trog had no other vulnerable point but its eyes, yet hitting that target was almost impossible under the best conditions.

These were not the best conditions.

The ringing in his head was fading. Standing, Diello staggered a bit, and the trog blurred into two monsters. Concentrating hard, he threw another rock, hitting its shaggy shoulder. The trog swung its attention to him. Diello waved his quarterstaff and jumped up and down, yelling to confuse it. But it was hard to confuse something this stupid. The trog turned back to Cynthe.

"Throw the money away!" Diello shouted. "That's what it's after!"

Cynthe released another arrow, but the trog batted it down and leaped at her, knocking her flat. Snarling, it went for her throat. Diello heard her scream of agony.

Desperately he jumped on the creature's back, hammering at the trog's head and yelling with every blow, ignoring the pain jolting through his fists. Cynthe was still screaming. When Diello managed to hook one arm around the trog's thick neck, he found it all gristle and sinew. He couldn't choke it enough to save her, but he went on squeezing with all his might while he tried to stab it with his knife.

Again and again he struck, but his bronze blade, designed for slicing rope and skinning small game, couldn't pierce the creature's tough hide.

Cynthe's screams stopped, and his heart stopped, too.

"No!" he cried.

Suddenly, a she-wolf sprang into sight, bounding right over Diello to bite the trog in the back of its neck.

The trog shrieked and reared up, shaking off both Diello and the wolf. Abandoning Cynthe—who lay torn and still on the ground—the trog swung its bloodied snout first in Diello's direction and then the wolf's. It chose Diello. He lifted his hands defensively, but the she-wolf leaped between them and held the trog back, snarling viciously with her teeth bared and a ruff bristling around her neck.

When the trog moved, the wolf attacked. They fought savagely, snapping and growling.

Diello scrambled over to his sister. Her tunic was torn, and blood soaked the shreds of her sleeve. His eyes blurred with unshed tears, and he sank to his knees beside her.

"Cynthe."

Her hand, filthy and streaked with blood, gripped his. Her eyes opened wide, staring at him. She was alive, fully alive! She was crying silently, tears streaking her dirty cheeks.

Tenderly, he used his knuckles to brush away her tears. "Lie still. Let me see—"

In a rush, she sat up and clung to him. "Oh," she breathed, pressing her face to his chest and sobbing.

He stroked the back of her head and closed his eyes in grateful relief. They were two halves of the same being, inseparable. It had always been that way, no matter how much they quarreled. Just thinking about living without her made him feel cold and lost. He held her, both glad and scared, his throat knotted with the effort not to cry.

But already she was pushing him away, reaching for her bow as the fight raged on nearby. When the snarling animals moved in her direction, Diello pulled Cynthe out of their path.

"My quiver." She shoved her hair back. "Hurry!"

He fetched it for her. They couldn't just run. They had to kill the trog if they were to survive. Even if they gave it the gold now, it had drawn Cynthe's blood. It would not give up until it finished them.

The quiver held only one arrow. The others must have spilled out during her struggle. Diello gulped and handed her the lone arrow.

Cynthe's fingers curled back, unable to take it. She looked as desperate and scared as he felt.

He needed to be strong now for both of them. He touched her cheek lightly. "You can do it," he said with absolute conviction.

Determination flamed in her coppery-green eyes. She nodded, and when he handed her the arrow, she took it.

Diello watched her nock the arrow to her bowstring.

The trog was winning its fight against the wolf. Its musk scent was rank in the air, nearly choking Diello. The she-wolf was a sizable animal, larger than any wolf he'd ever seen before, but no match for the trog. She was bleeding from a torn ear, and although she harried the trog, nipping at its bowed legs and dodging its lethal claws, she was obviously tiring.

"Get ready!" Diello yelled.

His sister drew her bow and held her aim, waiting with the patience of a hunter, strong and true.

The trog clawed the wolf along her side, and she yelped, falling. The wolf struggled to her feet, staggering with her head low. Gaunt sides heaving, she growled, her eyes intent on the trog. It hesitated, watching the wolf before rising from its crouch and turning deliberately on Cynthe.

And still the girl held back, waiting until Diello feared she'd lost her nerve.

Her arm, he thought, seeing blood drip on the leaves at her feet. *She can't hold the bow much longer.*

He was in agony for her to release the arrow. He wanted to yell, "Now!" but dared not utter a sound. *Cynthe knows what she's doing*, he assured himself. The wolf had bought them time, and maybe a chance of escape, but if Cynthe missed her mark they would all die.

The wolf crept forward, hackles raised, fangs bared. Her bushy tail stuck out stiffly behind her. Although torn and bleeding, she was not yet beaten. She growled and sprang, biting at the trog's leg.

The instant the trog shifted its attention to the wolf, Cynthe's arrow hit its left eye deep. The trog toppled over, crashing onto the ground, and did not move.

Diello stared at the fallen monster.

"Hurrah!" he yelled. "You got the brute! Hurrah!"

"Quiet!" Cynthe said. She was shaking and sat down. "No shouting."

"I can't make any more noise than we already have," Diello replied.

Slapping his sister on her shoulder, Diello approached the trog cautiously. It was dead, the arrow still projecting from its eye, but he kicked it to make sure. Only then did Cynthe come to retrieve and clean her arrow.

"Good aim," Diello said. He kicked leaves in search of her other arrows, but didn't find them. "The best marksman in the shire couldn't beat you. You've never done better."

Smiling, she rubbed her face with the back of her hand, leaving new smears of blood and dirt across her cheek. "Thanks. But where did that wolf come from?"

"I don't know." Diello turned to the she-wolf.

The animal lifted intelligent blue eyes to his, then crumpled to the ground. He ran to kneel beside her.

"Diello, be careful!" Cynthe called.

"It's all right," he said. "She helped us, remember? Without her, we'd be dead by now."

"She could be dangerous, too."

"I don't think so."

The wolf lay on her side, breathing hard, making no effort to get up. Her wounds were terrible, more than Diello could hope to bind. Still, he tore off one of his sleeves and pressed the cloth to where the blood seemed to be flowing the most freely. When the wolf did not snarl or snap at him, he pressed harder. "You poor creature," he said, stroking her coarse fur. "How good you were to help us."

"Think not of Shalla," the wolf said.

Diello dropped the cloth and scrambled back. Cynthe was beside him in an instant.

"Did she speak?" she whispered. "Really speak?"

"Yes," Diello said. He was staring hard at the animal, noticing now that her pelt was not the usual gray of a wolf, but rather a light gold that appeared almost to sparkle in the dappled sunlight.

The wolf opened her eyes and twisted her head so that she could look at him. Her eyes, even glazed in pain, were remarkable. He thought she was going to speak again, but she just lay there, silent and suffering.

"Are you playing some trick on me?" Cynthe asked.

Diello shot his sister a scathing glance and ran to the stream to bring the wolf water in his cupped hands. She lapped weakly and went on staring at him with her strange eyes. It was like looking at a person wrapped in the body of an animal.

"Thank you," the wolf said. Her voice was gruff and peculiar, almost a growl, yet he could understand her words clearly. "You are kind." She closed her eyes again, resting.

"How can she speak?" Cynthe asked. "What manner of creature is she?"

"I think she must be a samal wolf," Diello replied, recalling legends his mother had told around the fire when winter snows kept them housebound. "They have the power to speak, and other magical gifts as well. Aren't they descended from the Far-Seeing People, the first inhabitants of Embarthi? There's a story about how they came to live in wolf form."

"Never mind stories. Samal wolves are myths—"

"Not in Embarthi. Not among the Fae."

"We aren't in Embarthi."

Diello gently stroked the wolf's neck. "Look at her paws, how torn and cracked they are. She's traveled a long distance."

"That doesn't mean she's come from Embarthi, or that she's a samal wolf."

"Believe what you wish," Diello said. "But we both heard her. How would you explain it?"

"I don't know," Cynthe admitted. "Look, she's been suckled. She must have pups somewhere. Poor thing. She's so thin."

"We've got to help her," Diello decided. "We can't just let her die here like this. Perhaps Mamee can heal her."

"Yes," Cynthe agreed, moving closer. "We can make a travois from some of these broken saplings and drag her home."

"No," the wolf said, her eyes still closed. "Think not of me. You are found. Danger closes around you. Beware."

"You've been looking for us?" Diello asked nervously.

"Lwyneth's scent is on you. You are her son?"

"Yes," he said in wonder. "How—"

"I am Shalla. Once Lwyneth called me friend, and I considered her my pack-sister. Because of the bond we shared, I have broken laws and come to warn Lwyneth, to guard her and her pack. Her enemies are closing in. Diello, son of Lwyneth, warn your dam that she is found. Betrayal . . . *betrayal!* She and all her pack must flee before nightfall." The wolf looked at him beseechingly. "And when you are safe in hiding, ask Lwyneth to forgive me for failing her on the Dark Day. Tell her that Shalla stayed her friend to the very end. But first, warn her. Danger comes."

Diello bent closer. "But—"

A great sigh escaped the wolf. Her head fell limp to the ground.

"She's dead," Cynthe said softly.

Diello touched the wolf and knew that his sister was right. "What did she mean?" he asked. "What was she trying to tell us about Mamee?" He stared at Cynthe. "She knew my name and Mamee's. She knew us!"

"Do you think she was warning us of a goblin attack? But the *cloigwylie* at the farm will keep goblins away."

"Not as many as we saw today," Diello said. "And that gor-goblin broke my protection like it was nothing. He could—"

A mournful yip in the bushes cut him off. He swung around, listening hard, and heard a faint rustle and another snuffling yip.

Cynthe pointed. "Over there." She hurried in that direction.

"Cynthe, wait!"

But she had already jumped the stream and shot into the brushy thicket. She emerged a moment later, carrying a snarling wolf pup by his scruff. "Look at this."

Twisting and struggling, the pup snapped with his sharp milk teeth.

"Put him down," Diello said.

Cynthe released him, and the pup ran to his mother, nuzzling her in a bewildered way that broke Diello's heart. He watched the pup paw at his mother's muzzle, then sit down and tilt back his head, trying to howl. Diello couldn't bear to listen to those squeaky attempts at grief. Turning away, he joined his sister, who was washing her wounded arm in the stream and wincing.

"Is it bad?" he asked, realizing with a pang of guilt that perhaps he should have been tending to Cynthe's hurts first. "Has the bleeding stopped?"

"Mostly," she said, shaking her arm and sending droplets of water everywhere. "Except a little here where the claws went deep."

Diello bound it for her, doing a good job even when she flinched and sucked in her breath. She didn't protest, but tears filled her eyes by the time he finished.

He thought she was braver than anyone, even Pa. "It must hurt like the devil."

She shrugged. "It does. Maybe I'll have my first fighting scar."

Envious, he nodded. "Unless Mamee's salve heals it too

well." He paused, seeking the right words. "You were lucky."

Fresh tears swam in her eyes before she blinked them away. "I know."

"I'm sorry I gave you the gold to carry," Diello said.

She scrambled to her feet, flinging back her hair. "Easy to say now. I told you not to take it."

"Cynthe—"

She pointed back at the thicket. "There's another pup in there, you know."

Giving up on their talk, he went to look and found the creature lying dead in a nest of leaves and matted grass. It was a pathetic scrap of skin and bones inside a coat of lovely gold fur. He rejoined his sister. At her quizzical look, he shook his head.

She was feeding the surviving pup bits of the second bun she'd bought at the fair. Cynthe was cooing to the little wolf, and the pup was nuzzling her hand eagerly. They were already bonding, and Diello couldn't help but wish the other pup had lived so he wouldn't be left out.

Then he felt petty and selfish, and he joined Cynthe in stroking the pup. The little fellow was almost white, with a faint golden tinge to his fur. He still carried much of his fuzzy baby coat, although Diello could feel wiry, more protective hair growing in. A tuft of fur grew atop the pup's head between his tall ears, giving him an almost comical look. He had the same intelligent blue eyes as his mother.

"Poor mite," Cynthe said, feeding the pup another piece of bun. "Look how hungry he is. Is he too young to wean?"

"No point in asking that now." Diello sat back and

rubbed his forehead. A tender lump was rising there. "His paws are as torn as his mother's."

"We can't leave him behind to fend for himself," Cynthe said urgently. "He's too young."

"I know. Too little to make it on his own, but too big for you to carry far, especially with that hurt arm."

"Never mind my arm," Cynthe said. The pup licked her hand. "See? He trusts me already."

"He wants more bread," Diello said, but he smiled as the pup licked Cynthe's hand harder, making her laugh. "I'll carry him for you."

"My arm's all right," she said. "He's accepted me. I want to carry him."

Diello gave in. "I'll make a sling."

He tore off the other sleeve of his tunic and the one left on Cynthe's. Tying them together in a loop, he slipped the makeshift sling over her shoulder and tucked the pup inside. It was a poor fit, but the baby wolf didn't seem to mind and snuggled against Cynthe's chest.

She stroked his tall ears. "We'll have to give him a name. Fuzzytop?"

"Not yet," Diello said, more forcibly than he'd intended. "And not that."

"Don't you like him?" Cynthe asked. "You bring home every—"

"This isn't the same," Diello interrupted. "I don't know whether Pa will let us keep him."

"He has to. He will, once he knows the mama wolf fought for us."

Diello started to remind her that it was unlikely Pa would

permit a wolf to grow up with the livestock, but he held his tongue. He wasn't sure *what* Pa would say. And he didn't want to leave the pup behind, either.

"See if you can get him to drink some water," Diello said. "I'll take care of his mother."

"You can't bury her. The ground's too full of roots. Besides, we need to go."

The little wolf was staring at Diello as if he understood every word. Diello said, "I'll hurry."

First he fetched the other pup and laid it beside its mother before carrying stones from the stream to cover their gaunt bodies. It wasn't a very good cairn, especially since he had to fill in the gaps with sticks and leaves, but it was better than nothing. It amazed him that Shalla had so willingly given her life to save him and his sister. Why should an animal come so far to help strangers? And what about the things she'd said? He wished he understood.

As he placed the last stone, his fingers rested on the she-wolf's golden pelt. Suddenly his mind was flooded with images of running, running, running, of hurrying through hills and forest, racing across unfamiliar terrain. And with every mile and league traveled, being driven by a growing sense of urgency and looming disaster. Then . . . attack, fighting savagely and killing, before running again, always running, barely taking time to hunt or eat or rest. And the goblins . . . green, mottled, stinking pursuers . . . tall, red-eyed, mud-colored ambushers. Beware! Beware! But keep running, no turning back . . . run to warn, to protect . . . *run. . . .*

The images faded, leaving nothing but a still, black void.

Diello sat back. His bones itched and tingled, but he didn't feel sick the way he had when he saw through the goblins' disguising spell. This was neither magic nor vision. Just the lingering memories of the she-wolf. But what he'd seen reinforced Shalla's warning, making her final words burn in his mind.

"Diello?" Cynthe asked. "What now?"

He looked at the sky, gauging the angle of the sinking sun. The memory of the Death Flock on the cottage roof, the shriek of the wind as it called his mother's name the past three nights, and now this bizarre warning from a wolf that could talk—there were too many ill omens to shrug off.

"She said to warn them—Mamee and Pa—before nightfall." He met his sister's eyes. "Do you think you can run?"

Cynthe nodded grimly. "All the way. Come on!"

chapter seven

the farmstead was gone.

Crossing the narrow footbridge over the creek, where the *cloigwylie* should have been, Diello stared numbly at a scene of devastation.

Twilight was folding her arms about the world, lengthening the shadows in the woods. Above the treetops, Sientha, always the first star to appear, burned low and bright in a purpling sky. The full moon and her small, crescent sister were rising in the east.

But where the cottage should have been standing, its lights shining a welcome from open door and windows, only ashes and rubble remained. The barn was also gone, with nothing left except its broken foundation walls.

Diello kept staring. *It isn't real*, he told himself. *It isn't real. It isn't real.*

Cynthe, who'd been lagging behind, stubbornly carrying the wolf pup the whole time despite Diello's offers to help, now halted beside him and gasped. "What—what's *happened*?"

As she spoke, the breeze shifted direction, bringing smoke and the stink of death. Diello could see the milk cows lying on the ground where they'd been felled, blood glistening on their cream-and-tan hides. With them lay the gray bodies of Ton and Poco, their plow oxen, a pair so gentle that even Amalina could lead them by their nose rings to their stalls. Pa had raised the oxen from orphaned calves, and Diello had fed them every night and morning of their lives—except today.

He knew then that this was no vision. This *was* real. And his chest began to ache.

"Raiders?" Cynthe asked, her voice tight. "Did the goblins do this?"

"How should I know?" he spat.

"We'd better stay out of sight," she said. "Circle around and see if we can find where Pa and Mamee are hi—"

A cloud of dark rooks flew up between the remains of the cottage and the barn. Their harsh cries filled the air.

The Death Flock! Diello broke into a run.

Cynthe called after him, but he ignored her. There was a hive of bees buzzing inside his skull, drowning out everything. The possibility that danger could still be lurking here didn't matter. He had to find them. . . . He had to *know.* . . .

Smoke hung thick in the air. Coughing, he stumbled over strewn possessions and slaughtered poultry. Nothing, it seemed, had been left untouched. He saw pieces of furniture broken and tossed aside, smashed crockery, torn bits of clothing, even food from the larder chewed on and discarded. The malice behind the destruction, the sheer cruelty, left him stunned.

He bent and picked up a splintered piece of wood. It was a spindle from Mamee's loom.

A soft, inarticulate cry came from his throat.

The Death Flock flew away in a loud rush of wings.

Cynthe caught up with him. Shrugging off her sling and leaving the baby wolf free to explore, she punched Diello in the shoulder. "Are you daft! Don't you smell the goblin spoor? If they catch us—"

"I don't care," Diello said. He moved away from his sister, determined to keep searching. The farm *cloigwylie* wasn't just broken, he realized. It was *gone*. And that meant . . . that *had* to mean . . .

At the rear of the cottage stood the stone cistern, positioned to catch rainwater runoff from the roof. Although their well was a good one, Pa preferred to save its water for the needs of the household and use stored cistern water to keep the garden going. One dry day of stress and wilt, he would say, meant poor growth and less harvest.

The cistern's stone walls were blackened by the fire. Chipped marks and cracks marred its sides where the raiders had tried to tear the structure apart. They hadn't succeeded, but the ground itself had been clawed, even dug up, in places. The sour stench of goblin hung rank in the air, mingling with the acrid smoke. Diello turned away.

That's when he saw her, lying partway between the cistern and the well.

"Mamee," he whispered.

His feet would not carry him to her.

"Mamee!" Cynthe cried out.

She raced past him to where their mother lay and dropped on her knees.

"Mamee!" she shouted, bending over and clutching her mother's dress. "Mamee! Oh, no. No!"

Diello watched her shake Mamee harder and harder. His mind seemed to have drifted far away, where nothing mattered very much. A world without Mamee in it was incomprehensible to him. He wanted to run as far and fast as possible to the end of the road, to the end of the woods, all the way to the end of the world.

A slap to his cheek snapped him back to the here and now. Cynthe glared at him.

"Do something!" she demanded, pointing behind her. "Touch her. Reach her while there's still time. Bring her back to us."

"I'm no healer," he protested. "I can't pull her soul back into her body if it's already—"

"You don't know she's gone," Cynthe said. "You haven't even tried."

"But I—"

"There's a chance. You *know* that. At least *try*."

Diello forced himself to approach his mother's body, unsure he could bear to experience Mamee's memories just before death as he had the she-wolf's. Yet could he do less for Mamee? Swallowing hard, he sank to his knees beside his mother and stretched out trembling hands.

Mamee's flesh was hard to the touch and icy cold. Her face was coated with powdery white dust, much like a slab of stone when it is first cut from a mountain quarry.

Her pallid slender fingers curled slack around a skein of thread that had unwound into a messy cobweb.

All around her were deep gouges in the dirt where her

goblin murderers had raked their claws, releasing the musky scent of victory.

Diello felt hot, sour bile rising in his throat. He bowed his head.

"Don't just stare at her," Cynthe said. "*Do* something!"

"I am."

But he couldn't get past how changed his mother was in death. How strange she looked, how still and cold she was.

Mamee's long silvery tresses lay tangled around her head. The copper streaks in them had faded to dark gray. Her hair was no longer pliant and soft but rough and rigid like dry twigs. In the gathering gloom, her skin should have been aglow, giving off that faint radiant light that made her luminous at night. But there was no glimmer, no fading sparkle. There had been no life within her for quite a while.

While we were fighting the trog, he thought bleakly, *she was dying.*

He found the courage then. *Mamee,* he called softly in his mind, in his heart. *Mamee, come back to us.*

But he could make nothing stir in Mamee. There was no thread of thought, no whisper of memory, no glow of love remaining in her. He tried stretching himself into the empty void, but he might as well have tried to hold the wind in his fist. He was too late. Whatever Cynthe hoped for was gone forever.

Wearily he dropped his hands to his sides. It was as if Mamee had never been a living creature at all, but something fashioned from stone and dust and twig. He feared that if he dared move her, she would crumble.

"Well?" Cynthe demanded.

Grief speared through his numbness. Unable to answer his sister, he reached up and held her hand. Her fingers trembled in his.

"No," Cynthe whispered. "There must be something. There *must* be!"

Diello bowed his head again. Cynthe threw herself across Mamee, weeping, while Diello sat there trapped in misery. Without Mamee, he was nothing.

A cold, wet nose burrowed into the curl of his palm. It was the wolf pup, nuzzling him anxiously and whining.

The panic inside Diello receded, and he noticed how hard and raggedly he was breathing. He was aware now that the sun was well down, no more than a fading coral glow among the trees rimming the farmstead. Soon the twilight would fade to darkness. *What if the raiders come back?* With Mamee dead and the *cloigwylie* gone, they had no protection at all.

He had to find Pa.

He touched his sister's back. Cynthe flinched as though he'd struck her.

"What are we to do?" she whispered.

"She'd want us to be smart and safe," Diello said. "She'd want us to be strong. I'm going to look for Pa. You start searching for Amalina."

Cynthe jumped to her feet. "Amie . . ."

"Start looking. We've got to hurry before it gets completely dark."

Cynthe nodded. But her eyes remained huge and desperate. "If they took her—"

"Don't think about that," Diello said. "She's probably hiding. You know Mamee put her in a safe place first if she—if she had time."

Before Cynthe could say anything else, he turned and headed off, pushing himself to move, to take action, to be a man. But of everyone in his family, Mamee was surely the one most likely to survive, which meant . . .

He shoved such thoughts away. Running to the remains of the barn, he was driven back by the heat still radiating off the embers that glowed like goblin eyes in the ashes. There was a terrible stink here. *Burned flesh*, he thought queasily.

Shielding his face with his arm, he retreated a bit, moving around to the east side where the paddock had been. The rails had been broken or tossed on the fire. The posts leaned crazily. Diello rubbed his stinging eyes. Pa was too smart to be caught in a burning building. Even hampered by his withered arm, Pa was tough and strong.

Where would Pa have gone? Diello's gaze swept around as he considered. What would be the *human* reaction? Pa did not panic. He would have a strategy.

During the attack, Pa's first concern would have been to draw the raiders away from Mamee and Amalina. So Diello headed across new field, stumbling over the trampled tender plants that he'd weeded only that morning with such resentment. He felt ashamed of the boy he'd been then, hating his chores and thinking how unfair it was to work on his birthday. Now he had no home, no mother, no—

Stop the self-pity. Find Pa. His father would know what to do—how to track down the raiders and make them pay for what they'd done. Or maybe Pa was wounded, in need of help, too hurt to call out.

Diello choked down a sob. *Just keep looking.*

He found Pa lying face down at the far edge of the field, almost hidden in the muddy ditch between the field and the woods.

All Diello's hope drained away.

With slow, quiet feet, he approached his father. No need to hurry now.

In some way he had known what he would find. The Death Flock had come twice today, and the Death Lord had walked through the farmstead, reaping as he pleased.

By the look of him, Pa had fought hard. His clothing was ripped, and blood stained the ground beneath him. His quarterstaff lay in pieces, and his hands were skinned and raw. He'd fought with his fists before he was brought down.

The twins had long suspected that far in Pa's past, he must have been a warrior, perhaps even a Shieldsman. From the day he'd first placed a quarterstaff in Diello's hand, he'd trained his son in a professional manner, with endless drills and a demand for perfection in footwork and technique. When Cynthe's talent with a bow became evident, Pa had been equally demanding in training her. But despite the old sword rusting in the barn, Pa refused to let Diello handle it. Nor would he discuss swordplay. He never answered questions about how he'd learned to fight, or what had happened to his arm, but he knew weapons all right, even if he refused to carry any blade more lethal than his whittling knife.

Whatever had changed Pa from a fighter to a farmer had

done him no favor this day. Bare fists and a quarterstaff were no match against goblin spears, fangs, and magic fire.

And poor Mamee, no longer possessing the full magic that any Fae should have. Neither of his parents could fend off the attack. It had been too strong, too ferocious. Why had they chosen to live out here, away from others? Most of the farmers lived in the village and tended their fields by day. Mamee always assured him that the *cloigwylie* was strong enough to protect them from anything, but it hadn't stood up to a creature as powerful as a gor-goblin, had it? Still, it should have warned them in time to flee. Pa had drilled each of them—even Amalina—to run and hide in case of goblin attack. So why had his parents stayed and fought? *Why?*

Diello gently rolled his father over. The broken shaft of a goblin spear protruded from Pa's chest. Blood soaked his tunic, the fresh, coppery smell of it flooding Diello's nostrils. The light breeze ruffled the brown tips of Pa's hair.

Cradling his father's shoulders, Diello pressed his hand to Pa's chest above the spear. He felt the weak, erratic thud of a heartbeat against his palm and jumped in surprise.

"Pa!" Diello cried. "Can you look at me? I'm here, Pa. I'm here!"

His father's eyes fluttered and opened. It took a moment for Pa to focus, and as he came around, his face contorted in pain and he whimpered. His hand moved instinctively to the spear, but Diello pushed his fingers away.

"You mustn't touch that," he said. "Pa, do you know me? It's Diello."

Pa's eyes closed again. He puffed out a faint sound.

Diello didn't know what to do. Remove the spear or

staunch the bleeding? He was afraid the first would kill Pa on the spot, yet there was no time to be wasted. Pa had lost too much blood already.

"Don't worry," he said. "I'll get help for you, even if I have to run all the way to the castle."

Pa blinked. His hand twisted in Diello's grip. "Son . . ." Diello could hear a sucking gasp in every breath Pa struggled to take. Blood flecked his lips and he coughed weakly, his head lolling across Diello's arm.

Diello touched his father's mouth, wiping away the blood. "Don't talk, Pa. Just rest. I'll—"

"Listen," Pa gasped.

"But—"

"*Listen*. The deed seal . . ." He fumbled at the neck of his tunic, and Diello slipped his fingers under the leather cord and pulled out the silver disk so his father could touch it.

That seemed to ease some of Pa's distress. He rested, his lungs dragging in those wet, struggling breaths as his fingers lightly stroked the disk. All his life, Diello had never known his father to remove it, not even to sleep or bathe. The deed seal was engraved with the survey marks of the farm and the name of Pa's ancestor who'd originally been granted the land by the king. Pa had told Diello many times that the deed seal must be guarded above everything, for without it, ownership of the farm could never be proven. The royal grant of land meant that Pa did not owe Lord Malques his fealty, did not pay an annual tax, and did not give a tithe to the Church benefice. It was rare to own land with such privileges, and Pa had always been proud of his family's legacy. Only the head of the family had the right to wear the deed seal.

Looking at the disk shining within the weak clasp of Pa's fingers, Diello began to tremble.

"Diello," Pa whispered. "*Listen.*"

Diello met his father's eyes as tears filled his own. "I'm listening, Pa."

"Guard it well."

The tears slid down Diello's cheeks. "I will. I promise, Pa."

"Swear it."

"In the name of the Guardian, I swear to protect the deed seal."

"With your life."

"W-with my life."

Pa sighed, fumbling with the disk. "Put it on."

"But you're going to be all right, Pa, as soon as I—"

"Hush. Put . . . on."

Diello obeyed. The silver disk gleamed pale against the dark surface of his tunic. He touched it, finding the metal warm from Pa's skin. His fingertips traced the engraved marks, and as he did so, a shiver passed through him. Something shining white flitted through his mind.

"*Eirian,*" whispered a voice. But it was all too quick and ghostly for him to understand.

"From me to you, Stephel to . . . Diello," Pa said formally. Then his eyes widened. "Did it touch . . . did you feel . . ."

"Eirian?" Diello guessed, more confused than ever.

His father sighed again, trying to smile. "Good. Guard . . . it . . . well," he murmured. "Eirian must return. We were . . . wrong. Guardian forgive me, so many traps . . . betrayal . . . wrong. I failed Lwyneth. I . . . failed. . . ."

Diello took his father's hand as if he could keep him there. "Pa, don't—"

"Protect your sisters," Pa whispered. "Help them. Be strong . . . for them."

"I will, Pa, but—"

Pa's hand went slack in his. Pa's eyes gazed at something Diello could not see.

"Lwyneth," he moaned. "My Lwyneth . . ."

Then there was only silence.

Diello sat with his father's head in his lap, still gripping Pa's work-callused hand. There was no magic in Pa, no Gift, nothing special about his last breath. Just a gradual cooling of flesh while Diello held him, and a quietness to his body, as if he lay at peace.

When Diello was a little boy, he would sit in Pa's lap by the evening firelight, secure against Pa's muscular chest, and he would press his small hand to his father's large one, comparing the shape of their fingers and the breadth of their palms. Now, by the moonlight, Diello saw that his hands were almost as big as his father's.

And he wept with all his heart.

chapter eight

A nearby rustling sound startled Diello. Reaching for his quarterstaff, he whirled around. But it was only the wolf pup in the shadows beneath the trees. The pup's blue eyes stared intently at Diello.

When Diello lowered his quarterstaff, the scrawny pup came and sat down by his foot.

"You know, don't you?" Diello whispered to him. "You understand how it feels to lose your family."

Somehow, saying the words aloud made it worse, but Diello rubbed his eyes dry with his sleeve. He was through crying. For now.

As he pushed himself to his feet, he felt peculiar and light headed. Then the sensation passed. Pa had placed a heavy responsibility on him and would expect him to do his best. It was up to Diello to take care of his sisters, to deal with the farm and put things to rights. As soon as Cynthe found Amalina—who *had* to be hiding—they would seek safe shelter for the night. Without the *cloigwylie* in place, the woods already seemed darker, more sinister.

He looked toward the trees and felt a stab of fear.

It was hard to leave Pa lying there in the grass and trampled weeds. Very hard. But Pa was too large for him to carry. Diello cut a square from his father's tunic and laid it over Pa's face as a temporary measure of respect.

"May your spirit walk in grace," he murmured and then stumbled away before he could start crying again.

He came upon Cynthe near the stone water trough, counting a handful of arrows as she fitted them one by one in her quiver. There was no sign of their little sister.

"Couldn't you find her?" His voice shook.

Cynthe jumped like a cat before she shot him a furious look and turned back to her arrows, sliding them into place methodically.

Diello clenched his fists, certain he couldn't bear it. "Where is she—"

"They took her," Cynthe said. She slipped another arrow into place.

"What? Are you sure?"

Cynthe shrugged, checking the shaft of another arrow before she put it in the quiver.

He wrested the quiver away from her and flung it on the ground. "Tell me!" he shouted. "Are you sure?"

Cynthe's shoulders went rigid. "Don't interfere. I'm going after her."

She bent and reached for the quiver, but Diello planted his foot on it.

"Careful!" she snapped. "You'll break the arrows."

"Forget the blighted arrows! How do you know they took her? Are you just guessing?"

"I can't find her. That's all," Cynthe admitted.

He caught his breath. "Then you don't know for sure."

"I *do* know! I looked everywhere, but I can't pick up any of her tracks. There's no trace of her, no place that she could be. Just goblin spoor everywhere."

"So we keep searching."

"I tell you I looked—"

Cynthe's voice broke off as she stared at the silver disk hanging from his neck.

Diello said nothing. When Cynthe's face crumpled, he hugged her tightly, feeling her body shaking.

"I held him as he died," Diello said hoarsely. "He made me put on the deed seal and swear to keep it safe. He . . . His last word was Mamee's name. He was calling to her as he died."

Cynthe pressed her face to Diello's shoulder. "I want them back," she whispered. "I want them back!"

"I know."

She straightened and pulled away, rubbing the tears from her dirty face with her sleeve. Her eyes were ablaze. "We'll leave at once. I can follow the spoor until—"

"No."

"We can't abandon Amalina!"

"But you don't know that they have her," Diello said. "Not really. So first we search some more."

"Why won't you listen to me? I did look!"

"Not well enough."

Cynthe kicked at the ground. "So you think she's dead?"

"No. Hiding."

"You're giving up. You'll let them get away with— with—"

"I'm giving up nothing, but we have to be sensible about this."

"Sensible!" She gathered up the rest of her arrows and crammed them in her quiver. "We need to move fast to catch up with them. They can't be that far ahead."

"Go after a horde of goblins? Catch up with a horde of goblins? Then what? Pa fought them hard, Cynthe, and he couldn't beat them. How can we?"

"Diello, they'll *eat* her."

"Don't you think I know that?" he yelled.

Silence fell over the clearing while they glared at each other. The pup paced back and forth, watching them anxiously.

Diello pulled his temper back under control. He couldn't let Cynthe make him so upset that he stopped using his wits. He'd had only *two* sightings of the Death Flock today, and he believed that Amalina was still alive.

"If the goblins took her," he said, "even if they carried her, wouldn't there be some tracks? You said you found none. *None*, Cynthe. That means Mamee protected her, hid her maybe with magic so she can't be seen. We have to puzzle out where she could be. Where exactly did you search?"

Cynthe gestured hopelessly at the destruction around them. "The hollow tree, the barn, the paddock, the cistern, the garden, the poultry house, the orchard. And part of the old field." She pointed north. "They left in that direction. I don't have to seek goblin tracks in the dark. Their spoor is stinky enough to follow."

Staring at where she pointed, Diello wanted to agree with Cynthe, to let her pick up the trail and lead him into the woods. But . . . how dark it looked inside the woods, so dark he couldn't see much past the hollow chesternut, so dark and silent the forest might have been emptied of everything that normally lived there.

Transfixed, he took a step forward, thinking, *Cynthe is right and I am wrong. Cynthe is right. She's right. She's right.*

The pup shot between his feet, tripping him. As Diello regained his balance, the deed seal swung on its cord, thumping against his chest. He started to tuck it under his tunic for safekeeping. The instant he touched the cool silver, a strong tingle ran up his fingers into his hand and wrist. He felt shivers through his arms and legs.

Someone was using magic on him, trying to lure him into the woods!

Tightening his grip on the disk, he felt its strange power flowing up his arm and spreading through his body. His vision grew stronger, despite the closing twilight. His hearing, always keen, grew even more so. His very bones thrummed with energy, and the shivers stopped. He didn't understand how the disk could have magic or whether Pa had known, but he couldn't wonder about that now.

Cynthe turned to the north and walked forward a couple of steps.

"No, Cynthe! It's the gor-goblin playing with our minds, trying to control us. They don't have Amalina. They want us to follow them. It's a trap."

"You're daft."

"I'm not." He remembered what the gor-goblin had whispered to him in the village: *Her spawn.* The gor-goblin had known Mamee.

Diello glanced toward his mother's body. How could the gor-goblin know his mother? And the creature had made him afraid today, trying to send him scuttling home.

To follow us? To find Mamee? That trick had failed, but the goblins had found the farmstead anyway.

Now the gor-goblin was trying to trick him and Cynthe again. *Why? What did he want?*

"It had to be the gor-goblin we saw today," Diello said. "This was no regular raid for food and money. They didn't want our things. They've spoiled most of the food deliberately, to drive us away from here."

"What are you talking about?" Cynthe asked. "Diello—"

He pressed the deed seal against her palm, not letting her pull away. He didn't know if she felt the same tingling sensation, but he saw the panic lessen in her eyes.

"They won't trick me again," she said, giving him a nod.

"I'll find Amie," Diello said. "You look for food. See if there's anything left in the garden. Rest awhile. And stop using your injured arm so much. I'll be back as quick as I can."

chapter nine

h e started his search with the massive hollow tree that was the twins' favorite spot. All his life, two gigantic trees had stood on this side of the farmstead, both planted by Pa's ancestor generations ago. One was the walner that had been felled by last night's lightning. The other was the chesternut, with low branches that spread out wide and broad to support its huge canopy. Its trunk was hollow at the main fork, like a huge bowl. Pa had often muttered that someday it would fall in a storm, yet here it stood, as stalwart as ever.

Perhaps a good omen?

"Amie?" he called. "Amie, where are you?"

There was no answer, and he dared not call again. He stood with his palm resting lightly on the rough bark of the chesternut and closed his eyes, seeking any good magic still in use. The woods seemed to crowd closer; the air was hotter, the breeze stronger, the mingled smells of goblin stink and smoke more intense. But there was Fae magic still active— the faintest, slightest thread of it . . . *there.*

He hurried toward the creek. Amalina was forbidden to go near the water by herself. But where else could a three-year-old hide? He slithered down the bank to an old willuth tree leaning precariously over the water, its supple branches trailing across the surface. Some of the tree's knobby roots had been exposed by the gradual erosion of the bank, and under the weathered roots was a shallow cavelike hole further excavated by Mamee. She had lined the sides and bottom with flat stones. That's where she kept her milk and butter cool, stored in pottery crocks surrounded by pans of cold creek water.

Peering in, Diello saw only the shadowy outlines of crocks and jugs. He fought down disappointment and made himself concentrate. Nothing here was smashed. The raiders had not come here.

The woods on the other side of the creek were quiet and dim. He heard the water rushing over the rocks. All he smelled was damp soil, leaves, and cool milk.

He tried to summon Sight, even though he wasn't sure how to do so. Right now, he *had* to control it. He had to see the truth.

Sight. He channeled all his raw emotions into this one urgent need. The deed seal, lying against his skin, grew warm, sending its tingling magic into his bones. The sensation was so strong it felt like pain, and yet it didn't really hurt. At the same time, he felt so light he almost didn't seem to exist.

Amalina, he thought, staring into the hole until his eyes burned and ached. And then, between one blink and the next, the illusion flickered away.

There she lay, curled among the dairy crocks.

She was sleeping, grasping an object in one chubby hand, the other tucked beneath her cheek. Her clothes and face were filthy, her lips greasy probably from eating butter.

A dried ring of milk encircled her rosy mouth. Her blonde hair rioted about her head, with one long curl falling across her brow.

She was safe. He had found her, and she was safe.

He pulled her out, waking her as he did so. She screamed before he clamped a hand over her mouth. Gathering her close, he whispered urgently, "Hush, Amie. It's me. You're all right now. Don't cry. It's me."

She clung to his neck, weeping.

The hiding spell that had rendered her invisible melted away, and with it went the last trace of Mamee's presence.

"Del," Amalina said, her voice choked with tears. "Del. Del!"

"I know, little one," he said, stroking her curls while his heart sent up a prayer of gratitude. "I'm sorry I scared you. I've been looking for you everywhere."

She wouldn't talk to him, just clung like a limpet, so he kept murmuring to her, his words meaningless but soothing. Eventually she lay more calmly against him, her small body heavy with trust and exhaustion.

The object she'd been holding dropped from her fingers and rolled across his foot. Picking it up, he saw that it was one of his bird whistles that Pa had whittled for a past birthday.

He felt a rush of loss, realizing that all his other belongings, all the things he'd known and cared about, were gone—burned up, stolen, or broken. Amalina made a dive for the whistle, but Diello kept a firm grasp on it.

"Were you playing with my whistles today?"

Amalina nodded her curly head. "Uh-huh. Didn't hurt them. I was careful, like I promised."

"You're a good girl, Amie."

"Very good. I like this one best 'cause it's *your* favorite."

It was the blue marpet, with its sharp tone that rose high before falling to a trilling coo. It had been made for his tenth birthday, and Diello still considered it Pa's best creation. Now, thanks to Amalina, it was safe in his pocket, like having a piece of Pa with him.

Diello kissed Amalina's greasy cheek, making her giggle. "Thank you," he said.

She patted his face. "My doll's all burned up, hotter 'n' hotter. Did you see the fire, Del?"

"I saw it." He hoisted her higher in his arm. "I think I saw Dolly, too. Let's go get her."

"Don't want her!" Amalina shrieked, stiffening in his arms as he carried her up the creek bank. She struck at him with her fists. "She's burned up. Don't want nothin' burned up!"

"Hush," he said, catching her hands. He wondered how much of the devastation Amalina had witnessed before Mamee hid her away. "Dolly isn't burned, but she needs mending."

Dolly was filthy and headless, but when he showed the tattered body to his sister, Amalina grabbed it and pressed it to her face. Her wails rose into the evening air despite his attempts to shush her.

Cynthe came at a run, dropping the vegetables she'd been scavenging from the garden. "Where was she? Is she all right? Did they hurt her?"

"She seems fine. Just scared, I think."

"Let me hold her." Cynthe pulled Amalina from Diello and soothed her while the wolf pup frisked at their feet. "Hush, Amie. Hush. Look at our new friend."

Amalina smiled, enchanted with the wolf. "It's a puppy!" she said. "Is it mine?"

"No. He's our *friend*," Cynthe said, setting Amalina on the ground so the pup could sniff her fingers. "He belongs to himself."

"What's his name?"

"We haven't decided yet."

Amalina petted the pup. "I want to name him Star."

"I like Fuzzytop."

"No," Diello said. "Those names are stupid. Don't make fun of him that way."

"I'm hungry," Amalina announced. "Where's Mamee?"

Diello flinched and met Cynthe's eyes. "Keep her away from the—"

Cynthe silenced him with a nod. Picking Amalina up, she swung around and started walking back to where she'd dropped the vegetables. "Look, Amie. I found tender marrows no bigger than my finger."

"Don't want marrow," Amalina declared. She began to cry again, a low grizzling whine of fatigue. "Want Mamee to make me 'lary sauce with walner nuts and bitty seeds."

There was no point trying to explain that Mamee would never again cook sweet, butter-rich camelary sauce for glazing her cakes. Diello scrounged some unripened pears, and they ate those and some meager raw vegetables without any appetite, afraid to cook over the lingering patches of goblin-fire and too cautious to build a fire of their own.

A gust of icy wind hit them, tearing at their hair and clothes, and swirling ashes, dirt, and bits of grass into the air. Shielding his face from the stinging debris, Diello staggered back, nearly lifted off his feet. Cynthe hugged Amalina, protecting the child's face with a fold of her tunic. The pup had disappeared.

Then, as rapidly as it had come, the gust was gone. Shivering, Diello lowered his arms and shook the dirt from his clothing. His legs were tingling, and the hair rose on his arms, prickling inside his sleeves. "Was that her—"

"Yes, the Death Wind," Cynthe said breathlessly. She put Amalina down. "It's come for her, and we don't have her platform ready."

Diello stood watching as his twin ran to the paddock, where pieces of broken fence rail lay scattered like a giant's game of spillikins. He knew what she intended to do. A tide of misery welled up inside him. He wasn't ready for Mamee's Death Wind to take her away. It had come much too soon.

But that first gust was only a warning, and there wasn't much time to prepare her. A proper funeral for Mamee would be to place her unshrouded body atop a tall wooden platform in an open place. As Fae remains became dust, the wind carried them back to Embarthi, the land of the Fae people. While the Death Wind blew, her family should sit together quietly, speaking the ritualized words of respect and blessing. And when the wind ended, there would be nothing left of her—not even her bones.

From what Mamee had taught them, traditionally the

Death Wind didn't arrive for a day, sometimes two or three, after the passing. *What is the hurry now?* he wondered angrily.

"Diello!" Cynthe called. "Help me!"

Amalina clutched Diello's leg. "Hold me. Hold me!"

He knew the child was tired, still hungry, and too little to understand. He pulled her hands away. "I can't carry you right now, Amie. Go into the garden and wait for us."

"No! I want to help."

"You can't."

She stamped her foot. "I want to help! I want Mamee! I want Pa!"

Another gust of wind—this one warm—buffeted them, swirling around so that Diello could hardly keep his balance. "*Lwyneth*," it called, the voice of his nightmares.

Who was sending the Talking Wind now? He wanted to curse it, to yell it was too late, but he saved his breath. From the opposite direction, another blast of chilling air struck him. This time, the Death Wind didn't gust and die down. It blew steadily, with increasing force.

"Diello, hurry!" Cynthe called.

He saw her dragging a board over to their mother's body, which lay beneath a blanket. Amalina was still whining, pulling at his tunic.

"Come on," he said, grabbing her hand and hurrying her along. He put her inside the garden and propped the broken gate in place. Amalina stood on the other side, peering at him and crying.

Harsh, icy wind whipped around him. Whether he liked it or not, Diello knew that he and Cynthe had scant time now to say the proper rites over Mamee.

"Stay there," he told Amalina sternly. "Don't come to us."

Amalina gave the broken gate a push, knocking it down. "I don't have to do what you say!"

"Yes, you do." Seeing the pup's fuzzy head pop up from beneath a bush, Diello pointed. "Look! There's the wolf. Stay with him, Amie, and I'll be back as quick as I can."

He left her squatting next to the pup, petting him and chattering. Racing across the clearing, Diello joined his twin as she was dragging another board up beside the first.

"One more board," Cynthe said, panting.

Diello snagged her arm and held her back, shaking his head. "No need."

"But it's not finished."

"We're too late!" he shouted over the howl of the Death Wind. It beat at them, billowing through his clothing as though to tear it to shreds, and pulling Cynthe's long hair from her braid so that blonde strands streamed out from her head. "The rites—"

"Say them quickly!" she yelled.

"But I don't *know* them."

"Say something. Say the prayer to the Guardian that she taught us."

Holding hands, Diello and Cynthe started to kneel at their mother's side when lightning cracked above them, splitting the heavens with such searing ferocity that Diello cried out. Purple spots blurred his vision as thunder boomed, shaking the ground.

Cynthe said something he couldn't hear, then he felt her hands urging him up. Competing winds, one freezing and one warm, pushed him this way and that. Instinctively he clung to Cynthe, using her weight to help him keep his balance. She was doing the same.

"What is this?" she shouted.

He heard the hissing crackle of more lightning and ducked to one side, pulling her with him. The bolt hit the ground with a bang.

"Let's get out of here!" he yelled.

"Where?"

"Our tree!"

"Too dangerous!" Cynthe shouted. "Get Amalina!"

But they ran no more than a step or two before another bolt of lighting speared down near the chesternut. For a moment Diello thought it had hit the tree, but when the bright light and noise faded, he saw that the old tree was still standing.

By then, Amalina was running to him. She flung her arms around his leg. "Del! I'm scared!"

He lifted her, letting her cling to his neck. He wanted to reassure her, but he couldn't even reassure himself.

"Why is this happening?" Cynthe asked, looking up. "This is no normal storm."

Diello looked up, too. There were no clouds in the sky; the stars and double moons were shining clearly. No, the warm wind, thunder, and lightning came from another source. *Were the storm and the Death Wind fighting each other?*

As if hearing his thoughts, a shadowy figure appeared in the air. It looked like the Death Wind was transforming itself into a creature with long, reaching fingers. It was so ghastly a creature that Diello averted his eyes. Intense cold flowed from it, nearly freezing his bones. *Don't look!*

"*Lwyneth!*" it sighed, its voice flat and toneless. "*I come for Lwyneth!*"

"*Let Lwyneth bide!*" crackled a deeper voice—a living one—through the thunder.

Diello looked at his mother's body. Cynthe had pinned the blanket over Mamee with sticks shoved into the ground. The Death Wind was plucking at the wet shroud, trying to rip it away.

"Stay here," he said to Cynthe. Handing over Amalina, he ran to his mother's side.

Somewhere in the darkness, the wolf pup began to howl. Cynthe called to him, and the pup fell silent.

Pushing against the wind, Diello reached out to yank the blanket away and release Mamee's dust. Rites or no rites, at least she would be able to go home to Embarthi.

A bolt of lightning struck just a few strides from him, and as he watched, it transformed into a narrow column of swirling light, hovering directly over Mamee's body. The column broadened and spread until dazzling radiance encompassed Diello. He cringed back, raising his arm as a shield.

"*Let Lwyneth lie!*" commanded that deep crackling voice in the storm. "*She lived by her choice. So now has she died by it.*"

Diello squinted through his fingers, trying to see who spoke, but the light was blinding. "Who are you?" he called out. "I can't see!"

The brilliance dimmed slightly, and a face appeared. It had the angular cheekbones and pointed chin of a Fae. Its eyes were as cold and white as snow. It might have been carved from purest marble. There was no mercy in it, no kindness.

"Who are you?" Diello asked again. "In Lwyneth's name, I demand an answer!"

"I am Clevn, mage-chancellor to the queen. Who are *you*, to question me?"

"Diello, Lwyneth's son!"

The pale eyes lost their stoniness. "A son!"

Diello felt his body rise off the ground as though the mage-chancellor was drawing him upward, then a sudden force slammed him down hard. Diello fell sprawling, the air knocked from his lungs. The stern, forbidding face and the intense light vanished.

"Diello!" It was Cynthe beside him. She tugged him upright, and he sat weak and dazed, leaning against her. She touched his face, his hands, his throat. "Diello, can you hear me? Diello!"

He blinked, realizing that both the storm and the Death Wind had gone as well. The air lay calm now, natural and warm with summer heat. He noticed also that he was splattered with dirt. His hair was stiff with it, and it filled the folds of his clothing. There was even dirt in his mouth.

Grimacing, he spat it out and wiped his mouth with the back of his hand. Only then did he see that the blanket still covered Mamee's body. The ground around her had been scoured clean until it was as hard and smooth as plaster. The blanket shroud should have been ripped away by the Death Wind, but it was exactly as Cynthe had placed it. A terrible feeling of failure sank through him.

"It's gone," he whispered. "Gone. It didn't take her."

"Diello, are you all right?" Cynthe asked. "Do you know my name? Look at me and tell me how many ears do I have."

He shifted his gaze to his sister. "I don't care how many ears you have, but you've got six warts on the end of your nose."

She stood, letting him get to his feet unaided. "I guess you'll live. But what happened? You were shouting words I couldn't understand. What did you see? Who were you talking to?"

He didn't answer. "Maybe it will come back," he muttered.

"What will come back?"

"Her Death Wind."

Cynthe's face grew sad. "No, I don't think so. Why didn't you pull away the blanket so she could go?"

He wasn't taking the blame for this. "You didn't see the face?"

"What face?"

"The face in the lightning, in the storm! It fought the Death Wind and drove it back. It wouldn't let me help her go." His voice broke, and he rubbed his face wearily. "It said she had died by her choice, and it wouldn't let her go."

The last of the goblin-fire was flickering out, the evil flames sinking lower in the ashes. In the dwindling light, Cynthe had become a shadow.

"Who was it?" she asked.

"He was Fae. He looked very old."

"Are you making this up?"

Diello scowled at her.

"All right." Cynthe shrugged. "It isn't fair that you have Sight and I don't. But this doesn't make sense. The Death Wind always takes the Fae home to Embarthi, no matter how far away they go. Mamee wouldn't have lied about that, would she?"

Diello had no answers. It seemed pointless to speculate, but he couldn't stop himself. All their lives, he and Cynthe had been trying to solve the mystery of their mother's past. And now her death had raised even more questions. "If she were exiled," he said thoughtfully, "doesn't that mean she couldn't go home?"

"Not ever?" Cynthe shook her head. "That's cruel, Diello. Not even an enemy should stop her Death Wind. It's wrong! Are you sure it wasn't a goblin face you saw in that vision of yours?"

"It was Fae. He said his name was Clevn."

Cynthe gasped. "The name Mamee mentioned today before we went to Wodesley."

"Mage-chancellor to the queen."

"What queen?"

"The Queen of Embarthi, I suppose."

Cynthe's eyes widened as she gnawed at her lip. "Do you think—"

Diello was tired of guesses. "We'll build Mamee's platform anyway," he decided. "There's time now to do it right. And we'll bring her flowers each day as she fades. That's the best we can—"

Amalina screamed. A cry of sheer terror.

Diello glimpsed his little sister running away toward the creek. Her scream rang out again.

Cynthe was already racing after her. "Amie, wait! Don't—"

Her voice chopped off in mid-sentence, and Diello saw why. An orange glow was flickering through the woods, here, there, on all sides. It was closing in on the farmstead, coming fast.

"Fire!" Diello shouted. "Come back! The woods are on fire!"

Cynthe and Amalina kept going. Diello started to shout again, but suddenly he couldn't seem to breathe.

It wasn't fire coming toward them, but torches bobbing through the trees.

Torches carried by goblins.

chapter ten

iello didn't know he could run so fast, but he nearly flew, catching up with Cynthe just as she caught up with Amalina. The child was still screaming in terror. Cynthe pressed Amalina's face against her stomach to muffle the cries.

Diello understood. Screaming could excite the goblins as much as the smell of fresh blood. "Amalina!" he said, trying to use the same stern tone as Pa.

She turned her tear-streaked face to his. Her mouth stretched open to scream again.

"Stop it!" he said gruffly, pointing his finger at her exactly as Pa would.

She grew quiet, hiccupping, her breathing ragged.

Diello could hear the goblins now. Large and small, half-glimpsed shapes in the shadows and torchlight, they ran in a curious, hobbling shuffle that covered ground rapidly. As they came, they sang a hoarse, guttural chant. Something in the sound carried an old type of magic—raw and elemental—and Diello felt the chant resonate inside him. It made him want to stand still and let them capture him.

Desperately, he shook it off.

Picking Amalina up, he repeated to Cynthe what Pa had once told him, "Run for the creek. Goblins are awful swimmers. They won't follow us into the water."

"It's not deep enough unless we go in near the—"

"Just do it!"

They ran in that direction, but more goblins emerged from the woods to the east, cutting them off.

Goblins were spreading out, trying to surround them. A faint whimper from Amalina made Diello realize that he was nearly squeezing her in half.

"Split up," Cynthe breathed in his ear. She took Amalina from him, shifting her bow to her other hand, and ran as fast as her long legs would carry her.

A shrill yell rose from the goblins, but before they could surge after her, Diello jumped up and down like a demented thing and waved his quarterstaff in the air.

He yelled, "Bet you can't catch me!"

Then he lowered his head and ran for the old field, trying to lead as many as he could away from Cynthe. His plan was still to reach the creek if possible. The water would help mask his scent if he dropped out of sight, and the current was swift enough to interfere with goblin magic, although it wouldn't protect him from a well-aimed spear. As he ran, his back was itching from the certainty that steel was going to pierce his spine and lungs at any instant.

Diello dodged and lunged and yelled to enrage them more. He saw that he couldn't make the creek now, for a cluster of laughing goblins blocked the footbridge, and others were stationed along the bank. Diello angled toward the barn, thinking he could gain on them as they circled the hot ashes. But the goblins came bounding straight through the burned site, kicking up ashes and scattering smoking timbers in their wake.

That's where they caught up with him, talons snagging his tunic. He fought, his fists and quarterstaff flailing madly. But even as he wrenched free, he found himself cut off by another goblin, one of the shortest breeds called bloidy-goblins. This creature's face was mottled green and tan, lips curled back to bare yellow, crooked fangs.

A second goblin closed in, and the pair began to circle him. Diello exhaled, planted his feet, and swung his quarterstaff like a club. He knocked the bloidy-goblin off his feet, sending him tumbling backward into a third one coming up to join the rest.

"Hah!" Diello shouted, but his triumph was short-lived. His tunic was gripped from behind. He fought the instinct to pull away and instead threw his weight backward, crashing into his assailant. At the same time, he jabbed hard with his quarterstaff and connected with something that said, "Ooof!"

The hand upon him fell away, and Diello spun to strike quick and hard again, the quarterstaff swinging and reversing deftly in his hands. Another goblin went sprawling, and another, but one more tackled him from behind, clawing at his back and shoulders. Ignoring the pain of those talons, he struggled to shake off this new opponent and even tried to slam himself backward against a tree. But his attacker was too wily for that old trick.

He felt teeth nipping at the back of his neck and lifted both his arms over his head in an attempt to pound the goblin with his quarterstaff. Talons gripped his throat. Diello froze, but the claws pressed harder, five pricks on his jugular, warning that his life could be ripped from him between one breath and the next.

The fight died in him. Diello felt the goblin's weight pressing on his shoulder. He heard him hiss and chortle in glee. His captor's fetid breath fanned across Diello's ear and cheek. He flinched once. The deadly talons dug in, breaking his skin and sending a trickle of blood down his throat. He forced himself to remain absolutely, unnaturally still.

Fragments of memory filled his mind, disjointed at first, then with more clarity. Pa had taught him what to do if he were ever ambushed by a goblin.

Rule number one was to avoid goblins at all costs. To be smart enough not to get into this kind of situation.

Diello frowned. That was a stupid rule.

Rule number two was to remain calm and quiet. Strong emotions, such as anger or fear, gave off scents that could make a goblin bite.

Rule number three was to spill no blood. The smell of Faelin blood was said to drive goblins wild.

Rule number four was to hum. When you were as quiet and as calm as possible, you were supposed to hum in a low, monotonous tone that—if pitched right—could actually mesmerize some goblin breeds, especially the small bloidy-goblins.

However, the goblin that had caught him was bigger than a bloidy-goblin, and all these instructions from Pa were nothing like reality. For one thing, he couldn't slow his thundering heart no matter how much he tried. Panic kept bubbling up into his throat like a scream, and he wasn't sure he could silence it much longer. For another, his captor had deliberately made him bleed, and now more and more goblins of various breeds, colors, and sizes were surrounding him. They clacked their talons, hissing and chattering in their language. Jostling and snapping their teeth, they stared at him hungrily. It was only a matter of moments before his captor tore out his throat. Just one bite and he would be ripped to pieces.

Diello tried to hum, but his throat was so dry he couldn't utter more than a squeak. Swallowing hard, he tried again, but no one seemed to hear him over the noise.

Then his captor was knocked aside, and Diello found himself flanked by two goblins as tall as he was. They were clad only in loincloths that revealed their scarred, scaled hides and a ridge of cartilage projecting from their spines. They were all knobby bone and sinew, as ugly as a nightmare, and twice as scary as the smaller goblins. Both had eyes filled with hate. *Gor-goblins*, he thought, tightening his grip on his quarterstaff.

One of them struck. As quick as he was to lift his quarterstaff in defense, Diello wasn't quick enough. The weapon was wrested from his grasp and flung aside. As Diello's arms were pinned behind him, the other gor-goblin—the taller of the two and the color of mud—drew a black-bladed dagger still sticky with blood. The creature brought the point closer and closer to Diello's face until his eyes crossed. He shut them, bracing himself for death.

The point of the dagger pricked his brow right above

his nose. Despite his fear, Diello opened his eyes. From this angle, the filthy dagger looked enormous. All the gor-goblin had to do was drive it deep into his brain. Diello stared, too scared even to tremble.

The gor-goblin laughed while the others around them howled and shrieked encouragement.

But Diello didn't die.

Instead, he was marched back across the farmstead, escorted by most of the horde. The two gor-goblins kept a firm hold on his arms, while the others swarmed close, jabbering and grunting in triumph. Some of them prodded him with their spears, and if he stumbled they all shouted with glee.

He didn't understand where they were taking him or why they hadn't killed him already. He supposed they intended to torture him first.

Pa had taught him never to let fear control him, so he tried hard now to stay alert and in command of himself. *I can be as icy cold as Mamee at her most furious. I can be as calm and brave as Pa.*

He wasn't dead yet, so he still might get a chance to break away. At least his sacrifice had let his sisters escape. If Cynthe stayed smart and careful, she and Amalina would be all right.

A quarrel broke out, and Diello saw the bloidy-goblin that had caught him shouting in a fury and being beaten about the head and shoulders by one of the gor-goblins. A mid-sized goblin, with a tall crest of hair atop a bald skull, was also shouting, pointing at Diello, and slapping his chest repeatedly.

Diello realized that they were arguing over who had actually caught him. Maybe they were arguing over who got to eat him. *I can't give up.*

They took him to the cistern, where torches on stakes had been stabbed into the ground, forming a rough ring around the water supply. Diello saw a tall figure clad in a long, hooded cloak. This individual seemed to be sniffing the stones of the cistern's walls, muttering to himself all the while. When Diello's captors pushed him closer to the ring of torches and the cloaked figure, he dug in his feet.

His resistance sent up a roar of satisfaction. Diello flushed, angry at himself for showing fear.

The gor-goblin with the black-bladed dagger called out, and the cloaked one spun around. The cloak was so thin and light that it floated and swirled with his movements before settling down around his legs once more. Diello could not see a face inside the dark hood, but he was conscious of being studied closely. He stared back—making himself remember Pa and Mamee lying broken and bloody—and kept his expression wooden.

Then the cloaked figure pushed back the hood, revealing cruel red eyes in a face of greenish-gold scales. Rootlike knobs spiked from his narrow skull, and a wedge of cartilage grew out of the back of his head to protect his neck. His nose was as long and pointed as a carpenter's awl.

This was the gor-goblin they'd encountered in the village square, the one that had tried to trick them into running home. He was taller than the rest of his horde and markedly silent. All the goblins seemed to be talking to him at the same time. At last the cloaked one lifted his hand, and they quieted, bowing their heads and shifting their feet uneasily.

Diello had never heard of goblin breeds allying themselves like this. The breeds stayed separate and usually fought one another as much as they fought Fae and humans. *Maybe it's the start of another invasion,* he thought anxiously, like the Great War that old Griffudd had told him about.

Griffudd was Faelin, a gray-bearded peddler who visited the farmstead once a year in early spring. Diello's parents, so cautious around strangers, so aloof from the villagers in Wodesley, always welcomed Griffudd as friend and guest. Diello remembered talks late into the night, "adult" talks that he and Cynthe were excluded from, but Griffudd also took time to spin legends for the twins, telling them about the Great War several generations ago, when the goblins had united and crossed Antrasia to invade Embarthi. They were driven back, however, and the goblins and the Fae had fought savagely on Antrasin soil, using the shires as their battleground. "That is why," whispered Griffudd, "many Antrasins dislike both Fae and Faelin now." Worse, after the Fae had retreated to Embarthi, the angry goblins had wreaked revenge on Antrasia—pillaging, killing, and mutilating both human and Faelin victims. They had taken skins as trophies to their gorlord—their supreme leader.

Diello took another look at that dark, supple cloak and shuddered.

One black talon crooked, and Diello was shoved forward. The gor-goblin studied him as before. Then the creature unleashed a guttural cough that Diello recognized as laughter.

"So," the creature hissed, "we meet once more, little

Faelin spawn." His voice was raspy, but he spoke Antrasin fluently. "You were clever to escape me in the village. You will not be so clever again." The gor-goblin leaned close and licked Diello's throat with a narrow, darting tongue. "There is no iron here to protect you."

Diello said nothing. In his mind, he prayed to the Guardian.

The gor-goblin flung back the folds of his cloak, revealing broad gold bracelets on each bony wrist and a collar of thick beaten gold at his scarred neck. He carried a mace, but instead of the usual iron bludgeon, his weapon was made of a skull stuck on the end of a polished bone shaft. At his waist hung a splendid, bejeweled scabbard, oddly empty. *Stolen loot*, Diello thought. The gor-goblin was clad only in a loincloth that hung halfway down his knobby legs and the long skin cloak.

Human skins. Faelin skins. Maybe my skin, soon.

Sitting before the hearth fire, snug and secure with his parents exchanging quiet glances over his head, Diello had thought Griffudd was merely spinning yarns for children. He'd never believed that goblins actually wore such garments.

He believed it now.

Can this be the gorlord of the Great War? he wondered. *Do goblins live that long?* But why would a gorlord—a sort of king—be raiding farmsteads like some ordinary bandit?

Diello considered the devastating destruction of his home, the deaths of almost every living thing, and he knew this wasn't about plunder. This monster was no bandit, but he *was* a murderer.

Great Guardian, Diello prayed, *guide me to find vengeance against these creatures and put my parents' souls to rest.*

"You will not speak," the leader declared, grabbing Diello's attention. The gor-goblin clicked his talons impatiently. "You fear me, perhaps? Fear me enough to lock your tongue inside your mouth? I smell your terror. I hear your heart beating faster and faster in its fragile cage of ribs. Do you know that nothing tastes better than the still-beating heart of a human child?"

"I'm not human," Diello said.

The leader spat at him, and only Diello's quick reflexes caused the spittle to miss his face. It hit the ground and sizzled in the grass. Flames flickered off the tips of the leader's claws.

"Mongrel! You *dare* boast of your Fae blood! You *dare* flaunt it to me!"

"I'm Faelin," Diello said with dignity. "I'm not ashamed of it."

The gor-goblin with the black dagger twisted Diello's arm behind him. The agony in his arm kept him from hearing what the leader shouted. Then his arm was yanked straight, and that hurt almost as much. Gritting his teeth and blinking back tears, Diello struggled not to utter a sound.

The leader watched him. "Defy me, and you are punished. You understand this?"

Reluctantly, still trying to catch his breath, Diello nodded.

"Now, spawn of Lwyneth the Betrayer, you will tell me—"

"Don't call her that!" Diello said. "You've no right to speak of her that way."

"Silence!" the goblin leader roared. He swung his skull-mace at Diello's shoulder, smashing him to the ground.

Diello lay there as waves of pain throbbed through his shoulder and chest. He tried to draw on his anger to stay strong. But it hurt so badly that if he could have found the will to move, he would have curled up into a ball.

They dragged him to his feet.

The leader's fangs gleamed yellow in the torchlight. "I am Brezog, gorlord of all goblinkind! I speak of the Betrayer as I please. You, Faelin mongrel, have no right to speak to *me*, unless I permit."

It's true, Diello thought. *Everything Griffudd said is true.*

Only what was the gorlord doing *here*? And how did this creature know Mamee by name? Was Brezog who she'd been hiding from all these years?

"I am Brezog!" the leader shouted again, holding his skull-mace aloft. "I slew Lwyneth and her consort, Stephel. I have tasted her blood and found it sour and foul, like that of all Fae demons. No more will she be called Lwyneth the Betrayer, but Lwyneth the Slain. I claim her kill! And you, spawn of her body, will tell me where she has hidden the—"

"You killed my mother!" Cynthe shouted.

Diello twisted around. There, behind the goblins, just at the edge of the torchlight, stood his twin. Aiming her bow in flawless archer stance, she released her arrow with a twang, sending it straight at Brezog.

chapter eleven

Brezog lifted one claw-tipped hand, and the arrow burst into flames just before it reached him. Crumbling to ashes, it fell harmlessly to the ground.

Roaring, the goblin horde swarmed Cynthe. She vanished in their midst, screaming as they pulled her down.

"Cynthe!" Diello tried to run to her, but he was held back. "Cynthe!" he yelled frantically.

Kicking and straining, she was half-dragged, half-carried and shoved to her knees beside Diello. She'd lost her bow and quiver. Fresh blood stained the bandage on her arm. With battle fire raging in her eyes, she spat insults around her with such vehemence that even Brezog flinched.

Diello was relieved to see her alive and still in one piece, but just then he could have cheerfully boxed her ears. Why hadn't she stayed hidden and safe? What did she think she could accomplish as a prisoner with him? And where had she stashed Amalina?

His feet were kicked out from under him. He tried to rise, only to be shoved down again. Shoulder to shoulder, both twins were forced to kneel at Brezog's bony feet.

"You addlepate!" Diello whispered furiously to Cynthe. "What's wrong with you? Why didn't you stay out of sight?"

"Shut up," she whispered back. "That thing's got to die for what it did to—"

The skull-mace smashed down between them.

Brezog studied Cynthe a moment. "Female," he said dismissively and turned to Diello. He hoisted Diello to his feet by his aching shoulder.

Diello had to bite the inside of his cheek to keep from whimpering. With Cynthe there, he was more determined than ever to show no weakness to this enemy.

"Let us go!" Diello shouted. "We don't serve you. Let us go!"

"You squirm like a mouse, Faelin morsel. Do you want your arm torn off? Do you want the marrow sucked from your broken bones? BE STILL!"

The command smashed through Diello's mind. *Magic*, he thought, trying to resist.

"Sword!" the gorlord shouted in a rage. "Where is it?"

"What sword?" Diello and his sister asked in unison.

Diello was shaken so hard he thought his head might snap off his neck.

"Fool!" Brezog snarled. "Do you wish to die like Lwyneth?"

Before Diello could answer, pain and a blinding flash of white exploded inside his head. Fire and chills coursed through his skull, and when he managed to open his eyes he found himself wobbling on his feet, still being shaken by the gorlord. His head was throbbing with spikes of pain. Somewhere, Cynthe was screaming.

"Sword!" Brezog demanded. "Must I break your skull to have my answer? Where is the sword?"

Diello blinked fuzzily. There was Pa's old broken sword, the one with the hilt snapped off. It hung in the barn, where the iron in its rusting blade wouldn't bother Mamee. Pa had used it to cut twine. Diello couldn't imagine what a gorgoblin would want with it.

"Speak!" Brezog commanded, the magic resonating painfully in Diello's bones. "The sword!"

Hate boiled up inside Diello, stronger and more violent than anything he'd ever felt before. He lifted his throbbing head and focused on the ugly gorlord.

"You killed my mother."

This time, when Brezog hit him, the pain exploded in his jaw, smashing his lip against his teeth. Diello spat out a mouthful of blood. It tasted horrid. Already he could feel his lip swelling, and it hurt nearly as much as his head.

"Fool!" Brezog shouted. "Eirian! *Eirian!* Where is it?"

The silver disk beneath Diello's tunic flashed warm against his skin. A fresh tingle of its magic ran through him, clearing his head a bit. *Pa died for Eirian. Whatever it is, I'll die for it, too. I promised.*

"Better," Brezog said, watching him closely. "Your face no longer lies. Now, be quick. Where is the sword?"

"You killed my parents! Be cursed for what you've done. I'll tell you nothing!"

The gorlord lunged at Diello, but Cynthe jumped between them, deflecting his blow. The other goblins jerked her back, pushing her roughly to the ground, but she jumped up again.

"We're farmers!" she yelled. "We don't have any swords!"

Brezog stared at her through narrowed eyes. Diello feared the gorlord might kill his twin on the spot.

"She's right," Diello said. His swollen lip slurred his words. "We don't know an'thing 'bout some sword."

The gorlord's eyes glittered at him. "Lies," he hissed. "For years I have hunted, sending my spies to follow a trail gone very cold." He shook the empty scabbard. "This is Eirian's and fits no other blade. Can you guess what it has cost me in bribes, in blood, to obtain? Yet it alone is not enough! Sword and scabbard must be together! I have searched across this land, finding nothing but silence and secrets until now. An Antrasin, weakened by drink, spilled the names of Lwyneth and Stephel for my spies to overhear. I had him tortured. The fool!" Brezog leaned down. "Then I ate his heart. All he knew, I now know. And I have tracked Eirian *here*."

"We don't have what you want, so why don't you leave us alone?" Diello yelled back. "You've searched, destroyed all that we have. Is that what you killed our parents for?"

"Our father had a crippled arm," Cynthe added. "What would he be doing with a sword? Why don't you go away!"

All the goblins shrieked and hissed and grunted. Then everyone fell silent, watching Brezog. Silhouetted against the orange torchlight, the tall gorlord clicked his long black talons on the shaft of his skull-mace. The warm breeze stirred the hem of his cloak.

He won't kill us as long as he thinks I'll tell him where the sword is, Diello realized. His resolve hardened. He could stand one more blow, and then he'd pretend to crack. He'd lie and send these rotten goblins off on a wild goose chase.

The gorlord growled deep in his throat. "Bring the little child to me."

Two mottled-green bloidy-goblins ran toward the woods. Diello and Cynthe shared one wild-eyed look, then Cynthe flung herself forward, only to be jerked back again.

"No!" she yelled. "Leave her alone!"

Brezog uttered his grunting laugh. "I'll eat the child's heart," he said, smacking his thin lips. "Little ones taste best."

All Diello's defiance trickled away.

"No," Cynthe pleaded. "She's innocent. Don't hurt her."

"Lwyneth's spawn can never be innocent!" Brezog turned back to Diello. "You can save the child by talking. Now."

"It—it's in the woods," Diello said. "My father kept it wrapped in leather, in an old cave. He swore us all to—to secrecy, and it—"

"Stop!" Brezog ordered.

Diello choked back the rest of his words, praying that this lie would work.

Brezog moved closer, his horrible cloak brushing against Diello. The gorlord's hand closed on Diello's sore shoulder again, and the pain was excruciating. Helplessly Diello twisted as his knees buckled under him. He heard the gorlord speak a command he didn't understand.

But his body obeyed it anyway, his eyes lifting to meet the gorlord's. There was nothing Diello could do. Mesmerized, he stared into those half-crazed eyes as something clawed its way into his mind. It was a slithering, repulsive touch. Diello tried to close his thoughts, but he was much too weak. An image of Pa's deed seal filled his mind. He struggled to think of anything else, but he couldn't stop the memory that Brezog was conjuring up. Pa's last words whispered through his head.

"Ah," Brezog murmured. "How touching."

The intruding presence withdrew. Diello found himself on his knees, shuddering in the aftermath. He vomited on the grass.

"Diello!" Cynthe tried to go to him, but the goblins restrained her. "Diello, what's he done to you? Diello!"

He felt he might be going mad.

Brezog raised his long, knobby arms. "Eirian is here!"

The goblins cheered, making Diello's head pound even harder. He had let Pa and Mamee down. They'd found the strength to defy Brezog, but he hadn't. He felt more wretched than ever.

"No!" Cynthe screamed. "Diello, *look*!"

The anguish in her voice reached him. Diello got to his feet and saw one of the bloidy-goblins returning from the woods, carrying Amalina. The child was limp in his arms—either unconscious or dead.

Diello's misery was forgotten as rage took its place. He turned on Brezog. "I've told you all I know. Let us go!"

The gorlord's skull-mace would have crushed Diello's head if he hadn't ducked. "No one tells Brezog! No one orders Brezog!"

Goblin hands pummeled Diello. Brezog grabbed him by the front of his tunic and pulled out the deed seal. The silver disk gleamed in the flickering torchlight, spinning on its cord.

"You can't have it." Diello reached out, only to have his hand smacked down. "You can't—"

Brezog's fist clamped on the disk. "Can," he said. "And will. Eirian belongs to me!"

A flash of white light blazed from the seal's surface, and Brezog howled in pain. The gorlord flung down the disk and blew on his palm. Diello could see the gorlord's scaled flesh already swelling with angry blisters. Smiling grimly to himself, Diello bent to pick up the seal, but Brezog shoved him back.

The gorlord pointed at Diello. "Kill him! Kill him *now*!"

chapter twelve

"Kill him!" Brezog shouted again.

The black dagger swung up, but before it could strike, a trumpet blared in the woods. Diello heard galloping hoofbeats coming their way.

Brezog whirled about, shouting commands. Cupping his hands, the gorlord blew a black mist across his palms and flung it at the goblins. A dark cloud shrouded each goblin, disguising them as humans.

Picking up the deed seal, Diello edged away. One of the gor-goblins noticed, and shoved him up against the cistern wall.

A group of armored horsemen in the baron's colors burst from the woods and came galloping into the open. They were double the number of goblins. Brezog snarled an order, and the goblins scattered.

Diello thought they were fleeing, but then he realized the goblins were forcing the Shieldsmen to spread out and some of the goblins were circling around behind the riders.

In an instant, fighting broke out across the farmstead, vicious and bloody. The guard holding Diello shouted something and joined the battle, brandishing his spear.

Cynthe grabbed Diello. "Let's get out of here!"

But Diello saw the bloidy-goblin scuttling away with Amalina still clutched in his arms. The goblin was making for the woods. Diello ran after him, but was nearly run down himself by a snorting war charger.

He ducked away, cringing as the horse reared. Hooves pawed the air above his head, and the rider swore at him. A snarling gor-goblin disguised as an Antrasin bandit leaped at the rider, whose sword whistled through the air. Screaming, the goblin sprawled on the ground, and the Shieldsman galloped on.

Diello jumped out of the path of another Shieldsman and saw that the bloidy-goblin had gained too much on him now. Cynthe was running after him, but even her long legs weren't going to catch the goblin before he reached the woods. She stumbled, falling to one knee.

"Amalina!" Cynthe cried in anguish.

Diello plunged through a gap in the melee, ducking once to avoid a slashing sword and nearly getting run through by a goblin spear. He scooped up Cynthe's bow and quiver from the ground, mercifully untrampled.

"Cynthe!" he shouted, tossing them to her.

Deftly Cynthe pulled out an arrow and nocked her bow. Just as she released the arrow, Diello yanked her out of the way of a horse.

Spitting mad, Cynthe punched his shoulder. "If you spoiled my aim, she's lost."

"No!" Diello said eagerly, pointing. "Look!"

Her arrow had thudded into the bloidy-goblin's back. He went down, crashing on top of Amalina.

For once, Cynthe couldn't outrun Diello. Reaching the child together, they rolled the bloidy-goblin over and pulled Amalina free. She was wailing hysterically as Diello felt her arms and legs to see if anything was broken. Other than a rising bump on her forehead, she didn't seem to be hurt. Red-faced, she howled louder when he tried to comfort her.

He glanced up at Cynthe, who was standing guard over them with her bow held ready. "She's fine," Diello said. "Just scared."

Cynthe nodded, her eyes intent as she released another arrow with a twang of her bowstring. "Got one!" she yelled.

"Watch out!" Diello shouted.

She and Diello jumped apart as a goblin crashed face down just steps from them. A club, made from what looked like a human thigh bone, fell loose from his hand. An Antra-sin dagger protruded from his back.

They ran for the safety of the hollow chesternut tree.

But the trumpet blared once more. The fight was already ending. With howls and savage curses, the gorlord fled into the woods with his remaining goblins. Most of the Shields-men chased after them. The rest swept back and forth across the clearing, some dismounting to check the dead and wounded, others trampling the ground even more as they surveyed the damage and their horses crunched heedlessly over the scattered debris.

The debris of our lives, Diello thought as he held Ama-lina. Cynthe found his quarterstaff and brought it to him, then stood close by his shoulder. No one seemed to take any notice of them.

"Isn't this Stephel's farm?" one of the Shieldsmen asked.

"Think so. That's him, ain't it, out there dead in the turnip patch?"

"Aye, poor fool. And the wife, too, over there. Made a right mess of the place, didn't they?"

"Bound to happen, living this deep in the woods. Asking for trouble, they were."

It was too late for Diello to cover Amalina's ears. She stared at him, her eyes bewildered. "I want Mamee," she whined. "I want Pa."

"I'm sorry," he said, his voice choked.

"They're gone," Cynthe said gruffly. "Like Busa."

Busa was a rabbit, the only survivor when Pa's plow accidentally dug up the nest. Diello had fed him drops of milk from a spoon, and soon the little rabbit thrived and grew into a feisty, rather arrogant pet that teased the farm cats. But Busa got clever at escaping his cage and was killed by a fox one night. The twins and Amalina had given him a grand funeral in the woods.

Now as Amalina's eyes widened, Diello said hastily, "Look at the sky, sweetling. Mamee is a star now, shining over us."

The child pointed at the twinkling lights.

"That's right," Diello said. "She will watch over you always."

"Want Mamee here. Want supper! Want my story! Will Pa come and tell my story?"

"Not tonight. Pa has gone away, too."

"Will you tell my story?"

Diello's throat knotted. "Yes," he replied. "But not right now."

Amalina fell silent then, putting her thumb in her mouth, and rested her head on his shoulder.

It was clear enough that no one had come here to rescue Diello or his sisters. By their talk, the Shieldsmen were chasing bandits that they'd tracked from two other farmsteads burned out this afternoon. Whether those were also goblin attacks, either to plunder or to hide their plan here, Diello couldn't determine. The Antrasins had simply followed the smoke. Now that they were here, they showed little regret for what had happened to Stephel and Lwyneth. As for Diello and his sisters, they might have been invisible for all the attention paid them.

Diello stared at Lord Malques's vivid blue-and-crimson banner. How desperately he'd wanted to grow up and become one of the Shieldsmen. Of course, it was forbidden for any Faelin to join their ranks, but Diello had let himself dream anyway, imagining he might perform some deed so brave and famous that the rules would be broken and he would be given his spurs. But after seeing the baron's man spit on Cynthe this afternoon, Diello's feelings had changed. And now . . . *now*, he felt twisted inside with both shame and resentment. Even if he wanted to feel grateful for being rescued, he couldn't.

"Boy!" called an authoritative voice. "To me!"

Diello saw one of the horsemen beckoning impatiently. He frowned, not budging.

"You, boy! Come here. Someone, send that boy to me."

Diello handed Amalina to Cynthe before approaching the man's stirrup warily.

The man had removed his helmet and sheathed his long broadsword. With his gauntlets held in one long-fingered hand, he sat at his ease atop his restive black charger. His hair was dark, falling smoothly to his shoulders. His beard was clipped short, showing a smattering of gray. He had a long Antrasin face with an aristocratic nose and deep-set eyes.

It was Lord Malques! Diello recognized him from the fair. Suddenly, Diello stood tongue-tied and gawking, feeling very unimportant indeed.

As for the baron, there was no kindness in his expression, no sympathy in his brown eyes. His lips were fleshy and red within the dark frame of his beard. They compressed in a faint sneer as his eyes lingered on Diello's slightly pointed ears.

"Faelin," he murmured.

Diello flushed, but reminded himself to be polite. "My lord, I must thank you—"

"Who owns this farmstead?"

"I—I—we do."

"What name?" Lord Malques snapped. "Do you think I know every vassal and farmer in this shire by sight? What name?"

"Stephel, son of—"

"Ah, I know Stephel. A man of valor and honor . . . once. So this is where he lives. Bring him forward."

Diello's hand curled into a fist at his side. "He—he's dead, my lord."

A man next to the baron leaned over and murmured in his ear. Lord Malques glanced toward the field and said, "Have him carried here."

"Yes, m'lord." The Shieldsman rode away.

Lord Malques returned his attention to Diello. "His son, I suppose. You have the look of him, but . . ." The baron glanced again at Diello's ears, clearing his throat uneasily. He gestured in the direction of Cynthe and Amalina. "These others?"

"My sisters."

"Hmm." Lord Malques did not seem interested in speaking to them. "Not the first good man turned fool by a pretty Fae face."

Diello scowled. "That's not—"

"How many bandits attacked here? I counted perhaps two dozen. Would you agree? Or was there a larger force, already moved on? Which direction?"

Taken aback by the rapid questions, Diello said, "They weren't bandits. They were goblins."

"Goblins?" Lord Malques laughed, gesturing at the dead bodies still disguised by Brezog's spell. "Nonsense! I have eyes to see for myself, boy. Keep your mind in reality. I'm sure these men thought they'd take advantage of the market-day fair, believing Wodesley and its farms ripe for their plucking. We'll get those that fled. Now, how many? Did they come from the north or west?"

"Does it matter?" Diello asked bitterly.

"Was their leader old Robbie Clot?"

"Robbie Clot!" Diello was astonished that the baron suspected a road bandit too old, and by all accounts too drunk, even to ride a horse anymore. "No!"

"I'm told the Ferrins have stooped to thievery of late. Is that true?"

Diello knew that Pa had "lost" some tools when Wilt Ferrin helped dig up stumps one day, but the baron was on the wrong track. "Sir," he began again. "My lord, you must listen. The goblins are disguised—"

"Let's have no more wild tales, if you please," Lord Malques said. "There hasn't been a goblin raid here in nearly five years, thanks to the vigilance of my Shieldsmen. It's true information I need, not a child's foolery."

Diello bit back what he wanted to say, too frustrated to find the words he needed. It was like talking to a stone.

"My brother's telling the truth!" Cynthe said, coming closer. "They *were* goblins, led by a gorlord calling himself Brezog. He wore gold bracelets and a cloak of human skin. He tortured Diello and threatened to eat my little sister!"

Lord Malques didn't even look at her. He beckoned to one of his men, who saluted.

"M'lord?"

"There's no useful information to be had here," the baron said. "Leave a detail of men to set things to rights. I shall be—"

"Our parents are dead!" Diello shouted. "Lwyneth and Stephel are dead. How can that be put right?"

He expected to be struck for his impertinence. Instead,

the baron stared down at Diello and Cynthe, and his demeanor softened as he looked upon Amalina, lying asleep across Cynthe's shoulder. "You children are alone here then? Does no one else live here besides you? Servants? Field serfs? Any adults at all?"

Sighing, Diello shook his head. "Just us. If you will kindly ask someone in the village to come tomorrow and help me burn the dead livestock, I—"

But the baron had turned away. "Sergeant Alton," he was saying, "you'll be in charge. See that the dead are given proper burial, and when that's done bring the children to the castle for the night. Faelin or not, they've nowhere else to go, poor mites."

"Aye, m'lord."

Diello was looking at Cynthe in horror. "Burial," he whispered.

"No!" she cried out, daring to touch Lord Malques's stirrup. One of the men pushed her back. "You don't understand," Cynthe insisted. "We don't—"

"That's all," the baron said to his men. Touching his spurs to his horse's sides, he rode away.

Cynthe glared after him. "But we don't bury our dead!"

The sergeant was a youngish man with a square honest face under a thatch of brown hair.

"If you please, sir," Diello said, "we'll need your help only to prepare our parents for—"

"Move aside, boy," Sergeant Alton said, refusing to meet Diello's gaze. "We've much to do and the night's getting on. Out of the way now. There's a good lad."

The men walked over to where Mamee lay under her shroud.

"Stop them!" Cynthe cried. "Diello, they mustn't!"

But Diello couldn't stop them. The men were as brusque as Lord Malques, not unkind but ignoring Diello as they brushed him aside and dug two graves near the garden. It was one thing to bury Pa—although a burning pyre would have been better—but Mamee could not be treated this way.

"I beg you," Diello said to Sergeant Alton. "Fae are *never* buried in the ground. They can't transform—uh, go back to—"

"Not now, boy," Alton said, gesturing for the men to continue lowering first Mamee's body and then Pa's into the graves. The damp smell of turned soil filled the air. "Your Faelin beliefs, as you call them, ain't nothing but a pack of superstitious twaddle and well you know it."

"But—"

"I been a believer all my life." Alton pulled out his crumix—a circle and cross worked in plain gold—and kissed it reverently. "I be sworn to the true way and the right way. You'd do a sight better if you believed in the Union. When times come hard and your heart is broken, see, like this . . ." His fingertip traced the cross. "But if you believe in Wholeness, in the Union, then all's well." He drew his finger along the circle's edge and smiled.

Diello stared at him blankly. "At least let us leave Mamee up in the branches of a tree—"

"In a tree?" Alton looked appalled. "To be pecked at by crows and left rotting for weeks? Is that what you want for your ma, boy? Why, that's downright blasphemous, not to mention unclean."

"But it isn't like that. She'll fade—"

The sergeant motioned him away. "I'll hear no more about it, you little barbarian. Shocking, you are. Shocking! Why, it be a kindness from his lordship to grant your type of folks the blessing of a proper burial. For Stephel's sake, I reckon, what with him and his lordship having grown up together, you might say. Yes, a kindness. Now that's an end to it."

Diello's head was spinning from what the sergeant had said, but he couldn't wonder about Pa and the baron now. "If you'd just listen—"

"In the Union lies Wholeness, and in Wholeness, Truth, and in Truth our protection," Alton recited. "Get back, you and your sister both. Leave us be to do our work."

Cynthe uttered something inarticulate and fled, carrying Amalina. Diello stood anguished as the men shoveled dirt on top of his parents. There was nothing proper about it, not for Mamee. There would be no way the Death Wind could ever carry her back to Embarthi. To stick Mamee down inside a hole was to exile her forever.

But she wasn't going back. He thought of the face he'd seen in the swirling light. *She was already exiled. Embarthi is forever closed to her. And the Death Wind won't return.*

He pushed the thoughts away, wanting to believe that somehow in the night or perhaps on the morrow, the Death Wind would return for her. There had to be leniency somewhere, no matter what lay in her mysterious past. If that force calling itself Clevn hadn't intervened, she would have been gone before these humans ever came.

Diello had been taught by Mamee that a human soul and body were two separate things that joined in birth and parted in death. He believed that Pa's soul was now safely consigned into the care of the gentle, always merciful Antrasin god Mercinth who would conduct it to the Fields of Peace. But Fae folk were different in that their souls and bodies were one. If the Death Wind did not take them to Embarthi, to be blessed by the Silver Wheel on the Isle of Woe and then conducted to the magical cloud Dweigana that floated in the sky, they could never be reunited with loved ones in the afterlife, and no living Fae could visit them.

Some exiles would lie scattered as dust, forever lost. Others would transform, become part of the sunset over the western sea, and a few might become lesser stars in the night sky. Diello supposed that Mamee might have been content to be a star, bright and shining against the darkness. But to stop the Death Wind completely, to leave her here to be buried, to be imprisoned in the ground to rot . . . it was unholy, cruel, and *wrong*.

He could hear Cynthe crying, the sound muffled as she tried to hide her tears. Amalina murmured sleepily when Cynthe laid her down, and the little one curled around her sister's feet.

We do not matter to these humans, Diello thought. *They insult Mamee and call it kindness. They're the barbarians.*

When the graves were filled, the men leaned on their shovels and wiped the sweat from their brows. Night lay upon the farmstead. All was cool, quiet, and still.

"Now, boy," Sergeant Alton said to Diello. "Come and say whatever words matter over your folks. And look sharp about it."

Diello stumbled over to the graves, his mind blank.

Someone prodded him in the back. "Go on, then. Make it quick, you little squint."

What could he say? It seemed wrong to pray aloud to the Guardian in front of these humans. He did not know what Pa would've wanted, except to please Mamee.

Suddenly Mamee's presence seemed to be with him. He felt something light run through his bones, and when he pressed his palm against the deed seal beneath his tunic, the sense of her grew stronger. He remembered a song she and Pa used to sing together in the evenings after Pa had enjoyed his cup of hard cider. Their voices blended well together— Mamee's so clear and true, Pa's deep and surprisingly melodic. And as they sang they would gaze into each other's eyes, smiling to themselves alone. Sometimes Pa would clasp Mamee's slender hand in his and kiss her fingertips.

It always made Diello happy to hear them sing. The world seemed right. For an instant he felt her soft fingers pressing against his hand. Her voice whispered through his thoughts, *Sing to us, Diello.*

Staring up through the treetops to the stars shining overhead, Diello began to sing, his young voice pure and crystalline as he wove the old Fae words into the melody:

> *Dance through the Breath of Night, my lady,*
> *Dance to meet your lord!*
> *Wear the moonlight for your mantle*
> *And trust music's sweet accord!*
> *Tho parting has been oft cruel,*

In the dawning with your beloved
Your heart shall have wings anew.
Then kiss him, my lady, with laughter sweet,
Caress him and take his hand,
And you and he shall rise and fly
To claim love's promised land.
Oh, dance through the Breath of Night, my lady.
Dance to meet your lord.
Wear the moonlight for your mantle
And trust music's sweet accord.

Near the end, Cynthe's voice—choked and quavering—joined with his. There was more to the old ballad, but Diello's throat closed and he bowed his head.

Mamee's presence seemed to be everywhere now. He felt that if he could just glance fast enough to this side or that, he would see her. And he yearned to do so, yearned to hear her voice one last time. . . .

"That's enough, then," Sergeant Alton said. "Time to be gone."

"Wait!" Cynthe protested. "This can't be all there is. We're not finished."

"Be done with it, lass. Your folks are gone. It's hard, aye, but so's the world. You ain't the first orphans made, and you won't be the last."

She stared at the man, not giving an inch. Her anger was like a blaze around her. Then Diello realized that her skin really was glowing.

Not strongly, not enough for humans to notice. He hoped.

She's coming into her power. He felt his bones tingling from the magic inside her. *She shouldn't go into a tempest, not here, not like this. She'll manifest her Gift before she's ready.*

He clamped his hand on her wrist, drawing her anger away, dampening it as he used to dampen her tantrums when they were infants. He hadn't done anything like this for a long, long time. He wasn't sure he even remembered how. Yet desperation helped him do it.

He saw the glow fading from her skin, the brilliance lessening in her coppery-green eyes. After what Brezog had done to him tonight, he could hardly bear to take in Cynthe's wild emotions. But he'd managed to quell the storm of uncontrolled magic rising inside her.

I must take care, he thought wearily. *I must watch her more closely from now on. As long as we're among humans.* It was awful to think of Cynthe going through tempests without Mamee to guide and control her. Yet this was a sure sign that her Gift would be manifesting soon.

Cynthe seemed unaware of what he'd done. As Diello dropped her wrist and stepped back, she shook her head, looking confused.

"Right, then," Alton said. "Let's go."

"I've got to take my wol—my puppy," she said. "Let me find him."

"Forget that! Next you'll want to pack up your burnt things and we'll be here half the night."

Alton called to the other men to bring up the horses. The animals shied from Diello. Jerking at his horse's reins, Alton ordered Diello to get on.

"There's nothing to be frightened of," the sergeant said. "Mount!"

Diello took one unwilling step, and the animal snorted in fear, its eyes rolling white.

"What now?" Alton cried, trying to keep the horse from bolting. "What are you doing, boy?"

Mumbling an excuse, Diello fled to the creek. The men shouted after him, but he didn't slow down until he slithered to the bottom of the bank and stumbled to his knees at the water's edge. He plunged both hands into the cold water, pushing his palms flat against the stones at the bottom. He had to expel Cynthe's raw emotions from inside him.

At first he couldn't get rid of her fury and heartbreak, but then the emotions drained from him, flowing down his arms as they trembled from the strain. The water boiled and churned around him until at last the stream carried all that potent feeling away. Gasping, Diello rocked back on his heels. It surprised him that he'd been so quick to know what to do. Mamee had never taught him that.

"Boy!" Alton called. "Where are you?"

Climbing the bank was difficult, for Diello's legs seemed filled with stones. His shoulder hurt. His heart hurt. His eyes were heavy and he longed for sleep. He didn't want to be brave and grown up. He didn't want to cope with anything else. He just wanted someone to take his burdens and let him rest. But there was no one.

Cynthe came rushing up to him. "Thanks for the diversion," she whispered. "I got a chance to look for Fuzzytop, but he must be hiding."

"Both of you!" Alton called angrily. "Enough of your pranks. Get over here now."

Diello led Cynthe back to the men. She said no more about the wolf, but her face was stony and mutinous. Diello knew she was worried that the pup would starve on his own. As for Diello, he was worried about Cynthe working herself into another tempest. The Antrasins would probably kill them in ignorance and fear. He'd have to talk to her, warn her to control her feelings better, but not here, not now.

This time, to his relief, the horses showed no distress around him. Alton was waiting there with a whimpering Amalina draped over his shoulder. Diello frowned, taking his little sister and attempting to soothe her.

"Want Mamee!" she cried, rubbing her eyes fretfully. "I'm hungry!"

"You've got the sense of a goose, the two of you," Alton said, "running off like that when we're set to go. And all for a damned puppy."

Cynthe stiffened but held her tongue. Patting Amalina's back, Diello bleakly met the sergeant's eyes.

The censure in Alton's face turned to compassion. Hesitantly he reached out and tousled Diello's hair.

"You're just a scrap of a lad, ain't you?" Then he cleared his throat and looked around at his men. "Mount up. Let's get these poor mites to the castle for their supper and a decent night's rest."

As they rode out, Diello glanced back at his parents' graves. He didn't think he'd ever have a night's rest again.

chapter thirteen

It was a long ride back to Wodesley, with the Shieldsmen talking among themselves above the steady clip-clop of hooves. Clinging to Sergeant Alton's back, Diello fought the urge to close his eyes and sleep. He didn't feel safe among the Antrasins. He wasn't sure he'd feel safe anywhere. He thought that Cynthe might be crying silently as she rode behind another Shieldsman. Amalina, quieted by Alton giving her a bit of sweet taffy to suck on, was cradled in a third man's arm, sound asleep beneath his cloak's protective folds. Now and then the trees parted enough for moonlight to filter down upon her small face.

Most of the village looked asleep, the cottages shuttered, hearth fires banked for the night.

Up the road, the castle loomed, a hulking shadow against the sky. For the second time that day, Diello ascended the tall stone ramp, crossed the moat's drawbridge, and passed through the gatehouse into the outer ward. The place looked more forbidding at night. Extra sentries were standing watch along the wall walks, their weapons glinting. The inner gatehouse looked even more massive and intimidating than the outer. Guards hailed Sergeant Alton and his men. It appeared that the larger group of Shieldsmen had ridden in just moments ago, back from chasing away what they supposed were bandits.

As they rode through the gatehouse, Diello glanced overhead at the murder holes and shivered, not liking the close quarters, the loud echo of voices and hooves, or the sense of being trapped.

But entering the inner ward took them to another world. The glass windows of the great hall and apartments now shone with light. Strains of music, laughter, and chatter carried on the air. The baron and his guests were feasting merry indeed. All was bustle at the stables. Shieldsmen were dismounting, spurs jingling. They were calling out orders to servants and laughing and joking. Stableboys rushed here and there, some unsaddling horses or rubbing them down, while others led the animals to their stalls for feeding. Several house servants in livery were asking questions about whether the bandits had been caught.

Sliding to the ground, Diello slapped horse hairs from his leggings and tunic as he looked around. He blinked owlishly, struggling to stay awake.

Cynthe edged up to him. "We shouldn't be here," she whispered. "They don't believe anything we say."

"I know," he murmured, "but we have to stay for the night. Tomorrow we'll go our own way."

"Boy!" Sergeant Alton was snapping his fingers for Diello's attention and ignoring Cynthe again. "No time for gawking. Come!"

Diello and Cynthe trudged along in the sergeant's wake.

They each held tightly to one of Amalina's hands, urging the child along as she stared and dawdled.

"Make way!" called a flustered voice.

Sergeant Alton pushed them to one side as a line of servants laden with platters of food filed from the cook-house into the great hall. The mingled aromas made Diello's stomach rumble. The doors to the hall stood open to receive the food bearers. Light and noise spilled out. He glimpsed rows of tables, where men and women were lifting their wine cups to greet the arrival of more food. Diello craned his neck, hoping to see the baron's table. But the crowd was too thick, and too many servants were coming and going.

A hand boxed his ear, and he was given a shove.

"Come along," Alton growled. "You can't go in there."

"I wasn't. I just—"

He broke off, since the sergeant wasn't listening. Silently they crossed the inner ward to the apartments.

But they never entered. A tall, lanky man in a very stiff blue tunic met them just outside the door, waving them away. He was the under-steward, with orders from Onner Timmons to see that no Faelin children slept under the baron's roof. The two men conferred in low voices before the sergeant shrugged and took the children instead down a dark, narrow walkway behind the stables to a row of stout wooden doors set in the base of the wall.

The under-steward followed them with a torch in one hand and a ring of large keys in the other. While they waited, he unlocked the door at the end of the row.

"This will do," he said.

Alton jerked his head for the twins to enter. "Hurry now."

Seeing that the door's weathered hinges were made of bronze, Diello let out his breath. But as the under-steward lifted his torch, sending ruddy light into the room, Diello glimpsed an iron bed jammed in one corner past a stack of wooden barrels. Cynthe edged closer to his side. The place smelled of straw, mouse, and moldy apples.

"We've prepared the storeroom for you," the under-steward said. "Swept it out and fetched a pail of fresh-drawn water from the well. There's a bed and plenty of straw and blankets if you want 'em. Your supper will be brought shortly. By the looks of you a good washing wouldn't come amiss. Go in now, and before you know it you'll have something to eat."

When Diello didn't move, Alton grumbled under his breath and scooped up Amalina, carrying her inside. He tossed her lightly onto the bed and came back out, beckoning to Diello and Cynthe.

"Come on. I reckon it be comfortable enough, with no one to bother you."

Amalina stood up in the middle of the iron bed and began to cry, scratching her arms. Diello hurried in and pulled her off. He could feel his own skin starting to itch, and as he brought her outside he saw red welts rising on her tender arms.

"Oh, look at you," Cynthe murmured to her. "Poor baby!"

"We can't sleep in there," Diello said to Alton. "The bed—"

"Now, see here, the lot of you," he said. "His lordship's

doing you a rare kindness, putting shelter over your heads for the night. Let's not be picky and thinking ourselves as fine as his lordship's guests."

"Oh, we don't mind sleeping in the storeroom," Diello assured him. "It's the bed."

"What about it?" Alton asked.

"A very kind gesture, we thought," the under-steward said, "not making you sleep on the floor like hounds in the kennel. Of course, if that's all you're used to—"

"We've always had proper wooden beds and chairs," Cynthe said indignantly, "and—"

"Don't take that tone with me, you Faelin wench. I suppose next you'll be demanding an apartment as sumptuous as her ladyship's." The under-steward laughed.

"No," Diello said. "The bed is iron."

"Iron!" Alton exclaimed, snapping his fingers. "Well, now. I never thought of that. It does something awful to Fae skin, don't it? Burns holes in it, or something." He peered at Amalina's welts. "That looks right wicked. I'm sorry, little one."

"If we could just be rid of the bed, please," Diello said. "The—"

"I suppose you want the door removed, too," the under-steward said.

"No. Just the bed."

Alton nodded. "Fix it as you like. But mind you're tidy. No strewing things about."

"Yes, sir."

"And don't you go prowling about the inner ward. No one's got time to deal with you tonight."

The sergeant looked hard at Diello, who prudently said nothing.

"Right," Alton said. "Now thank the under-steward for his kindness."

Realizing that neither man was going to help them get rid of the bed, Diello swallowed a sigh. "Thank you."

Alton looked directly at Cynthe. She frowned stubbornly until Diello nudged her with his elbow. "Thank you," she said.

Despite their lack of enthusiasm, Alton seemed satisfied. He took the torch from the under-steward's hand and plunked it into a nearby sconce bolted to the wall.

"Now do as the man said and wash up," Alton added. "A dirtier band of young 'uns I never saw. Mind you don't scare the maids when they bring your supper."

Watching the two men stride away, Cynthe planted her fists on her slim hips. "What does he expect us to do to them? Wear snakes on our heads and freeze them to stone?"

Diello didn't care. "Let's get rid of the bed. Find something to protect your hands."

They looked around without success and finally used the hems of their tunics to cover their hands as they half-lifted, half-shoved the bed farther down the passage in front of another storeroom door.

Cynthe whisked off the straw-filled mattress and dragged it back inside, where she sat down in a heap. "I feel dizzy."

Diello fought the weakness in his own knees. If he sat down he didn't think he'd ever stand again. "Supper's coming. It'll help."

Cynthe ran back outside into the darkness. Diello heard

her being sick. *The barrels*, he thought. They were bound with iron rings.

He wrestled with them, rolling them out, for they were too heavy for him to lift. By the time he finished, drenched with sweat and itching all over, Cynthe had returned. She gave him a trace of a smile and sank down in the far corner next to Amalina.

"What's all this mess?"

In the doorway was a pair of young women carrying full trays. They wore long white aprons tied over their livery and full-bottomed skirts that reached the ground. Glaring at the barrels scattered in all directions and the bed standing nearby, they turned accusing eyes on Diello.

"Did you do this?" the older woman asked. "What are you, touched in the head?"

"I just swept the place out, I did," announced the younger maid. "And helped carry that bed in for you. Dirty little beggars, ain't you never seen a bed before?"

Afraid they'd leave and take the food with them, Diello stepped forward. "Please," he said. "We're sorry, but—"

"I ain't serving no pig," the older woman declared. She slammed the tray on the ground, oversetting a jug of milk, and backed away.

The younger one banged down her tray as well. "Let's get out of here before they put the evil eye on us."

"Wait!" Diello called out, but the pair fled out of sight. He could hear them squealing with fright.

Righting the jug of milk, although it was nearly empty, Diello carried in the soggy trays.

"See?" Cynthe said quietly, taking one from him. "They're all stupid."

Amalina fussed about being washed, and they gave in, letting her pick what she wanted off the trays. She ate hungrily, then pointed at Diello.

"You be Pa," she ordered. "Tell me my story!"

Diello settled her against his side, while she held a heel of cheese in both hands. "Long, long ago," he began, clearing his throat, "there was a beautiful maiden—"

"Me!"

He kissed Amalina's temple. "The fairest in all the land. She lived in a palace of crystal, like winter ice, and all her subjects loved her."

Amalina nodded with satisfaction. "She had ducks, and a cat, and a dolly, and a big cow, and a pony."

"A pony?"

"Yes."

He smiled. "One day a stranger came, a valiant and handsome warrior from far away. He was on a quest, searching for . . ."

Amalina fell asleep, her lashes curling on her cheeks. He eased her down in relief.

Pushing up his sleeves, Diello washed his dirty hands and face. Cynthe washed, too, kneeling at the wooden bucket beside him. Then they sat on the floor with the two trays between them. Despite the spillage, there was a generous amount of food, with fresh-baked bread sopping but still edible, slabs of meat, cheese, a dish of morsels that smelled too sour to be appealing, and fruit pastries that were just as delicious with a milk-soaked crust.

Their backs were to the open door. Suddenly, Diello heard a furtive noise. He whirled around just as the large door slammed shut, cutting off the torchlight outside. He jumped to his feet, calling out, but the sound of a key turning in the lock silenced him.

There was no window in the storeroom, no light at all. Diello attempted to get his bearings. He moved cautiously forward to avoid stepping in their food and blundered into Cynthe instead.

"They've locked us in!" she said in outrage. "Like prisoners. They made us come here, and now they treat us like—"

"They're afraid of us," Diello said.

"They should be! I'd like to—"

"That won't help."

She sighed. "I miss the *cloigwylie*. Nothing feels right without it around us."

"We'd better finish eating."

"How? In the dark?" Cynthe snapped her fingers a couple of times, failing to flick fire from her fingertips.

"You could set us all on fire in here," he warned her. "There's a lot of straw."

"Would they care?" she asked.

"Cynthe, don't talk like that."

She snapped her fingers again, achieving a brief spark but nothing else. "I don't understand!" she cried. "Usually I'm good at this. I've always been good at this."

Diello hoped it was because she was too tired and upset—and not because of how he'd drawn her magic away earlier tonight. He hadn't considered what the consequences might be.

Cynthe began to cry, but when he touched her arm in comfort she snapped, "I'm sorry! I don't want to cry like a stupid girl. I don't want to cry!"

He groped around and found a piece of meat and the soggy bread. "Eat," he said with his mouth full. There was no other comfort he could offer.

Cynthe sniffed in the darkness. "I'm not hungry," she said. "I want to go home."

Diello chewed a mouthful of what now tasted like sawdust, and forced himself to swallow. The food seemed tasteless and bland, containing none of the flavors and spices he was used to.

Tomorrow will be better, Diello told himself. But as he listened to his twin crying herself to sleep, he didn't believe it.

chapter fourteen

In the morning, the rattle of a key in the lock woke Diello. He sprang up as the door banged open, dazzling him with a spill of sunlight. Squinting, Diello saw two shapes: a portly man and a lanky boy.

"Enough lazing about," the man said. "Up with you."

Diello slapped some of the dust and straw from his hair and clothing. He knew that voice all too well.

Onner Timmons.

Cynthe was slower to get up, wincing and cradling her injured arm. Diello started to inspect it, but the steward rapped his knuckles loudly on the doorjamb.

"Come out of there at once!" he said.

They filed out and stood before the steward and his attendant.

"By the nine mercies, could you be more unsuitable to appear before his lordship?" Timmons said. "Even the alms-house would turn you urchins away. You were supplied with plenty of water last night. Why didn't you wash?"

We did our best, Diello thought. But he didn't reply. Onner Timmons was a cheat and a toad. Diello wasn't going to tell him anything.

159

Besides, he was hungry, stiff, and sore. He had a puncture on his shoulder where one of the gorlord's talons had dug in deep, and it felt hot and swollen. He would have given a tooth for some of Mamee's healing salve.

Next to him, Cynthe had straw sticking out of her tangled hair, and her clothes were wrinkled and grubby. Her eyes were red-rimmed and dull with grief. As for Amalina, all dirt-streaked face and golden ringlets, she was staring up at the steward with big blue eyes while she sucked on her fingers. The more Timmons nagged and criticized them, the closer she pressed herself to Diello's leg. He took her hand reassuringly.

Timmons sniffed. "Now, have you paid attention to what I've said?"

Diello met the man's black, close-set eyes. "Aye," he said shortly, sounding a lot like Pa. "You're telling us how to behave in front of his lordship. But why need we see him? Can't we just go—"

"As I've already explained, his lordship has *sent* for you. How I'm to get you clean and presentable enough before the Audience bell rings, I don't know, but remember that you're not to speak unless he speaks to you first. Volunteer nothing, and by the mercies do not dare to interrupt him. Do you understand? If he ignores you, do nothing to bring yourself to his attention."

"That's daft," Cynthe said.

"Del!" Amalina said, tugging at Diello's hand. "I'm hungry!"

"There isn't time," the steward said, shooing them ahead of him to the inner ward. "Go with Hant here."

"Del!" Amalina said, jumping up and down.

"Please, sir," Diello said as Onner Timmons turned away. Right then, if the steward had served them sugared plums off a silver tray he would have refused, but where Amalina was concerned, Diello could swallow his pride all day long. "Please. The little one is hungry, and she doesn't understand. May we have something for her?"

The steward hesitated. Around him, the grooms were filling mangers with grain or armfuls of long-stemmed, sweetly fragrant grass. Beside the stables, a pair of young boys was emptying pails of scraps and peelings into a wooden trough. Flies buzzed everywhere as squealing, grunting pigs shoved one another to plunge their snouts greedily into the food.

"If the brat must eat," Timmons said, "give her scraps from the pig trough. Just see that you hurry!"

"Scraps!" Diello said.

"From the pig trough!" Cynthe added.

"Well, it's irregular," Timmons admitted, his black beady eyes darting to each of them. "Those pigs are being fattened for Lady Bethalie's birthday celebration in a few weeks' time, but since it's for the child, I doubt the swineherd will begrudge you."

Diello curled his fists. "You old—"

A page came hurrying up and bowed to the steward. "Excuse me, Master Timmons," the page said, "but her ladyship wishes to know if there will be dancing this afternoon, as she requested. She bids you come at once to consult with her about the music."

Onner Timmons lifted his pudgy hands and let them fall. "And have I not assured her ladyship twice already that the dancing will be to her liking? Hant, see to these urchins, and make sure they're in the hall before the Audience bell."

"Yes, Master Timmons," the lanky boy said.

As the steward hurried away with the page, Hant gave Diello and his sisters a friendly grin.

"Well, now," he said. "If you're quick enough at that water trough, I think we might have time to go past the cookhouse. Eh? Come on."

So they washed up, knowing there wasn't much they could do to look presentable. While Diello scrubbed a wriggling Amalina's face, Cynthe unbraided her blonde hair and let it hang loose and long down her back.

Hant watched Cynthe groom her hair with such open appreciation that Diello felt a strange, hot sensation burst inside his chest.

"Aren't you done yet?" Diello asked her.

"Almost." She pulled at another snarl and winced. "My arm's sore today."

"I'll braid your hair while you wash that gash," Diello offered. Amalina raced away from him, only to be caught by Hant, who tickled her as she squealed.

Cynthe smiled, her gaze lingering on the boy. Hant was maybe sixteen with a deep voice, and hands and feet oversized and awkward compared to the rest of him. "I checked under the bandage," she said absentmindedly. "It's healing well enough."

"You need a clean cloth on it."

"I can see to that," Hant said. "I'll ask Cook to spare some lint." He smiled at Cynthe, and a dimple appeared in his cheek.

Her smile widened, but she looked unusually shy. "Thank you."

Diello couldn't believe she was interested in this long-necked human. He braided her hair as fast as he could, tugging so hard she flinched.

"Not so rough! You're doing it wrong."

"Sorry," he muttered, but he wasn't.

Cynthe turned a little red, but Hant just laughed.

"Cook has a soft spot for me," he said. "Let's see what we can do for that arm."

So they followed him across the inner ward, past the chapel and barracks to the cookhouse, where a number of people were hard at work, chopping and slicing and peeling and scrubbing and stirring and kneading. An enormous fire blazed inside an oven of iron and stone. Although all the windows and the door stood wide open, oppressive, sweltering heat poured out. Everyone inside the cookhouse was soaked with sweat and red in the face. And they all seemed to be in a tremendous hurry.

Hant went in alone and approached a fat woman clad in a voluminous white apron stained down the front with what looked like gravy and maybe blood. Diello and his sisters hovered at the doorway, staring in at a table groaning beneath a mound of peeled taties and pan after pan of trussed game hens glazed with butter, sprinkled with herbs, and ready to be popped onto the spit. A dog was trotting on a creaking wheel, turning the long spit, where more game hens were already roasting. The air smelled of meat and hot, sizzling grease, freshly cut bread, and baked raisins. Sniffing appreciatively, Diello found himself drawn even closer to the doorway. His stomach rumbled and growled.

"I want that!" Amalina said. She darted inside the cookhouse before Diello could stop her.

He went after her, crossing the threshold. Amalina gripped the edge of the table. Standing on her tiptoes, she reached for a steaming bun.

"Amie!" he said, just as the cook turned around and saw them. "Don't!"

Ignoring him, Amalina jumped for a bun, but her arm was not quite long enough. She jumped again, her pink tongue sticking out from her mouth in determination. The whole tray of buns shook with a clatter and teetered on the edge of the table without falling.

"Thief!" the cook shouted.

Now everyone was yelling. Amalina blinked at them, then whipped her curly head around to Diello. "Del!" she said. "Help me!"

But he was watching the wrathful cook. "Come out of there, Amie," he urged.

"No! I'm hungry."

"No one steals from my cookhouse," the cook declared.

Hant was laughing. "Leave the little mouse alone, Cook. She's not hurting anything."

A corner of the cook's mouth quirked into a smile. "Ah, now. You'd have me handing out treats to every hungry mouth in the place, you would."

"It's just a little mouse," Hant said. He glanced at Cynthe, who was pushing past Diello. "Perhaps two mice."

"Cynthe, no!" Diello whispered, but Cynthe took the

bun that the child had managed to grab and broke it open for her, sending fragrant steam into the air.

Clapping her hands in excitement, Amalina gobbled it. "Good," she mumbled. "Good!"

Cook beamed. But when Cynthe tucked her hair behind her pointed ear and reached for a bun of her own, the cook smacked her hand with a wooden spoon.

"Ow!"

"Get out of here, you Faelin wench!" she screeched. "I won't have my loaves and cakes falling because of your bad luck. No, nor my custards soured. Get out! Get out!"

Smacking Cynthe again with the spoon, the fat woman drove her out, sending her stumbling over the high threshold. Cynthe missed the stone step, lost her balance, and crashed—arms flailing—into Diello.

He stood her up hastily, intending to rescue Amalina next, but the cook was bending down to the child and cooing, handing her a second raisin bun and breaking it open for her.

"There you are, poppet," she said, her broad, red face smiling kindly. "Do you want currant jelly on your bun?"

Cheeks bulging, Amalina nodded. The cook rapped out an order, and one of her underlings hurried to spoon bright red jelly from a stone jar. Amalina was escorted outside, her mouth and cheeks now streaked with jelly. Still chewing, she grinned up at Diello and raised her sticky hand in triumph.

"Del! It's good!"

He made himself smile. It looked good. It smelled good. But with Cook scowling at him and Cynthe, it was obvious that only Amalina was getting any breakfast this morning. Hant emerged from the cookhouse, also chewing.

At Diello's resentful grimace, he grinned and slipped Cynthe a bun from his pocket.

She accepted it, lifting her chin. "Aren't you afraid I'll give you warts or something?"

"Nah. Grew up with Faelin folk for neighbors, didn't I? Now come along," he said, handing her a roll of clean lint with another of his dimpled smiles. "If you lot aren't where you're supposed to be, there'll be a right fuss. Oops! There's the Audience bell. I know a shortcut. This way!"

He took them through the apartments, which were dim and shadowy from a lack of windows on the lower floor. The stone walls made the air cool despite the warmth outside. Mats woven from sweet-smelling rushes covered the stone floors, muffling their footsteps. Clustered together, they followed Hant through a number of passageways. They peeked through doorways into stately rooms, where Diello glimpsed tapestries depicting people and scenes from history and folklore. He marveled at the chairs—not the solid plain type that he'd grown up with—but fine seating with delicate legs and beautifully carved arms, each upholstered in costly fabric that shimmered in the dim light. And there were books, actual books of leather bound around vellum pages, some of them stacked casually on tables where anyone might touch them. All the door panels displayed heavily carved flowers or fruit. Diello knew his father would have appreciated the wood artistry, and surely Mamee would have loved how beautiful everything was, especially the fabrics.

"What's all this for?" Cynthe whispered.

"Don't touch anything," he said, taking firm hold of Amalina's sticky hand.

Hant hurried them along. "No time for looking," he said.

All this beauty made Diello understand why Onner Timmons had been so unkind to them, so contemptuous of their appearance. The inside of the castle was like a dream. And they were too dirty and poor to be inside it.

As they passed the foot of a magnificent winding staircase, Diello could hear voices, laughter, the soft strumming of a lute, and a dog yapping in staccato bursts. At the end of a long passageway was a massive set of double doors fitted with strap hinges. No decorative carving adorned them. They looked thick enough to withstand a siege. A Shieldsman stood at attention on either side, each holding his pike across the doors.

Hant halted. "The Audience has started. We can't get in that way. Come!"

Holding Cynthe's elbow, he hurried all of them around a corner and through a servant's door concealed in the paneling. They found themselves in a crude, narrow passage that ended at another door. Hant eased it open, pressing his eye to the crack. The sound of murmuring voices came through.

"Right," Hant whispered. "Go in and stay at the back of the hall, against the wall. Edge along it quietly and join the others waiting for their turn." He grinned at Cynthe and winked. "Nothing to be afraid of. His lordship's a stern old bird, but fair. You'll see. Oh! No weapons but belt knives allowed inside."

He plucked Cynthe's bow from her hand and took

Diello's quarterstaff. "I'll give them to the guards. You can have them back when you come out. Now, in you go."

With that, he opened the door wider and let them each squeeze past him.

The great hall was like nothing Diello had ever seen before. The size of it alone was jaw dropping. It could have held two cottages and their barn besides. The ceiling soared high overhead, supported by arched beams. Banners hung from the beams, their colors bright and bold in the light streaming in from one broad glass window set near the ceiling. Antique swords and lances hung on the walls in patterns. Benches were arranged in rows on either side of a central aisle leading arrow straight to a dais at the far end. There, Lord Malques sat upright and solemn on a high-backed chair. He wore the square flat hat of a magistrate and a tunic of rich, dark-red cloth banded with silver. Large glittering jewels adorned his tapering fingers, and more jewels were studded into a gold chain that stretched across his chest.

Diello forgot to move quietly along the back wall as Hant had instructed. Instead, he stood and stared until Cynthe pinched him.

"Come on!" she whispered.

Up at the dais, Sergeant Alton and a handful of Shieldsmen were giving a report to the baron. The sergeant's hauberk was clean, his armor polished, and his chin shaven. The baron was leaning forward in his chair, asking the men questions in his brusque manner.

Diello and Cynthe pressed against the rear wall. Even so, the others awaiting Audience moved away from them. A soft whisper wound its way through the group and up to those sitting on the benches.

Amalina tugged at Diello's hand. "I don't like it here," she proclaimed loudly.

He bent swiftly to shush her. "Amie, promise that you'll be a good girl now. Stay very, very quiet. Will you?"

Amalina glanced around, looking the room over before she turned her face up to his. Although he'd wiped the jelly away, the corners of her mouth were still stained. "Promise," she said, giving him an emphatic nod that bounced her curls.

Cynthe managed to look both scared and defiant and kept nervously hooking her hair behind her ears, only to pull it forward to cover them. Diello wished that he could remember Onner Timmons's exact instructions.

One of the suppliants standing nearby was holding his cap in his hand. He was obviously a farmer, his face seamed and weathered by years of outdoor labor. His clothing was scorched and tattered, and he reeked of smoke.

Burned out like us. Diello gave the man a respectful nod of greeting, but the farmer backed away from them, spitting on the floor as he did so.

Diello was tired of it—the insults, the looks, the general contempt—all of it. He stiffened his spine and refused to be afraid anymore. He had just as much right to stand in this hall as any Antrasin. They couldn't shame him away.

Then his keen ears heard "Stephel" and "deed seal." He stretched to listen to what Alton was saying in time to catch the sergeant's announcement that they had searched carefully for the seal without success.

"Probably the bandits stole it, m'lord," Alton said.

"He's wrong," Cynthe whispered, turning to Diello in excitement. "You have—"

He shook his head in warning.

Cynthe frowned. "Why—"

"Hush," he whispered.

"If he's worried about our ownership of the farm, we can prove—"

"Stephel's children!" a clear voice called over the assembly. "Come forward!"

Everyone turned to stare. Swinging Amalina into his arms, Diello walked up the aisle. He was almost to the dais when a clammy sensation ran up his spine. The strength left his knees, and he knelt awkwardly, setting Amalina down. Twisting away from him, the child wandered down a row of empty benches, patting them and smiling. She began to sing softly, one of the aimless tunes she liked to invent.

A few coughs and chuckles rose from the onlookers. Still on his knees, too dizzy to rise, Diello tried to breathe deeply.

There was dark magic in use here!

Cynthe gripped his shoulder, inadvertently touching that sore spot where Brezog's claws had pierced his skin. Diello hissed, but the pain cleared his head. He struggled to stand, unsure whether his legs would hold him.

Get her, Cynthe mouthed to him. She pointed at Amalina, who'd wandered to the end of the row, executed a wobbly spin, and was making her way back, still singing softly.

Fighting off another wave of dizziness, Diello could only shake his head. He saw puzzled alarm in Cynthe's eyes.

Hoping to find the source of the magic, Diello looked around. At first glance, he saw no one capable of exerting such strong power.

A broad-shouldered man with a reddish beard appeared at the back of the dais, approaching Lord Malques's chair from behind. He leaned down to whisper into the baron's ear. Lord Malques gave him a curt nod, then murmured a comment in return.

There was something not quite right about the newcomer, something blurry, a bit strange. . . . Diello stared very hard at the man and tried to summon Sight. He blinked, and then saw the dark veil of a disguising spell.

Brezog was behind the spell—the goblin as bold as brass right here in the Audience hall of Wodesley Castle, whispering who knows what in Lord Malques's ear! The baron nodded a second time, his expression growing slack and vacant.

Patting the baron's shoulder, Brezog turned his red eyes on Diello and grinned.

chapter fifteen

Diello knew he had to tell Lord Malques who this man really was, but he didn't know how. He could barely think under Brezog's gaze. He felt like a fox caught in a hedgerow, waiting for dogs to tear him to pieces.

But more than scared, he was angry. His mind filled with memories of Mamee's ashen face, of Pa's pain-wracked final words, of the scrape of shovels against the summer-dried ground and the dull thud of soil filling the . . .

"What's wrong?" Cynthe asked. "You look like you've seen a wraith."

Diello whispered raggedly in Fae, "That's the gorlord up there. In disguise."

Cynthe trembled. "Which man?"

"The red-bearded one next to the baron."

"What do we do?"

"I don't know." Brezog's disguising spell must have been very strong today, for Diello kept seeing an image of the red-bearded man over the gorlord's true features. Diello's stomach was churning. He was thankful he'd had no breakfast or he surely would have brought it up here in the baron's fine hall.

Cynthe nudged his arm. "Don't just stand there, gasping like a landed fish. Tell his lordship!"

"He won't believe me."

Alton glanced over his shoulder. "Hush, both of you."

Although he spoke softly, the order held such authority that Diello couldn't defy it. Then he saw Lord Malques laugh and pat Brezog's forearm in friendship. It was too much. Diello pushed forward.

"My lord!" he called out. "That man is—"

Brezog's taloned hand squeezed into a fist, and Diello's throat closed off. He strained to speak, but he couldn't utter a sound. He watched as Lord Malques continued to chat with Brezog. The baron smiled, apparently having no suspicion of being tricked.

"What are you doing?" Cynthe whispered. "Why don't you speak up?"

He could barely hear her for the thunder in his ears. He had to breathe, had to breathe *now*, but Brezog kept on choking the life from him. And no one—not even his twin—realized what was happening.

"Say something!" she urged him. "Warn him! What are you waiting for? All right then, I'll do it." She stepped forward. "My lord, take care! You're in—"

Her voice choked off, and she turned bright pink, then red. Her fingers clawed at her throat. Brezog was squeezing his other fist.

Diello's vision dimmed. He saw Cynthe's lips moving soundlessly. She writhed. The grayness was closing in.

Amalina came running to Diello, treading on his foot. Her hand clutched his, and the awful crushing pressure around his throat vanished. He wasn't sure how Amalina had broken the spell, but he dragged in a lungful of air, and another, and another.

"Cynthe," he croaked out. "Amie, help her."

Amalina took her hand. "Cynnie, you have to breathe now."

Cynthe sucked in a breath and started coughing. Diello pounded on her back for good measure, and she in turn pounded on his. Diello shut his eyes, drawing in the sweet, good air, and hugged both of his sisters tight.

Amalina pressed her palms to his cheeks. "Del," she said, her blue eyes huge with worry.

"I'm all right," he whispered, kissing her soft hands. "Thank you, sweetling, whatever you did. Cynthe?"

Looking wan and shaken, Cynthe smoothed Amalina's curls, then swung around to face the gorlord, who was scowling at them.

"Have you no sense of proper conduct?" Alton asked in a low voice. "Stop larking about. This be no time for foolery."

Is he blind? Can't he tell the difference between playing and choking? But before Diello could answer him, there was a stir at the door.

"Make way!" rang the herald's voice. "Make way for Lady Bethalie!"

All proceedings stopped. Everyone turned to watch the baron's wife enter the hall. Brezog bowed to Lord Malques and retreated several steps behind the baron's chair, where he could watch everything, including Diello and Cynthe. The gorlord's hatred poured through the disguising spell, nearly flooding Diello's senses.

"I'll do the telling," Cynthe muttered in Fae. "No goblin's going to choke me and keep me—"

"Quiet, you two," Alton said. "I ain't telling you again."

Lady Bethalie came up the long aisle, smiling and nodding her head graciously to the assembly as she passed. Very fair, with long honey-gold hair braided with ropes of pearls and another strand of fat pearls draped around her elegant neck, the lady was obviously much younger than her lord husband. As she walked by in a rustle of silk and lace, Onner Timmons escorted her, with a fawning expression on his fat face. Her ladies and attendants followed, chattering among themselves and enjoying the interruption they were causing.

As Lady Bethalie approached the dais, Alton and his men bowed low in unison, leaving Diello and Cynthe standing there uncertainly next to the benches. Amalina clambered on top of a bench and jumped up and down.

"Look at the pretty lady!" she cried, clapping her hands.

Diello pulled her into his arms. "Hush."

"Why?"

He put his lips against her ear so his breath would tickle her. "You have to be quiet."

Amalina giggled.

Lady Bethalie stopped and pointed at Amalina. "Who is this child?" she asked.

Diello's arm tightened around his sister. Excited by all the attention, Amalina granted the baroness and her entourage a wide smile and waved.

Lady Bethalie lit up, and she clapped her hands together much like Amalina. "What a little darling!"

Onner Timmons leaned close to her ladyship and murmured, frowning, but Lady Bethalie shrugged dismissively.

"Faelin?" she said. "Well, no matter. I wish to hold her. Bring her to me."

Diello backed away with Amalina, but the attendants were already crowding around them.

"Give us the child," they said. "How dirty she is! Someone clean her face and hands. Be quick!"

They tugged at Amalina, who turned shy and clung to Diello's neck. He kept a protective hand on her curly head. "No," he protested hoarsely. "She doesn't like strangers."

"Stupid boy," said one of the women. "This is a great honor. The baroness won't hurt her."

Onner Timmons was already snapping his fingers at a serving woman who hastened forward with a basin of water.

Before Diello could protest further, Amalina was whisked away from him, cleaned efficiently despite her howls, and carried up the aisle to the baroness, now sitting on the dais next to her husband with her pink silk skirts arranged prettily.

Cooing and clapping her hands, she took Amalina on her lap and bribed the child with a sweet pulled from her pocket. "Ah, she likes comfits. I thought she would. Such blue eyes! Is she not a pretty little thing, my lord?"

Lord Malques cast his wife an indulgent smile. "The two of you make a charming sight, my dear."

His tone made Diello wince and Cynthe roll her eyes.

Laughing, the baroness went on playing with Amalina as order was called in the assembly and proceedings resumed.

The baron beckoned to Diello alone, but Cynthe stepped forward with him. Together, they faced Lord Malques.

Diello managed a bow of sorts. He poked his sister's arm, and she bobbed a curtsy that looked strange in her boyish clothing. Some of the onlookers laughed, and Cynthe's face turned as pink as Lady Bethalie's dress.

The baron neither laughed nor smiled, and Diello liked him for that. Still, it was hard to withstand this man's somber scrutiny. Brezog had retreated somewhere, making it impossible for Diello to keep an eye on him.

"Had Stephel any other sons besides you?" Lord Malques asked.

And so the questions began. Legal questions. Personal questions. How old was he? How long had the farm been in his father's family? How many hectares made up the property? What were its boundaries? How much livestock? Was there a license paid to grow crops? Were the taxes paid? To what amount?

Diello struggled to answer, to make it clear there were no taxes owed, ever, and wondered why he was being asked things that Onner Timmons could tell the baron.

"As for your mother, the Fae woman, was theirs a legal marriage or a common-law joining?"

"Marriage!" Cynthe cried.

The baron's eyes barely flickered in her direction.

"They were married, my lord," Diello said.

"By Antrasin law?"

Diello floundered a moment. He heard someone

snickering, and heat flooded up to his hairline. His fists grew tight at his sides.

"Well?" Lord Malques asked. "Was their marriage recorded by Antrasin law?"

Cynthe opened her mouth, but Diello pinched her.

"You must forgive me," he said, imitating his mother's cool, aloof Fae tone. "I was not present on that occasion and so cannot answer your question."

Laughter went up around him. Even Lady Bethalie chuckled. "He speaks with the wit of a born courtier, my lord."

Lord Malques still didn't smile. His gaze bored into Diello.

"Legal rights of inheritance are not to be trifled with," the baron said. "If you do not know that, boy, then learn it now. It is not appropriate to jest with the authority of this court."

Cynthe leaned close and whispered furiously to Diello in Fae, "Speak up. Show him the deed seal and prove you're the rightful heir. Then we can go. Let him deal with the gorlord."

As though he'd overheard, Brezog came back, standing behind Lord Malques's chair. *Are they in league together?* Diello wondered.

The gorlord stared over Lady Bethalie's shoulder at Amalina, who was now playing with the baroness's pearl necklace. Diello tensed, fearing that Brezog would try to grab his sister and carry her off in the middle of this crowd. What would the gorlord do if Diello tried to warn the baron again?

The baron cleared his throat. "Your attention, boy."

Diello looked up at Lord Malques. He felt he was play-ing a game with rules he didn't understand. "Yes, my lord?"

"Where in Embarthi did your mother hail from?"

Diello had been taught by his parents how to answer if ever he was questioned too closely about Lwyneth's origins. "She grew up in Antrasia," he lied. "She came from Eber-on-Tamesley, in Bannethshire."

"Surely that is untrue," Lord Malques said. "Was your father not driven from his duties in Embarthi by scandal and misconduct? Was your mother not the root of that scandal and the cause of Stephel's disgrace?"

"No!" Cynthe cried.

"No!" Diello echoed.

"More untruths." Lord Malques stared down at Diello. "I knew Stephel from boyhood. I saw his rise and his dis-grace. And that Fae woman was the cause."

"My mother came from Eber-on-Tamesley," Diello insisted, trying not to focus on what the baron said. "She was Fae, yes, but born and reared in Bannethshire."

"Hmm." Lord Malques seemed almost disappointed. He drummed his square-tipped fingers on his chair arm. "Ban-nethshire, eh? Of course. All the way across the kingdom, as far from here as possible." He gave Diello a less-than-pleasant smile. "A long way to seek a bride, especially for a farmsteader."

There was something in the baron's tone that Diello didn't understand, and he had nothing to say. Pa's coaching hadn't prepared him for questioning like this.

"Did he never mention his service to the king? Or his time in Embarthi?"

Diello hesitated. "No, my lord."

"No, I imagine not. What man wants to tell his son of how he came to be stripped of his knighthood and honors, or how he nearly brought this kingdom to the brink of war with Embarthi? What man, having once been a Knight of Carnethie, wants to explain his downfall?"

"Carnethie!" Diello said in astonishment while Cynthe squeezed his arm. "But that's—that's a—"

"*Pa?*" Cynthe said. "How is it possible?"

Although he and Cynthe had been long convinced that Pa was once a trained warrior, they'd thought he'd served as an ordinary Shieldsman. But Carnethie was the supreme order of knights, reserved only for the bravest and most valiant warriors in Antrasia. Noble birth was not required, but no knight could belong to the order unless the king chose him personally. And Pa—*Pa* had been such a man.

All this time, Diello chided himself, *I thought he was just a farmer.*

"Stephel," Lord Malques went on bitterly, "who came home to Wodesley and begged me for permission to change his name. I would not agree. Why should I let him hide from his dishonor? Now, let us sort the lies from the truth, boy. Your mother was—"

"The daughter of a jeweler, from Eber-on-Tamesley," Diello lied, more confused than ever.

Brezog's eyes shifted from Amalina to Diello.

The image of a sword filled Diello's mind. It was white, shining with a radiance that made him feel stronger. How he yearned to actually see it, to hold it.

I am Eirian, it whispered. *Come to me.*

With difficulty he concentrated on the baron.

"Is the man still living?" Lord Malques asked. "Any other family there?"

"Our uncle lives in Eber-on-Tamesley," Diello said. "He's a jeweler there, like his father before him. His name is Owain."

"And you know your uncle well?"

"No, my lord. We've never visited him, and he's never come here."

"Ah, a stranger," the baron said. Brezog made a gesture behind him, and Lord Malques's eyes grew glassy. He rubbed his temple and sighed.

Hoping the interview was over, Diello asked, "Please, my lord, may we go home to our farm?"

"Ownership of the farm is now in dispute," the baron said. "You intend to seek a claim, then?"

"Yes, I—"

"Do you have your father's deed seal? It should have been in Stephel's possession. Without it, your claim can never be validated."

It was like being impaled with one of Cynthe's arrows. Diello began to announce that he had the seal and could prove his rightful claim then and there, but Brezog gripped the back of the baron's chair and Diello hesitated. Magic— Brezog's magic—was pressing him to speak up. *But why does the gorlord want the deed seal, especially after it burned his hand last night?* He heard again his father's voice, making him swear to protect it, and knew the baron would take the deed seal from him and give it to Brezog.

"Say something!" Cynthe whispered.

The baron's hand twitched on the arm of his chair, and Diello could feel the magic that the gorlord was exerting, sending prickles running up his arms, making him shiver. Under his tunic, he could feel the deed seal against his flesh. Most men would have kept theirs in a strongbox for safety, but not Pa. It was strange that the goblins hadn't stolen it from Pa last night, except they probably couldn't touch it. *Brezog knows I have it,* Diello thought. *Why doesn't he have Lord Malques take it from me? Or do I have to give it to them?*

It was the only explanation he could think of.

Lord Malques rose to his feet, towering over Diello. "Do you have it?"

"I—I—no."

"Are you certain, boy? Certain you haven't seen it, or know where it might be?"

"Show it to him," Cynthe hissed. "What's wrong with you?"

I promised. A deathbed promise is sacred.

He heard himself say, clearly and truly, "My lord, I cannot answer you as to where it might be."

Cynthe's face filled with disappointment and fury. Would she give him away? But she held her tongue.

"A pity," the baron said. "You have insisted on truth when a lie would have served you better, and lied when you should have spoken the truth. This ties my hands completely."

"I don't—"

"If my authority isn't sufficient to awe you, then we shall rely on the gods." The baron pulled his gold crumix from beneath his tunic. "Stephel was once my dear friend. That he should raise his son to lie to me is shameful."

The shame should be on you, trying to steal our farm.

"Pa always spoke the truth."

"Clearly he did not, since you are filled with his falsehoods." Lord Malques held out his crumix on his palm. "Touch this, and tell me the truth."

A hush fell over the assembly. Even Lady Bethalie stopped playing with Amalina to watch.

Diello knew there was no actual magic in a crumix, yet Pa had taught him to respect other men's beliefs. Faith could be a powerful force, and humans held the crumix sacred, for it symbolized their circle of gods as well as Antrasin unity with these deities.

Brezog pointed his finger at Diello.

"Come here," the baron growled. "Hurry up."

Diello ventured closer to the dais.

"Place your right hand on it," Lord Malques commanded.

Diello touched the crumix with his fingertips, but the baron caught his hand, pushing the object into Diello's palm.

"Now," the baron said, "the truth! Swear to me on this holy crumix. If you lie, your tongue will shrivel up and you will be struck mute for the rest of your life."

Diello tried to pull his hand away, but Lord Malques gripped harder, nearly crushing Diello's bones in his fist.

"Swear!"

"I—I swear," Diello whispered.

"Will you give me Stephel's deed seal?"

"I c-can't." Diello's tongue was so dry it hurt.

There was no flash of light, no flesh-searing heat. The baron dropped Diello's hand and sat back, pressing his fingers to his brow.

Diello felt his tongue gently with his teeth and flexed his aching hand. The crumix had cut into his palm, leaving an angry red mark, but that was all. Were they done at last?

He looked at Brezog, but the gorlord was focused on the baron.

Lord Malques lifted his head. "Now hear the findings of the magistrate. Without a clear establishment of title, by Antrasin law no underage child can—"

"I'm thirteen!" Diello said. "That's of age . . . or close enough."

The baron's mouth tightened. "No Faelin child of any age can inherit human property. Your insistence in claiming this Fae woman as your legal mother—"

"She is!"

"Were you not of mixed blood, you might stand a chance of inheriting. Under the terms of a court-appointed guardianship, of course."

"We own the farm," Cynthe jumped in. "We—"

"The seal would give you the right to appeal this court's decision," the baron continued. "It would then be for the king to decide whether your claim is valid."

"This appeal," Diello spoke before his sister could blurt out more, "can we, as Faelin, carry such a petition to the king?"

"Why do you ask?" the baron countered. "You've sworn on sacred oath that you don't have the seal. Did you perjure yourself? Have you thought of where your father kept it?"

The questions were like a bog, filled with trickery and traps. "I just want to be *clear*," Diello said. "Can Faelin appeal?"

Lord Malques looked reluctant to answer. "No, they cannot."

"So," Diello said, "even if I had the seal, it wouldn't change the law. We can't inherit, and we can't appeal. What justice is this?"

A muscle twitched beneath the baron's eye. Diello wondered if he was fighting the gorlord's spell. "A relative such as your uncle Owain—if proven to be a solid citizen of Bannethshire of long standing and good character—might be able to claim the property on your behalf. Still, this man's existence is questionable, and he's of Fae lineage. Our laws would not favor his suit."

"I don't understand," Diello said. "Fae folk own property in Antrasia!"

"I'm afraid it is your father's family that matters here. Since you have no paternal relatives—*human* relatives—to assume guardianship and aid you, there is little to be done now except for me to grant the deed to the owner of the adjoining lands."

"But—but *you* are that owner!"

"That is true."

Diello swept an indignant look around the hall, but he saw no face scowling in disapproval, no hand rising in objection. Except for Cynthe, the onlookers all seemed to admire the baron's audacity.

"This isn't right!" Diello shouted.

Cynthe was tugging at him. "Show them. Show them!"

Diello reached for the cord around his neck. *How could Pa have ever called you friend?* But he couldn't help but look from the baron's face to that of Brezog's. The satisfaction blazing in those horrid eyes stopped him.

It's not the baron's fault, Diello thought, dropping his hand to his side. *Brezog is making him do this. But why should a gor-goblin care about my inheritance? What does he want with the seal? What does this have to do with Eirian?*

Once more, he felt the pressure of Brezog's will against him. His bones hummed and ached, except where the seal hung over his chest. Diello felt its magic flowing through him, countering the gorlord's dark power. When Brezog's coercion receded, Diello continued to tingle all over. He raised his chin and saw the glee in Brezog's face turn into anger.

Choke me if you want, Diello thought, *but I will never give it to you.*

chapter sixteen

ynthe seemed to finally understand that there was more going on here than Diello could say. She gripped his hand.

"Are we dismissed, my lord?" Diello asked.

"Not yet. Now that you are both orphaned and homeless, by law, you will be indentured."

"Be a serf?" Cynthe squeaked. "Indentured for life, like a—like a criminal? But we are freeborn, my lord! Who could make such a law?"

Diello couldn't believe it. If indentured, he would live, work, and die by Lord Malques's order. He would have no rights, no will of his own. He would have to lick Onner Timmons's boots and obey the steward every day of his life.

He was convinced that Brezog—now pacing back and forth behind the baron's chair—was manipulating Lord Malques to be this cruel as punishment for his refusal to surrender the seal. *But how do I accuse the gorlord, when they can't even see what he really is?*

"Is there anyone in the village who would be willing to take you in?" Lord Malques asked. "Master Timmons, are there no Faelin families who might extend them charity?"

"The Ferrins, perhaps."

"No!" Diello and Cynthe cried together. Diello would rather run away than live crammed in that filthy hovel with eight other children who were never fed enough. Wilt Ferrin was a lazy man who drank and beat his family.

"My lord," Diello pleaded, "we don't deserve to lose our freeborn rights. We won't steal or make trouble for the village. We'll put no burden on anyone else for our welfare. Our father taught us how to take care of ourselves. We'll work hard and—"

"Begging cannot change the law," the baron cut in. "Without family, you lose your rights of birthrank."

"We *have* family," Diello said. "Uncle Owain."

"Ah yes, the mythical uncle."

"He's real!"

"For your father's sake," Lord Malques said coldly, "for the friendship we knew as boys and for the regard my father once held for him, I shall grant you an exemption and not indenture you."

Diello let out his breath. "Thank you."

"I don't want your gratitude. Everything depends on whether your uncle will agree to house and take responsibility for you . . . all."

"Of course he'll take us in," Diello said.

"Then I grant you permission to travel from this shire. But if your uncle is not found or if he will not acknowledge kinship with you because you are Faelin, back you must return."

Diello and Cynthe exchanged a quick glance. Of course, their uncle didn't really live in Eber-on-Tamesley, and Diello had no intention of going there. But the baron didn't need to know that.

"We'll make our way there at once," Diello said. "We'll set out today, in fact."

"Not alone. You are too young to travel so far on your own."

Timmons stepped forward and murmured in the baron's ear. Lord Malques nodded approval. "It seems that tomorrow we are sending a group of boys to be apprenticed. They will pass near Eber-on-Tamesley. You and your sisters will ride along."

"No, thank you," Cynthe said. "We don't need help."

If she isn't careful, we might end up indentured yet. "What my sister means, my lord, is that although we could journey there on our own, we accept your offer with thanks."

"It's best that you go to your uncle as soon as possible," Lord Malques said. "Put yesterday's misfortune behind you and look to your future." He gestured for them to move aside. "That is all."

The Audience was over.

Brezog turned and vanished through a door at the end of the hall.

Diello held out his hand to Amalina. "Thank her ladyship for her kindness, Amie," he said. "It's time for us to go."

Grinning, Amalina tried to scoot off Lady Bethalie's lap, but the baroness would not release her.

"I like this child. I shall keep her."

"Good-bye, pretty lady!" Amalina said, handing back Lady Bethalie's pearls. "I have to go with Del."

"No, dearest," the woman cooed to her. "Remember what I promised you?"

Amalina nodded. "I 'member."

Diello tugged at his sister, but the baroness still held Amalina tight. This fine lady, with her pearls and her pink silk, couldn't be serious. Could she?

"My lord," the baroness said loudly, interrupting the next suppliant, "this dreadful boy dares argue with me. Will you allow his impertinence?"

"Certainly not, my dear," Lord Malques replied. "But the child belongs with her family, don't you agree?"

"To live hand to mouth as an unwanted orphan? These older children are scarcely better than hooligans, but the little one has charming potential. Once she's old enough, she can be trained into a pretty waiting maid. I shall see the poppet well advantaged."

"No, my lord!" Diello cried. "Please!"

The baron gestured to a black-bearded man in armor. "Warden, see the boy and his sister removed from the hall."

"Yes, sir!"

As the warden started forward, Cynthe turned to Lady Bethalie. "You can't keep her, my lady. She *has* to come with us. She's our sister!"

"Nonsense," Lady Bethalie said. She stroked Amalina's bright curls. "This sweet child is too young for a journey halfway across the kingdom. You should thank me for my interest in her welfare."

"As my lady says," the baron added. "This is best for the child."

"But she's not yours," Diello insisted.

A strong hand gripped his sore shoulder. "Hush, my lad," Sergeant Alton murmured in his ear. "Don't be a fool. The lady's favor is not to be thrown away. Think of the advantages she'll give to the little mite."

Diello wrenched away from him. "She's trying to steal my sister as the baron has stolen my land!"

The puckered look on the sergeant's face told Diello he'd gone too far. But he didn't care. Defiantly, he stood his ground when the warden gestured for him to leave the hall, but Alton grasped his arm and marched him down the aisle.

"Get her, Cynthe!" Diello called. "Amie, come on!"

But the warden intervened, scooping Amalina out of Cynthe's reach. A Shieldsman pulled Cynthe back, squirming and struggling, as the warden handed Amalina to one of the baroness's attendants. Diello saw Amalina striking the woman's shoulder with her tiny fists. Her wails filled the air.

"I want Cynnie. I want Del!"

Diello struggled harder, but Alton manhandled him through the door.

"Del!" Amalina shrieked.

Diello's heart felt like it was cracking in two. He twisted his head around for one last look back, but Amalina was gone, her wails growing fainter in the distance.

Diello appealed to the sergeant. "This is wrong. It's wrong!"

Shoving him past the guards, a grim-faced Alton waited until Cynthe was ejected from the hall. The massive doors slammed behind them.

"Amalina!" Cynthe cried. She kicked her captor in the shins.

Alton shoved Diello against the wall, then took Cynthe away from the Shieldsman and pinned her expertly next to her brother.

"Now you settle down, the pair of you," he said. "It's done, and let that be an end to it."

"No!" Diello and Cynthe shouted.

The warden came through the doors. He was a hawk-faced man with a scarred cheek.

"Sergeant Alton!" he said. "Have the boy whipped for his impertinence."

"Yes, sir!"

It was too much. Diello no longer cared what happened to him. "They can't take her from us like that. They can't turn her into a servant and—"

"Sergeant, you have your orders," the warden said, and he strode back inside.

"Right, then," Alton said. "Let's get this done."

Diello drew back with his fists clenched.

"Now, now, none of that," Alton said, his tone much softer now that the warden had gone. "If you'll be calm and cause no more trouble, I'll see it's just one lick."

Diello stared at him, hating him, trusting nothing he said.

Cynthe stepped between them. "If you whip my brother for speaking the truth, then you must whip me as well."

"That's enough," Alton said, glancing over his shoulder at the guards, who were laughing. "I am trying to treat you fairly," he added in a low voice, "but if you keep spitting at me like a she-cat, then I've got no choice but to be harsh."

"What right has the baron to treat us so?" she demanded.

"Every right! But these ain't his lordship's orders," Alton replied. "They're the warden's. He'll have discipline in the castle no matter what. As for you, boy, I reckon it's your choice. Take what I've offered or make this hard for yourself. Have you ever seen a man's back flayed to bloody bits?"

"I'll take the one lick," Diello said.

"And so will I," Cynthe declared.

Shoulder to shoulder, they faced the sergeant.

He nodded. "Then move along."

They were hustled out across the inner ward to a much-scarred post fitted with iron rings. Diello didn't want Alton to think him a coward, but he didn't know if he could bear to be shackled in iron.

Cynthe saw the post and shivered. "No," she whispered.

"Don't be losing your nerve now," Alton said. A few idle Shieldsmen gathered around, joined by curious stableboys and some of the pages.

The sergeant opened a nearby wooden chest and withdrew a whip, shaking out its coils expertly. "Face the post, boy," he ordered Diello. "Put your hands on the wood. There's not much point in shackling you for one lash, but I warn you to stand still."

As he spoke, he snapped the whip to one side, cracking it in a way that shot Diello's heart into his throat. *I can endure this. I will show these Antrasins that Faelin are braver than they are.*

Cynthe touched his arm, meeting his look in silence before she stepped aside. Diello faced the post and gripped it with trembling hands.

"One lash for impertinence to his lordship!" Alton called out.

The whip whistled through the air and cracked against Diello's back. The sting filled his spine with fire. He held back his scream with gritted teeth and shuddered until he could draw a breath.

"Punishment delivered," Alton said formally. "Step aside."

Diello pushed himself away from the post. The pain made his eyes water. He blinked fiercely, not wanting anyone to think he was crying.

"Next!" Alton called out, coiling his whip.

Her eyes squinched up with determination, Cynthe moved to take Diello's place.

Diello looked at Alton. "Let me take her lash."

"No," Cynthe said. "We're in this together."

"I will take her lash," he insisted.

"Right," Alton said.

"I told you no!" Cynthe cried. "That's not why I—"

Alton beckoned to one of the Shieldsmen. "Milt, move her out of the way."

The man obeyed, grabbing Cynthe around the middle and lifting her aside.

Diello turned to face the post. The anticipation was much worse this time because he knew exactly what was coming. His knuckles whitened as he gripped the wood, and he braced himself as best he could. He had to do this, had to take it, because no sister of his would ever feel an Antrasin lash.

The blow, when it came, was as harsh as the first. It drove his chest against the post, and reawakened the pain in his back. A grunt escaped him, and he tasted blood as his teeth sank into the inside of his lip, but he didn't cry out. *Straighten up! Look strong!* he told himself.

Instead, he pressed his sweating forehead to the post and closed his eyes in relief that it was over.

"Punishment delivered," Alton announced. "Milt, take this pair to the storeroom and lock 'em in. That should keep 'em out of trouble until they're hauled off on the morrow."

As the Shieldsman urged Diello and Cynthe forward, some of the onlookers grinned at them or gave Diello friendly pats on his shoulder.

"Well done!" someone called out.

Diello pulled his shoulders straight and lifted his head higher, glad that he'd taken the punishment like a man. He'd protected Cynthe, keeping his promise to Pa. He'd lied on the baron's crumix and gotten away with it. So far. He touched his teeth to his tongue again to make sure it wasn't shriveling. Come the morning, they would be well quit of this place and not a moment too soon. If only they had Amalina. No amount of praise or respect could make up for that. There must be something he could do. But what? They didn't even have their weapons.

Hustled to the storeroom, the twins were shoved inside. The door banged shut, plunging them back into the dark.

chapter seventeen

losed up in the stifling room, Diello's newfound confidence crumbled. His back stung and throbbed, and the humiliation of the whipping post haunted him. Stumbling to the door, Diello kicked the panels hard.

"So break your foot and cripple yourself," Cynthe said through the darkness.

He gave the door another kick, and another. He wished he could strike the steward, or the baron, or Brezog. He wanted to hurt someone, anyone. He was tired of being treated like a child, small and ineffectual, cheated and ordered around by liars and thieves. He wanted to smash them all, and make them fear *him* for a change.

He kicked the door until the pain in his toes made him stop. Groaning, he put his sore back to the door and slid down it. He rested his chin on his knees, trying to think. There had to be a way out of this. But he couldn't find it yet.

Cynthe rustled around in the straw. Then he heard her snap her fingers. She snapped them again. He heard a sizzle and saw a spark.

Alarmed, he crawled toward her. "Be careful!"

She snapped her fingers a third time, and there was a tongue of fire licking at the pile of straw that she'd made. Cynthe sat on the dirty floor with a sour smile on her face.

"There!" she said, feeding the feeble flame another handful of straw. "I'd like to see those stupid Antrasins flick fire. They don't know anything!"

Without a word, Diello started scraping a bare ring around Cynthe with his foot, pushing all the straw on the floor well away from the flames.

She watched him, making no effort to help. "You think I'll burn us up?"

"You might," he said. "You're careless when you're angry."

"And you're a toad."

"We could burn to death in here, or die of the smoke. No one would hear us, much less let us out."

She got to her feet, picked up the wooden stool, and smashed it to pieces against the wall. Gathering the kindling, she placed a piece over the fire and watched the flames lick the wood. The room, warm to begin with, was growing very hot. Smoke boiled and eddied, curling upward toward a crack in the stone where a glimmer of daylight showed.

"Look," Diello said. "I'm furious about Amalina, too, but you don't have to roast us alive."

"Stop giving me orders!"

"I'm not."

"Who told you to be so bossy? Are you in charge?"

"If you want to blame someone, blame the goblins and the baron and the baron's wife, but don't blame me."

She snapped her fingers, and a spark shot past his head.

"I'm the oldest. I'm the tallest. I don't need protecting, and I don't need your help."

"Is that what this is about?" he asked. "Me saving you from a whipping?"

"Did you think I'd cry? Did you think I'd lose my nerve and beg Alton not to strike me as hard as he did you?" Cynthe gave Diello a push. "I was *trying* to take a stand with you, you daft ninny!"

"You're the ninny, getting angry over something so stupid," he muttered.

She draped her arm across her brow and pretended to swoon. "Am I supposed to tell you how brave and noble you were? Well, I won't! I think you're horrid for meddling."

"Meddling! Too bad you didn't get a lashing. It might have taught you something. Like gratitude."

"I'm not grateful to you. Who let the baron steal our farm? Who acted dumber than a tree stump and refused to show him proof of ownership? And who let him and his lady steal our little sister? A waiting maid indeed." Cynthe spat on the floor. "You should have stood up to them."

"How? What chance did I have?"

"You should have taken twenty lashes if it meant saving our property and our sister."

"And I'd have done it!" Diello shouted. "But what was I supposed to do? The baron wasn't listening to me, no matter what I said. And I believe Brezog was clouding his mind, controlling him."

"Maybe." Cynthe rubbed her throat, remembering. "But all you had to do was show them the seal. Or let me do it!"

"Brezog wants it! He tried taking it from me last night

and couldn't touch it, so here he was today, ready for Lord Malques to get it for him."

"If that's true, then why didn't the baron just take it away from you?" She raised her hand. "Wait! I forgot. You never showed it to him. You let him think it was lost, so he could do anything to us he wanted."

"You heard what he said. Even if I'd produced the seal, Faelin can't inherit."

"I don't believe that," Cynthe cried. "It isn't fair!"

"Nothing's fair when the laws aren't written for us," Diello said. "They don't protect us. That's the way it is, whether we like it or not."

"I hate the laws," she muttered, turning her face away. "I hate being Faelin!"

Something in her voice warned him. And even in the firelight, Diello could see that her skin was glowing. He gulped, glancing around, and hoped there was enough water in the wooden bucket.

"Cynthe," he began, forcing himself to sound calm. "You shouldn't get so angry. Try to—"

"Try to what? Calm down?" She poked the fire with a scrap of wood, sending up a shower of sparks and a big gout of smoke. The air in the storeroom was growing close and thick. Diello struggled not to cough. "Why should I calm down, Diello?" she went on. "Mamee always said that in Embarthi the first-born daughter is honored, but here, because I'm a girl, no one pays any attention to me. No one lets me speak for us in public. No one cares what I say or think. I'm not even allowed to take punishment with you, punishment that I deserved just as much."

"Neither of us deserved to be whipped," he said. "We aren't serfs. They had no right."

"Yet how they praised you for it."

He stiffened. "I didn't ask them to."

"You did the Antrasin thing. You made me into nothing," she said. "You were not Faelin out there, Diello. You acted like a human."

From Cynthe, there was no worse insult. "I have to look after you. I didn't want you to get hurt."

"Did Pa make you promise to protect me?"

Diello nodded.

"Pa and his human ways. I don't need that, Diello. I'm a better archer than you, faster than you. Who are you to speak for me or tell me what to do?"

Her skin was glowing brighter. The fire leaped up when she spoke, crackling and popping.

"You're getting too upset," Diello said. "You'll go into a tempest if you're not careful."

"Fine!"

Diello looked for cover, but there wasn't any. The bed and barrels were gone. There was nothing in the room except a few dusty heaps of straw, the old sack of a mattress piled in the corner, and the wooden pail of water. He eased toward the pail.

"Stop!" Cynthe cried. He froze, not liking the way her eyes were glittering at him. "I know what you're thinking," she said, "but I like my fire just as it is. I wish I could burn down this castle. That's a good exchange, isn't it? They take our farm and sister, and I take their castle."

"You can't burn down a stone fortress," he said.

"I can try."

There was more than fury in her voice, more than grief. Diello didn't believe she could really carry out her threat. She'd been flicking fire for only a few weeks now. Still, the reckless anger in her voice and the crackle of the flames made him nervous.

"What about Amalina?" he asked, trying to distract her. If it was a tempest building inside her—a real one—he wasn't sure he could manage it. *Oh, Mamee,* he thought, *if only you were here.* "What happens to Amalina if you set the castle on fire?"

"Anything that happens to her is *your* fault. It's all your fault!"

"That's an awful thing to say."

"I wasn't fooled by your show of bravery at the whipping post. Why weren't you brave where it counted?"

"You want to judge me? Then judge this: Pa made me swear to keep the seal safe. Not the farm, Cynthe, but the *seal.* I think there's something special about it, something unusual. It seems to have magic in it."

"Not likely!" she scoffed. "Pa had no magic, and he wouldn't carry anything that did."

Only a day ago, Diello would have agreed with her. Now he didn't know what to think. *Pa was a Carnethie Knight and he never told us. He pretended to be a simple farmer. He pretended to have scant use for magic, yet he carried this.* Diello rubbed the seal through his tunic.

"I don't think they can take it by force," he said. "Lord Malques knew I was lying about it, but he seemed to want me to give it to him. That's odd, isn't it?"

"What difference does it make?"

Diello shrugged. "All I know is that I promised Pa, and I intend to keep that promise. If you think I was going to show it to Lord Malques, especially with Brezog standing at his shoulder, ready to trick him out of it, then you're the one that's daft."

Her glow dimmed. "Do you really think he would have given it to Brezog?"

"I do."

"So it was Brezog making Lord Malques be so mean to us?"

"Yes."

"Oh. I knew he was spying, but I didn't think of that."

"No, Cynthe, you don't think," Diello said, forgetting he was trying to calm her down. "You just act. And lately you always believe I'm wrong about things. Maybe you should trust me sometimes, the way you used to."

"Trust you?" Her stare turned dangerous again. "Why should I after what you did to me last night?" The glow in her skin grew brighter than ever. "You thought I didn't notice what happened when you held my arm. Do you think I'm stupid?"

"I was trying to help you."

"By betraying me?"

"No one betrayed you."

"You ruined my Gift," she snarled. "Just when it was coming, you had to be jealous and destroy everything."

"Jealous! Of what?"

"Maybe you found your Gift first, but Sight makes you sick half the time. Why wouldn't you resent me for having a Gift that's truly useful?"

"How is it useful?" he retorted. "Exactly *what* is your Gift?"

She hesitated.

"Hah!" he said in triumph. "You don't know, do you? That's because it hasn't manifested yet."

"It did! It tried to, until you ruined it."

"I didn't ruin anything. It wasn't your Gift anyway, just a tempest."

"How do you know?" she yelled.

"I just do. Did you ever think that my knowing might be part of *my* Gift? And all I did was make it stop coming right then, the way I used to stop your nightmares when we were little."

"Well, you had no right to do it. Interfering and making all the decisions—" She stopped, a strange expression on her face.

"There wasn't time to ask you," he said. "And if I delayed your Gift, then I'm *not* sorry, because it didn't need to manifest in front of the Shieldsmen. Use some sense, Cynthe! They barely tolerate us now. How do you think we'd have been treated then?"

"It was my Gift!"

"It was a tempest! And we didn't need it then, just like we don't need it now."

Cynthe lifted her shaking hands. They were throwing off sparks of light. "Too late, because it's back. My Gift is here!"

"Cynthe, be careful—"

"Stop telling me what to do! This time I'm—" She jerked like a puppet on strings. "What is it? What's it doing to me?"

Her body jerked again. Diello gripped her shoulders, trying to hold her steady. He could feel tremors running through her. Her teeth were chattering, and her eyes were rolling back in her head. Her skin kept shooting off sparks that stung him when they landed.

He tried to draw the excess magic away as he'd done before, but it wasn't working. The magic today was stronger, too wild for him to catch. He'd have to talk her through it. Not that he knew a lot, but the most important thing was for her to stay calm and not panic.

"Cynthe, listen to me. Can you control it?"

"I don't know!" she wailed, pushing away from him. She ran crazily for the nearest wall, only to bounce off it and come running back. She seemed unable to stop herself. "It's building inside me. I don't know what to do!"

Diello backed away from her, fending her off when she came careening into him. He could feel a gathering tension in the hot room, like the air being charged before a strike of summer lightning. His hair was rising off his skull, standing up in spikes. His skin was itching and prickling until he wanted to claw at himself. It was worse than last night. He couldn't control this, and he found himself pressing his spine against the stone wall as he watched her, more scared than he wanted to admit. This wasn't the way it was supposed to happen.

Something was very, very wrong.

"Slow down," he said as she smacked into a wall, stumbled, and started running again. "Get in a corner and stay in it if you can. Concentrate on gathering the power into your control."

"I can't! You're interfering somehow." Cynthe's face contorted, and now she was crying. "I feel like I'm going to explode. It hurts. It hurts! Mamee said it would never hurt. What's wrong?"

Diello caught her and tried to hold her wrists, but the energy coursing over her skin repelled his hands. Trying again, he finally got a good grip on her. Power jolted up his arms, making them ache all the way to his shoulders. He wasn't sure how long he could hold her.

But just as she'd been willing to go to the whipping post with him, he was willing to hang on now even if she shook him to pieces.

As long as he could remember, he and Cynthe had been waiting eagerly for their Gifts to manifest. Mamee had always assured them that it would be a wonderful experience and that their Gifts would help their lives in many small but beneficial ways. They had wished and dreamed for more, of course, longing to know what it was like to control real, potent magic—despite Mamee telling them over and over that they would never have it. Faelin, she would say, did not have *true* magic, and that was the way of the world. But she'd encouraged them to anticipate the moment when their Gift would come. She promised that it would be as simple as one day not being able to flick fire and the next day making flames come to life with a snap of their fingers. Mamee had warned them that some girls experienced a few tempests before their Gift actually manifested—she'd described it as a "swirl of magic," like being caught in a weak whirlwind. Tempests didn't seem to happen to boys, and Mamee had said that Cynthe might escape them, too. But she wanted

Cynthe and Diello to understand what could happen just in case. Over and over, she'd emphasized that they weren't to be frightened of a tempest, that it was a lovely transition both natural and happy.

But Mamee could not have been more wrong. Diello had never known his mother to be mistaken about anything. And now she wasn't here to help. Again, he tried to pull the magic into himself, but something inside him repelled it.

Cynthe's head was flopping about as she spasmed. "You're m-making it worse!"

"I'm trying to control it."

"Well, stop!" she cried. "Let it go. Diello, let it go!"

He was afraid to, afraid of what so much pent-up power might do in the storeroom. She was glowing so brightly she might have been on fire herself. The sparks flashed and crackled around her head. Her back arched, and her arms tried to flail, but Diello held them close to her sides, hugging her with all his strength.

"Control it, Cynthe!" he urged her, feeling that wild power coursing through his own bones now. He was shaking from the force of it. His body seemed to want to separate in all directions. Desperately, he concentrated on helping his sister.

"Try, Cynthe!" he said. "You've got to!"

"Let it go!" she yelled through chattering teeth. "Let it goooo!"

At last he did, and the release of power hit him like a battering ram, knocking him backward into the door. Winded and gasping, he huddled on the floor while bolts of raw magic zoomed through the air, spraying rainbows of color.

With her arms outstretched and her head lolling back, Cynthe called out something, but he couldn't understand her. The power roared through her, shooting colors from her eyes and open mouth, and blazing in a corona around her head.

Diello felt like his skin was being scraped off his body. He couldn't catch his breath. He couldn't hear, could barely see. The walls were shaking and cracking on all sides, dribbling down bits of dust and stone, and on the floor their water bucket was jiggling and sloshing.

Water.

He pushed himself toward it, crawling through the swirling energy currents that pulled at him from all sides. Picking up the bucket, he resisted the urge to plunge his hands in the water and protect himself. Instead, he turned around, ready to dash Cynthe with it.

He saw her levitating above the floor. The rainbow swirls of magic lashed his hair back and whipped his clothing as he watched her floating higher and higher off the ground. The Fae were said to fly, but Faelin never did. Even Mamee, after she lost most of her magic, couldn't do it.

But here was Cynthe, rising into the air right in front of him as if she were a feather caught on some eddy of the breeze. With all his heart he wished that he, too, could do that.

Cynthe's little fire, forgotten, licked its orange tongues toward a nearby pile of straw, which suddenly ignited. Flames raced through the heaped straw and caught the mattress with a whoosh.

Smoke and sparks filled the room. Diello dashed the

water on the blazing mattress, putting it out with a great belch of dark smoke that drove him back, coughing. He kicked the wet, charred straw toward the stone wall, where it could do no more harm, and stamped out any last embers.

Some of the water must have splashed on Cynthe, because the magic vanished, like a snuffed candle. She tumbled to the floor with a thud and lay there, while the glow faded from her skin.

For an awful moment he thought she was dead. But then she wrapped her arms around herself and began to rock from side to side on the floor.

"Cynthe?"

She didn't seem to hear him. Eyes closed, she went on rocking. Diello smoothed her hair back from her face, wishing she would look at him. She was keening a high-pitched breathless noise.

"Cynthe."

Could she be suffering from the Dark Embrace? It was magic gone wrong, and happened sometimes to Faelin who had more human blood than Fae. Old Griffudd had told them about it once in a hair-raising story of a Faelin cobbler who sold his soul to the Death Lord in exchange for magic and paid a terrible price: He'd been driven insane. When they'd asked Mamee about it later, she'd assured them that such a thing would never happen to them.

Maybe she lied to us, Diello thought. *Like Pa.*

He was shocked at his own disloyalty, but he was so worried he didn't know what to think or believe anymore.

Someone is bound to come and let us out, he thought.

Someone must have noticed the shaking walls and all the noise.

But so far, no one was unlocking the door to check on them. Maybe everyone was too afraid.

Diello gave his twin a gentle shake. "Cynthe! Can you hear me? Are you all right?"

She opened her eyes. They were no longer coppery green—they were a blank silver. Diello leaped away from her.

Afraid of being plunged again into total darkness, he fed the embers a piece of the broken stool and blew to encourage them back to life. By the time he sat up and dared to look at his sister again, the silver hue in her eyes had turned back to green.

"Diello?" she whispered. "What was that?"

"A tempest," he said, his voice squeaking. "Do you hurt anywhere? Do you remember falling?"

She stared at him with a growing smile. "Was I flying?"

"Floating. Well, almost flying." He held up his hand. "You were this high off the floor."

"Really?"

He nodded.

She scrambled to her feet, and he did the same.

"My Gift is flying!" Cynthe said. "*Really* flying. I can't believe it. I've always wanted that more than anything, but I didn't think it would ever happen."

"You'll have to practice."

"Yes, a lot!"

"But not right now," Diello cautioned her. "You'd better rest."

"Who needs rest?" She jumped, but no higher than

normal, and when she came down her knees nearly buckled under her.

He caught her and moved her over to the dry side of the room. "Sit down awhile. You may have another tempest or two before the Gift really takes hold."

Cynthe nodded, her eyes dreamy now, a smile still curling her lips. "I'm going to fly," she said. "I didn't think Faelin ever could."

"That must be why the tempest was so strong. It's a very strong Gift." He paused, then asked wistfully, "What did it feel like?"

"Like—like riding a rainbow. Wild and free, with nothing to hold me down. I was scared at first because my whole body felt like it might shake apart, but I'm in one piece." She held up her hands and laughed. "Just before everything went black, I felt as if I might soar to the sky, and never find my way back."

He touched her fingers. They felt cool and normal, but he knew that nothing was going to be normal again. Cynthe would need real training. Flying—and possibly having other major powers—was a far different situation than casting a minor spell to make her arrows fly faster or her cooking taste better (if she ever learned to do more than boil marrows). Cynthe needed skilled guidance. Mamee had told them that young Faelin often saw their magic come and go sporadically for the first several months. Diello certainly never knew when Sight would work for him, although in the last day or so he seemed to be better at controlling it. But if Cynthe got hurt because they didn't know what they were doing—if she were, say, high off the ground and then lost her magic—*please, Guardian, what am I to do?*

"Diello?" Cynthe asked in a small voice.

"Yes?"

"I'm very happy, but I—I think I'm scared, too."

"I know," he said softly. "But don't be."

"I—I need to go to Embarthi, don't I? Will Uncle Owain help us? If we can find him there?"

Diello sighed. "I suppose."

"Will he teach me? Will any of the Fae teach me what to do?"

"I don't know." By all he'd heard, the Fae folk weren't much more accepting of Faelin than humans were. Mamee and Pa had lived as exiles, and even though Mamee had never complained about life at the farmstead, it was obvious to all of them how deeply she missed Embarthi. If her family had rejected her, and driven her away because she married Pa, why should her brother welcome them? Diello guessed that Mamee had more relatives, but she had never told her children their names or talked about them. Still, where else could they get the help and training Cynthe needed?

"Diello."

"Yes?"

Cynthe leaned forward and clasped his hand. "I hope you'll manifest the same Gift. We're twins, after all. We could have the same ability."

He felt a flicker of hope. "Maybe."

"I'm sure of it," she said, but he knew she wasn't. "Oh, if only it were already working. Then I could jump right over the walls of this castle."

He nodded, wishing things could be that simple. "You're not very patient, but this is something you'll have to practice."

"It's easy to be patient when you know what you're working for. I can start off slowly by jumping out of trees. I shouldn't go too high too soon because I'll have to learn about wind and not let it tumble me out of the sky the way it does the young eagles. But I'll be good at it. I know I will."

"Yes. But right now, I think you should rest."

"I will. I'm so tired." Cynthe let her eyes fall shut, only to open them again. "I'm sorry I called you all those names earlier. I was just being ratty."

"I know."

"You told the baron a fearsome big lie," she whispered sleepily. "And on his crumix, too. That was really brave of you."

"His crumix has no power over us," Diello said. He touched his teeth to his tongue, but it was still all right.

"What about Amalina?" Cynthe asked, her excitement gone.

"Don't worry about her right now. Get some sleep. Magic really saps your strength."

"Like you know." But she smiled, to show she was teasing. "There's a lot to do now. We'll have to plan."

"We've time. We'll talk more later."

Still smiling, Cynthe closed her eyes.

Watching her sleep in the ruddy firelight, Diello let some of his fears drain away. It was the first good thing that had happened to them in a long time, even if it did raise a lot of new questions. No matter what Lord Malques said, he and

Cynthe were not going to Eber-on-Tamesley. They had to find Uncle Owain—who lived somewhere in Embarthi.

The idea of such a journey was daunting, but thrilling, too. It was the kind of adventure he'd dreamed about all his life. He would have to think about supplies and distance and whether they had a good chance of reaching the land of the Fae before winter set in. But for now, they had to think about getting out of here and rescuing Amalina.

One thing at a time, Diello told himself.

And by the time Cynthe woke up, he intended to have a plan of escape.

chapter eighteen

Later that day, a Shieldsman came and released them. Reeking of smoke, they stumbled gratefully out into the sunshine, where a wary servant fed them pickles and cheese for lunch. The Shieldsman returned their knives, although he refused to acknowledge their demands for the quarterstaff and bow. He allowed them to explore the inner ward, and as long as they didn't venture too near the gatehouse, the hall, the apartments, the cookhouse, the stables and barracks, the chapel, or the mews, they could do much as they pleased.

"This is impossible," Cynthe complained, leaning against a laden cart parked near the well. "We can't get to Amalina if they won't let us indoors."

"That's probably the idea."

"So what do we do?" she asked, slinging her long braid over her shoulder. "Shall I create a diversion while you run into the apartments?"

Diello squinted up at the wall walk, where sentries on duty strolled by. One was staring down at them right then. Diello cleared his throat and tried to look innocent. "I think they're expecting that."

Cynthe followed his gaze and grinned. "They're watching us, aren't they?"

"Pretty closely, I'd say."

"Are you saying there's nothing we can do?"

He glanced at his twin. Since her nap, she seemed back to her usual self. In fact, she was brimming with good humor and mischief. *Anyone looking at her would suspect her of being up to something.*

"You!" yelled a man's gruff voice. "Get away from the well!"

Diello and Cynthe hastened away and found themselves a new spot next to Lady Bethalie's garden. The stone wall was short, reaching only to Diello's chest, so it was easy to peer over. Flagstone walks laced the garden, meeting at a fountain at the center. There didn't seem to be any food grown in it. What a luxury to have only flowers, he marveled, admiring its beauty despite himself. Every plant and shrub was bursting with blossoms, the growth so lush it reminded him of Mamee's vegetable patch. He watched a gardener pushing a wooden barrow piled with horse manure while another gardener spread it around the plants.

Cynthe hooked her elbows over the top of the wall and hung there, kicking her toes on the stone. A ginger cat came strolling along the top of the wall and rubbed against her before jumping down inside the garden and crawling under a shady bush. She started to scramble after the cat, but Diello stopped her. He needed to talk to her about Amalina, and she wasn't going to like it.

"Wait," he said. "Let's stay in sight so they'll leave us alone."

"What's wrong? Don't you have an escape plan?"

"I've got two."

"Aren't you clever? What are they?"

He hesitated, then squared his shoulders. "The way I figure it, the plan with the best chance of success means we can't take Amalina with us."

Cynthe's mouth pinched tight at the corners. "Leave her behind," she said flatly. "Leave her with these thieves and liars."

Diello had gone over it in every way possible, and it had to be faced, however much they both disliked it. "She's too little. It's going to be very hard, traveling so far. It will be dangerous."

"We'll help her," Cynthe said. "She's not exactly safe here with these people."

"I know that, but getting her out of the castle is probably impossible."

"So you're giving up, abandoning your own sister? Throwing her away like something unwanted, something that's too much trouble to bother with?"

He winced. "It's not like that."

"Then how is it?"

"Look, I'd carry Amalina a thousand leagues on my back, but we'll have to move fast, take chances that she can't. They like her here. They'll treat her well until we can return for her."

Cynthe shook her head. "You can't honestly believe what you're saying. If we're lucky, we might just reach Embarthi before winter sets in. If we find Uncle Owain and he's willing to help us, we might return by next summer.

Anything could happen to her in a year. She might even forget who we are!"

"I've already thought of all that," he said.

"What's your other plan?"

"It's not much. And very risky—"

"Tell me! I'll do anything if it means getting her out of here."

He leaned closer, lowering his voice. "We need some way to be invisible, to get inside without anyone seeing us."

Cynthe punched him hard in the shoulder.

"I'm serious," he said.

"And I'm not? Where are you going to acquire a *cymunffyl*? We can't pretend we have that kind of magical power, Diello. We have to think of something that will really work."

Diello watched some of the pages hurry by. "You're the hunter, Cynthe. How does a rabbit hide?"

"It sits in plain sight, its fur blending in with the undergrowth behind it." She nodded. "I see! We're going to steal livery and sneak in."

"Hush! Not so loud." Diello crouched at the base of the wall and pulled her down to his level. "I'm going in. You're staying out here."

"No, I'm not. We're in this together."

"Will you just listen? The sentries—*everyone*—are watching us too closely for us both to sneak about. I need you to stay in plain sight, and we'll have to make them believe I'm with you. Fill my tunic with straw and prop it over there in the shade." He pointed.

Cynthe stared at him skeptically. "They may be human, but they aren't stupid."

He flushed. "I told you it wasn't a very good idea. If you can do better—"

"I can." She pulled back the bandage on her arm and picked at the cut until it started bleeding. Hooking her elbows over the wall, she scrambled onto the top, where she crouched a moment before standing up, holding her arms outstretched and teetering slightly.

One of the sentries shouted at her. Ignoring him, she looked down at Diello. "When I fall off, fetch Hant to help me."

Diello grimaced. "What do you want with a lunk like him?"

"Don't call him that. He's been nice to us," she said, wobbling. "He'll take me to the castle infirmary if I ask him."

"Yes, but—"

"Stop arguing and get ready. I'll be inside then, won't I? And I'm the hunter."

"Who found her the last time?" he asked. "Besides, the infirmary isn't where she'll be."

Cynthe shrieked and tumbled off the wall into the garden. Peering over, Diello saw her lying among the crushed flowers with her arm beneath her.

"Cynthe!" he yelled.

She winked at him before closing her eyes and unleashing a shrill wail of agony.

Well, they were in it now. Hampered by his sore back, Diello climbed onto the wall, only to be jerked down by a Shieldsman.

"What's all this racket?" the man asked as Cynthe went

on shrieking and sobbing. "Weren't you told to stay away from her ladyship's garden?"

"My sister!" Diello tried to twist free of the man's grasp. "She's fallen. She's hurt."

The Shieldsman stared over the wall at her.

"She needs help," Diello said urgently. "She's *bleeding*!"

"Serves her right for not doing what she was told," the Shieldsman muttered. "Come on, girl! If you can yell that loudly, you have enough strength to sit up."

Cynthe didn't move, but her anguished screams fell silent.

It wasn't going to work. Diello gave the man an angry shove. "Don't talk to her like that. She's—"

"Here now!" Sergeant Alton said, rushing up to them. "What's happened? Report!"

"Cynthe fell off the wall," Diello said before the Shieldsman could obey the order. "Please help her."

Alton swore beneath his breath and hurried for the gate. "Shieldsman, with me!"

Diello edged away through the gathering onlookers. He had no intention of searching for Hant now. Ducking past one of the stableboys, he collided hard with a tall, lanky form, bounced backward, and nearly fell. *Hant.*

"Careful!" he said, steadying Diello. "What's going on?"

"Cynthe's hurt!" Diello said, pointing to where Alton was emerging through the garden gate, carrying Cynthe.

She had her face pressed to the sergeant's shoulder and was cradling her arm. Looking horrified, Hant rushed up to them and gently touched Cynthe's shoulder before Alton ordered him out of the way. Cynthe lifted her head and gave Hant a small, helpless smile. Diello couldn't help but admire his twin's performance. *She's as good as any mummer,* he thought.

Alton—with Hant hovering anxiously—didn't carry Cynthe into the apartments. Instead, he took her inside one of the watchtowers. It was just as Diello had feared: the infirmary was nowhere near the living quarters. Even so, Cynthe had created a wonderful diversion. Everyone seemed to have forgotten about Diello for the moment.

He lost no time in crossing the yard, ducking out of sight behind a cartload of fodder, and making his way past the cookhouse to the laundry. When the washmaids weren't looking, he grabbed a stained livery tabard awaiting cleaning and pulled it on over his head. Picking up a large basket, he carried it inside the apartments, holding it on his shoulder to hide his face from the guard at the door.

Inside, he paused to draw in a few steadying breaths and ease his aching back before starting up the opulent staircase. Just as he reached the first landing, a voice called out, "You there! Oaf! Use the servants' stairs!"

Diello swung about and saw a guard pointing at a door almost concealed in the wall paneling. Gulping, Diello slipped into a dank, gloomy passage so narrow he could barely keep the basket from brushing the walls. He met other servants. Most of them pushed past him without a glance. Each time he passed a door, he paused, wondering if he should go through it. Amalina could be anywhere. And without the dab of *cloigwylie* Mamee had kept on her at the farmstead, Diello had no trail to follow.

A maid gave him an impatient push from behind. "What are you dawdling for? Are those clean sheets for her ladyship's bedchamber? Get upstairs with them."

He made his way up a tight spiral of stone steps, struggling with the basket. By the time he reached the top, he was panting and his palms were slippery. If he could just find Amie. *Please, Guardian, let her be quiet when she sees me and not call out my name.* He hoped to hide her in the large basket and carry her out of here, but if he were caught . . .

Easing open the door at the landing, he peered into a long gallery furnished with carved chairs and finely woven carpets. Tall windows admitted streams of sunlight. He saw no one, but in the distance he could hear the chattering of feminine voices. The same dog was still yapping as before.

His feet made no sound on the rugs as he crept along. There were three doors along the wall opposite the windows. He pressed his ear to the first one, heard nothing inside, and cautiously opened the door. It was a bedchamber, sumptuously appointed with a massive bed hung with velvet draperies. A manservant folding an undertunic turned his head toward the door.

Diello jumped back, shutting the door hastily, and hurried to the next one. This time, his damp fingers slipped on the latch. He steadied his hand and pushed it open, peering inside.

Another bedchamber, this one lavish and feminine in hues of soft rose. Biting his lip, Diello started to retreat before he reconsidered. The voices were coming from the last chamber adjacent. Possibly it was some sort of sitting room for Lady Bethalie. No one was here in her bedroom right now, although he had the feeling that at any moment someone might walk in and discover him.

Still, this was his chance to search.

He slipped inside, putting the basket on the floor, and tiptoed across scattered silk carpets and fur rugs. Skirting the carved, gilded bed, he saw a door on his left standing ajar. Through it he could glimpse her ladyship's attendants sitting on embroidered chairs and floor cushions. They were nibbling delicacies off a silver tray and conversing. Carefully, Diello hurried past the doorway, praying that no one saw him.

To the right stood another door, one carved from oak. It was narrow and tightly closed. He listened, but no sound came from within. It wasn't locked, and when he swung it open, wincing as his fingers brushed the iron latch, he saw a small bed, just the right size for a child. A shelf held a set of wooden balls in a bowl and a draughts board. A doll with an embroidered face and gown of fawn silk lay on the floor.

Lord Malques and Lady Bethalie had no children of their own, so this must be Amalina's room.

But Amalina was not there.

Diello picked up the doll. It looked flattened, perhaps trod upon. As soon as he touched it, a rush of images filled his mind: a cloaked figure, intense terror, and darkness like a smothering blanket.

Dropping the doll, Diello stood trembling. He was trying to sort out the meaning of what he'd just experienced when he heard a muffled gasp from behind him.

He spun around, and saw Lady Bethalie staring open-mouthed at him.

"Where's Amalina?" he asked hoarsely. "Where's my sister?"

"Sister?" she repeated. "What mean you?" Her voice was slow, as though drunk. "And . . . how dare you enter my chamber, you—you thief!"

"Where is she? Who took her?"

With a blank expression, Lady Bethalie fingered her pearl necklace and made no answer.

"Amalina!" he shouted. "What's become of her?"

Lady Bethalie didn't seem to hear Diello. Pointing at him, she screamed.

chapter nineteen

that night, Diello and Cynthe sat on crude wooden bunks in a shed jutting out behind the mews. *Servants quarters*, Diello thought, gazing around. After what they'd done to the storeroom, the warden had ordered they be moved here where they couldn't endanger the castle's stores and provisions. The tiny space was just enough to hold two bunks and a wooden stool. The door was rickety, made of sun-warped boards with cracks between them, and hung on leather hinges. A window too narrow to fit through let in a few stray beams of moonlight. But after that horrid storeroom, it was like a palace.

"I hate them," Cynthe said, slapping her hand against the wall. "I hate them all!"

Sitting cross-legged on his bunk, Diello gently flexed his shoulders to ease the throbbing ache in his back. After being caught in Lady Bethalie's room, he'd been whipped again. But even worse, no one could tell him and Cynthe where Amalina had gone. At first, he thought it was because they were angry at him for snooping. When he pointed at the child-sized bed and toys, an attendant slapped his hand and scolded him for trespassing in a room reserved for the babies Lady Bethalie had never borne.

"You have hurt our sweet mistress," the woman said. "Intruded on her privacy and distressed her."

"I just want my sister!" Diello cried.

"Why would we have her? Get out!"

Then the Shieldsmen had come and taken him outside.

"Hant," Diello had whispered at the whipping post after his punishment. "What have they done with Amalina?"

"Who?"

"My little sister. You got the cook to give her breakfast."

"Better move along," Hant said.

Diello caught his sleeve. "*Please!* What's happened to her? Why won't you tell me?"

There was only puzzlement in Hant's eyes. "Tell you what? That I think she's pretty?"

"Not Cynthe! *Amalina.*" Diello held out his hand. "This tall. Curly hair. Three years old."

Hant rubbed his jaw thoughtfully. "Little, you say?"

"Yes! You were playing with her this morning, tickling her."

A peculiar blankness smoothed Hant's features. He shook his head.

"You can't have forgotten! If you're forbidden to tell me anything, at least admit she's here somewhere."

Hant blinked slowly before he said, "Never saw any little one. There's just you and Cynthe, and always was."

"But—"

"Hush up! Get moving."

Now, picking a hole in the blanket folded atop his bunk, Diello could feel his worry like a stone pressing down on his chest. *It's as if she never existed.*

"Where could she be?" Cynthe asked for the countless time. "Do you think they sold her? Was she naughty and they punished her? Is she dead?"

"No," he said. "Not dead."

"How can you know that?"

He thought of the feelings he'd gathered from the doll. "She's not dead."

"Then what's happened to her?"

Diello sighed. He feared Brezog was behind this, and the idea was so unbearable he couldn't speak of it.

His twin chewed on the end of her braid. "Maybe I'll be flying *tomorrow*. I'll escape this place and look for her."

"Fine. You do that."

"It could happen," she said. "It could!"

"Grow up, Cynthe. While you're flying, what if the castle archers attack you?"

She opened her mouth, but didn't speak.

"Don't say they wouldn't do it, because we know they would. They'd be afraid, and they'd knock you from the sky to your death."

"All right," she said. "This morning, when that woman took Amie, I thought things were as bad as they could get. Now—"

"Stop moaning," he said. "It doesn't help."

"If only I could fly now!" Cynthe cried out. "Fly and fight! Why does everything have to take so long?"

Diello didn't answer. What was there to say?

"Do you think Pa and Mamee are watching over her? No, what am I saying?" Cynthe pressed her hands to her face. "Mamee can't transform because they buried her. She can't even fade."

Diello bowed his head. His eyes were stinging. "Don't think about it," he whispered.

"I have to," Cynthe said, lowering her hands. "When we find Amie, we're going to kick these Antrasins tail over ears. Right?"

"Right." He spat on his palm and held it out. "I swear it."

She spat on her hand and clasped his hard. "Double sworn!"

But their bravado sounded hollow. Cynthe stretched out on her bunk and started picking at the new bandage she'd gotten in the infirmary.

Pulling out the deed seal from beneath his tunic, Diello balanced it on his palm, where the moonlight could shine on its engraved surface. There was more to this than ownership of property. What connection could there be between the deed seal and the mysterious sword that Brezog wanted?

"What are you doing with that?" Cynthe asked from her bunk. "You might as well throw it away."

Diello shrugged. He didn't intend to resume the old argument. "I want to understand it," he said.

"What's to understand? It's just a record of property."

"No. You saw it burn Brezog's hand last night. There's magic in it. And Pa made me promise to safeguard it."

"You told me that already," Cynthe said, yawning loudly.

"He made me swear an oath on my *life*, Cynthe. There

was a ritual to it, like he was passing some great responsibility to me. And he said Eirian had to be returned."

"What's Eirian?"

"I'm not sure. But it seems to be the sword Brezog wants."

"Maybe you're just making up a mystery so you don't feel guilty for losing the farm," Cynthe said. "It's done. We've got other things to worry about now."

Diello tightened his grip on the disk. "That goblin is still after us," he insisted. "We have to figure this out before Brezog comes back."

"He won't," Cynthe said. "He'll pester the baron now, not us. The land's not ours anymore, remember?"

"It isn't about the farm," Diello said. "It's about this seal. Remember how Pa wouldn't take it off?"

"Not even in the swimming hole," Cynthe said quietly in the darkness. "He'd carry it in his mouth while he swam, just in case the cord broke. Diello, I know you don't want to grow crops all your life, but we have to keep the land. Otherwise, Pa and Mamee were never there. They never mattered, and they'll never be remembered. Do you understand what I mean?"

"Have you changed your mind about going to Embarthi? Once we find Amalina, do you want to petition the King of Antrasia?"

"Don't be daft. Like we could."

"It would be a waste of effort," Diello agreed, hiding his relief. "There's more I have to tell you. Pa said that he and Mamee were wrong."

"About what?"

"I don't know. I think it had to do with Eirian."

"Back to the sword again? Why don't you stop thinking about it and worry about Amalina instead?"

"Maybe they're connected."

She sat up. "Are you saying Brezog took her?"

He hadn't meant to worry Cynthe more, but now he was glad to share the burden of his suspicions. "I think he did."

Cynthe scrambled off her bunk and rushed at the door. It didn't budge. She struck it with her fists and kicked it before turning around. "If he did, she's dead."

"I don't know that!" Diello cried. "And neither do you. He could want her for a hostage, something to bargain with."

Cynthe paced across the shed. "Why should he? He's big and nasty and has a lot more magic than we do. And if he took Amie away, then he can take us. There's nothing here to stop him."

"Except the magic in the seal. And we aren't fooled by his disguise spells."

"If you're trying to make me feel secure, you're failing. Could we have a weaker defense?"

"It's worked for us so far."

Cynthe snorted, but she said, "All right. So the gorlord wants this thing he thinks we have."

"Eirian."

"Pa didn't own any sword called Eirian."

"How do you know? Carnethie Knights are stationed across the kingdom, and many of them serve beyond Antrasia's borders. Pa must have traveled the world before he brought Mamee back here from Embarthi. He could have carried a sword with that name."

"We've seen Pa's sword. He stopped taking care of it and let it rust. It was ordinary anyway, nothing the gorlord is after."

Diello thought about the vision that had glimmered in his mind. "Eirian is long and thin, with carving on the blade." He angled the deed seal in the moonlight. "It shines like this, only brighter."

"You're making that up."

"No, I've seen it."

"Where?"

He wasn't sure how much to tell her. The moonlight made the silver disk look molten. The engraved words seemed to glow.

"I'm waiting for you to invent the rest of your tale," Cynthe taunted him. "Where have you seen this sword Eirian?"

The disk glowed brighter.

"Where, Diello?" Cynthe sat down on her bunk. "Can't you think of a whopper, now that you've started this fable?"

"I've seen the sword in my mind," he admitted. "It exists . . . somewhere."

"What a fib! Mamee always said you should have been a bard."

"She *never* did."

"A troubadour then, singing away with crystal bones."

"Stop it," he said. "Having crystal bones isn't about music or singing and well you know it."

"Then stop talking about Eirian. I don't care about some old sword that—"

"Cynthe!" Diello was certain that the disk was now shining far more brightly. "Say the sword's name again."

"Why?"

"Just say it!"

She sighed. "Eirian."

The engraved words flashed. Diello swung off his bunk and knelt before her, holding up the deed seal.

"Eirian," he said, but nothing happened.

Cynthe bent over it, her head against his. "Eirian."

The writing shimmered and glowed. The words seemed to be shifting about. Diello felt a tingle in his hands.

"Are the letters moving?" Cynthe whispered.

Diello touched them, and felt warmth flow up his finger. "Look," he breathed. He bent closer, peering at the archaic Antrasin wording. The phrases—*parceled ground, three hectares in size, shall mark its corners by the gray stone in the northwest and the quince hedge in the northeast, be it known by all that Cribble Creek serves the east boundary*—pulled apart, scattering into gibberish.

Then they faded, and other words appeared, taking their place.

The new writing was ornate. Diello recognized it as Fae script. "You're doing something, Cynthe."

"How? Why doesn't it respond to you?"

"I don't know. Say the sword's name again!"

"Eirian," she murmured, and the Fae words bathed his hand and wrist in soft, clear light.

"What is it?" Cynthe asked. "What does it say?"

"You read Fae script better than I do."

"But how is it—"

"Never mind how," he said. "Read it!"

"I can't . . . Is that an E?"

"Keep going."

"I . . . R . . ." She stopped. "Eirian?"

The disk flashed so brightly they shielded their eyes. When Diello looked again, the Fae words were glowing in the air between them. Mamee's lessons in reading Fae came back to him, and the words became clear:

Eirian
All seek you
None find you
Locked in a wheel that cannot roll,
A circle closed, a mountain's cup.
Slumber in your chamber safe,
Where the sky's tears guard you.
Apart, yet together,
Separate, yet unbroken,
Come not to life again, Eirian,
Lest you cut the world into pieces
That cannot be mended.

"There's no sense to it," Cynthe said as the glowing words began to fade from the air. "It's just a jumble of words and phrases that don't mean anything."

"Of course they do," Diello said. "I think it's a riddle."

"Can you solve it?"

"It has to be a clue to where Eirian is hidden."

"That last bit's a warning," Cynthe said. "What kind of sword is it, do you think?"

"I don't know." Diello rubbed his eyes. "But our parents

died for it, and Brezog wants it very, very badly. We need to go home and see if we can find it."

"Better we find Amalina first."

"No. We know that Brezog has her. He wants us to bargain for her with the sword."

"Can you read minds now, like he does?" Cynthe asked. "Are you *sure*?"

"No, I'm not sure."

"So you could be completely wrong."

"What other explanation makes sense?" he demanded. And when Cynthe had no response, he went on, "We need to find the sword."

"If it's that important, we should leave it where it is. Trick the gorlord somehow."

Diello slipped the cord back over his head and tucked the seal away. "If we have the sword, we probably could defeat Brezog."

"You can't use a sword! There's too much iron."

"It's magic—"

"Yes, and even if you could hold it, what do you expect to do with it? Fight all the goblins by yourself? You aren't even trained."

Diello struggled to keep his temper. "What do you suggest?"

"Like I said, we trick him. We're clever enough to do that."

"You realize Amie's life could be at stake?"

"Of course I do! But I'm not going to give that old goblin a magic sword that our parents died protecting."

"That's just it. It's a *magic* sword. We'll have the advantage."

"No. As long as Brezog has Amalina, *he* has the advantage," Cynthe said. "Don't forget that."

"Even so, its power could make all the difference. Besides, once we get Amalina back we still have an obligation to return the sword to where it belongs."

Cynthe pulled off her moccasins and flung them at the foot of her bunk. "Return where? Did Pa tell you where to take it?"

"No."

She loosened her braid and let her hair hang over her shoulders. "Does the riddle say where to take it?"

"Well . . . no. But—"

"We can't do everything at once," she said. "Let's stick to what's most important. Getting Amie back."

"I know, but even if we escape and rescue her somehow, that doesn't mean the sword is safe."

"Brezog searched everywhere and tore our farm to pieces, but he didn't find it. So it's secure enough for now."

"What if Lord Malques won't let us back on the farm to search for it when we return? Or what if—"

"If Pa had told you where it was and where to take it, then I'd say yes, we must fulfill his last wish right away," Cynthe said. "But he didn't. And he wouldn't want us to put it above Amalina's safety." Her voice wavered. "I hope you're right about why Brezog's taken her. I hope there's still a chance."

"Believe it," Diello said. "We have to."

Cynthe sniffed and pressed the back of her wrist over her eyes.

To distract her, Diello started the game of questions and answers that Pa used to play with them. "What's first?" he asked.

Cynthe sighed. "Escape."

The familiar ritual soothed Diello, too. "Can it be done?" he asked.

"Yes."

"What's second?"

"Gathering supplies at home. And looking for my wolf."

"Can it be done?"

"Yes . . . But we'll need a lot of luck to find anything still usable. I hope he hasn't starved."

"Luck needed," Diello said sternly, still imitating Pa. "So noted. What's third?"

"Tracking Amalina."

"Can it be done?"

She hesitated.

"Can it be done?"

"Yes," she said with determination. "Once we pick up the trail, we'll—"

"So noted," Diello interrupted. No matter what Cynthe believed, he was convinced that Brezog would soon be tracking *them*. He wondered if Brezog was watching them now, but he didn't sense the use of magic nearby. "What's fourth?"

"That's enough to worry about," she mumbled, her eyes closing. "Saving her and going to Embarthi. . . . Uncle Owain will help us with the sword later, once we find him."

Her voice slurred over the last words, and her breathing

grew heavy and still. Diello settled himself gingerly on his bunk, lying on his side to spare his sore back. He stared out the tiny window at the night sky.

"I won't forget my promise, Pa," he whispered, curling his fingers around the seal and feeling the light tingle of magic. "I'll find a way to outwit Brezog and save Amie somehow, but no matter what Cynthe says, Eirian isn't safe anymore. Help me to find it, Pa. Help me to solve the riddle fast, before we leave the farm forever."

chapter twenty

In the morning, they were brought a breakfast of fruit and bread plus clean changes of clothing. Washing in the pail of water provided, Diello shook his damp curls and pulled on his new tunic. Although he didn't want to accept Antrasin charity, this tunic was a lot better than his ragged, filthy one. He liked the color, too, a mulberry hue brighter than what Mamee had always made for him. It fit him well.

Cynthe held up her simple new gown of light blue, measuring it against the length of her body without much enthusiasm.

"It looks long enough," Diello said, curious to see if she'd actually wear it. At home, the only time she ever put on girl's clothing was for Mamee's birthday.

She now tossed it aside in disdain, rolling up his discarded tunic and cramming it through her belt. "Mamee's cloth is worth mending," she said. "I won't wear their horrid clothes."

Shrugging, Diello went on eating his breakfast of berries. The fruit was tasty, but he longed for the heartier fare of fried ham, egg pudding, griddle cakes, or piping hot fruit pastries he was used to at home.

Instead of eating, Cynthe took out her bronze knife and hacked off her braid.

Diello nearly choked on a berry. Her straight blonde hair swung loose and wayward along her jaw line. The ends were rough, but the effect was remarkable. In her tunic and leggings, she looked nothing like a girl at all.

She tossed aside her long braid and turned to face him, grinning as she ran her fingers through her short hair. "It's so light! I feel like my head is . . . Don't look at me like that. It had to be done."

He understood. If they found their little sister and their escape plan worked, their long, hazardous journey to Embarthi would be safer for Cynthe if she masqueraded as a boy. But still . . . the sudden sacrifice of her hair bothered him. It had never been cut before. Diello had always admired it, even been proud of it in a way. Cynthe would sit at night drying her hair by the fire, and Mamee would brush it for her until it crackled. Cynthe had complained about the inconvenience and refused to let it flow loose down her back, but it had been a thing of beauty.

Now, seeing her throwing it aside like trash . . .

A Shieldsman came to the door. "Let's go. Now!"

Cynthe gathered her quiver, slinging it over her shoulder, and sauntered out with a show of bravado on her face.

Diello bent to pick up the braid. It was surprisingly heavy; he could see why she'd been so often impatient with it. His precious bird whistle and the tinderbox already filled his pocket, so he scooped up the dress that she'd tossed aside and wrapped it around the braid, bundling it into a narrow roll. He knew that Cynthe would think him a fool for keeping her hair, but he wanted it anyway. And even if she didn't wear the gown, they could use it for bandages. He thought of Amalina, hoping she was unharmed.

"Boy!" the Shieldsman shouted. "Outside!"

As Diello emerged, Cynthe shook her head at him. "You're daft," she said as expected. "My hair doesn't matter."

He didn't try to explain.

"Come on!" the Shieldsman said. "Don't dawdle."

The castle guard was being changed atop the walls. Diello and Cynthe were marched under the portcullis teeth in the gatehouse and entered the outer ward during the exchange of sentries. Precise shouts rang out as the sentries saluted one another. Diello would have liked to watch, but their escort pushed them along. The castle gates were not yet open for the day's business. A weathered wagon harnessed with a pair of stout horses stood parked near the gates. It had tall slatted sides and a wooden bench running around its interior. The back was open, and steps hung there by a pair of short ropes. No other boys were present yet.

Their escort pointed to a spot near the wagon. "Wait here, and keep quiet."

The sun was barely up, casting a feeble glow across the ward and leaving many shadows. Diello yawned as he rubbed the last bit of sleep from his eyes. But then he forgot all about being sleepy as guards brought up a ragtag group of boys. Most of them looked to be about the twins' age or younger, except for three older youths that towered over everyone. One of these bigger boys had a knife scar across his face, pulling one corner of his mouth into a sinister, permanent grin. He boxed a smaller boy's ears for sheer meanness, and pushed forward in line with an arrogance that Diello didn't like.

If their plan failed, and he and Cynthe had to ride all the way to Bannethshire with a bully like this . . .

Diello wished for his quarterstaff. If only Cynthe still had her bow.

"That scarred lout is trouble," she murmured in his ear.

He nodded.

A Shieldsman gestured at them, sending them over to join the group. "All of you, form a line now, and no pushing!"

While Diello and Cynthe obeyed orders, joining the back of the line, a ruckus broke out at the front, leading to a lot of noise and confused milling about. A couple of the youngest boys scrambled into the rickety old wagon for safety, but the rest went on shouting and jostling.

As far as Diello was concerned—the sooner they got in the wagon, the sooner they'd be out of the castle—and he and Cynthe could get away. So he shouldered his way through, but just as he reached the steps, someone bumped into him. Diello found himself pinned against the splintery side of the wagon by the boy with the knife scar. The other side of the boy's face was swollen and red, with a half-healed brand of T burned into his cheek.

T for thief.

"What're you looking at?" the bully asked.

Diello tried to squirm free, but he was punched hard in the stomach. Gasping, he felt the bigger boy fingering his pockets and taking the contents.

"Hey!" Diello yelled.

The whistle and tinderbox were dropped on the ground as the bully grabbed Diello's bronze knife from its belt sheath.

"What kind of little sticker is this?" he growled, throwing it down in disgust.

When Diello crouched to retrieve his things, the bully's knee thudded against his jaw. His head was still ringing as he was yanked up and the front of his tunic was twisted until it choked him. He gripped the bully's wrist, trying to loosen the throttling hold.

"What else you got?" the boy demanded. "Money? Something I can sell?"

"Quiet!" yelled one of the Shieldsmen, momentarily silencing the din. "Get lined up. Stand shoulder to shoulder. Now!"

Diello used the distraction to twist away from his tormentor and grab his belongings. He slid his knife into its sheath. The blue dress had been trampled by the boys. He wadded it between his hands, hoping no one realized he was carrying a girl's dress, much less Cynthe's hair. But he still couldn't bring himself to throw it away.

He decided that from now on he'd stay at the back of the herd.

"How's your jaw?" Cynthe asked, joining him.

"Not broken," he mumbled, embarrassed.

A familiar voice hailed them, and Hant sauntered up in his friendly way. The lanky boy smiled at Cynthe, but looked startled by her hair. "That's a change," he said.

Her face went pink, and she touched her neck. "Do you like it?"

"Um . . ." Hant thrust a rucksack into her hands. "I

thought you could use this, being—well—being without things of your own now." He smiled, showing his dimple.

Cynthe gave him a nod of thanks, then felt the sack's weight. "What's in it?"

"Oh, just some bits and bobs. But make sure you don't go sharing none of it with this mob. Bunch of troublemakers, they are, and good riddance to bad rubbish!" Hant's smile faded a bit. "I wish you didn't have to go with them."

"We'll be fine," Diello said, stepping between the tall boy and his twin. "Thanks for your kindness."

Hant went on gazing at Cynthe. "I'm glad you weren't much hurt yesterday." He took her hand in a gentle way and held it, while Cynthe's blush deepened. "Take care of that arm now." He kissed her cheek lightly. "And stay off walls."

With a nod of his head, he strode off. As Cynthe watched him go, pressing her palm to her cheek, Diello took the rucksack from her and stuffed the dress inside it, tying the strings securely. He hoped Hant's "bits and bobs" meant food. They would need it when they set out.

"He's nice," Cynthe murmured, still looking in Hant's direction.

Diello grunted, hoping she wasn't going sloppy on him, and slung the rucksack over his shoulder. "Yesterday, you were saying you hated all Antrasins. Except for Pa, of course." He raised his eyebrow. "And except, maybe, for Hant."

With fiery cheeks, she turned away, but not before he saw her lips curving in a private smile.

The labor peddler arrived. He was an old man with a paunch and bowed legs that made him lurch from side to side when he walked. Long hanks of greasy gray hair straggled down his neck from beneath his broad-brimmed hat, and his homespun tunic was stained from more than one meal. He even had greasy finger marks on the sides of his leggings, from the habit of wiping his hands there. With a bristly chin, pouches beneath his eyes, and red veins covering the end of his bulbous nose, he looked a right old sot to Diello, who was hoping that would make it easier to escape when the time came. But the peddler's eyes were sharp, missing nothing, and he pursed his mouth mean and tight. Diello vowed not to underestimate him.

Lurching up with a whip in one hand and a sheaf of papers in the other, the peddler poked at the bully. "Get aboard, Peck," he ordered. "I know all about you, and I'm warning you now I'll brook no trouble this trip."

The tall boy crossed his arms and stayed where he was. "Don't fancy going."

Braided leather whistled through the air as the whip uncoiled. It cracked across Peck's chest and shoulder. Yelling, Peck stepped back, but was struck again.

"Keep yer place in line!" bawled the peddler.

Peck took his place while everyone else stood frozen and wide-eyed. The peddler looked up and down the line of silent boys before cracking his whip in the air and making them jump. "Get aboard. One at a time. One at a time! And don't be all day about it!"

Peck climbed in first, going to the front of the wagon because the peddler's helper was prodding him with a long pole between the side slats. As soon as Peck reached the front, the helper bound his wrists with rope, tying him to one of the slats.

Diello's hopes sank. If they were all going to be bound as prisoners, then he and Cynthe didn't stand a chance.

But only the three large youths were tied at the front. The others were allowed to choose their places on the wooden seats. They shoved and jostled about, as the wagon rocked, creaking on its leather springs.

A tap on his shoulder made Diello jump. Sergeant Alton was beside the wagon, holding Cynthe's bow and Diello's quarterstaff. He handed them over.

"I came to wish you a good journey," he said.

Diello was too surprised to speak. He hadn't expected any kindness after the events of yesterday. Cynthe gripped her bow, running her fingers along it.

Alton cleared his throat. "See that you show a right proper gratitude to your uncle for giving you a home. Be respectful of him and don't give him no trouble."

"What's this?" the peddler asked, coming up to them. He poked Cynthe with the butt of his whip. "No weapons allowed. Faelin are trouble enough without having more ways to afflict honest working folk."

"These children ain't on your list," Alton said, his tone suddenly authoritative. "They're going to Eber-on-Tamesley as freeborn passengers. Aye, and there's no apprentice contract on 'em. Mind that, and see they don't end up sold in the labor market by mistake."

The peddler shuffled through his handful of greasy papers, peering shortsightedly and mumbling to himself. "Right you are. Ah, names of Dell and Cynt?"

"Close enough," the sergeant replied before Diello could correct the peddler. "Now you listen. His lordship's agent in

the town will have instructions to collect these two and see
'em delivered safely to their uncle. He be a respectable fellow, with means. A jeweler by name of Owain. You follow
me on this, old man? They ain't your usual riffraff, and don't
you treat 'em as such."

"Oh, of course. Of course. No need to worry yourself
about this pair. Fine boys, eh! I'll coddle 'em like bottles of
the best wine." Grinning widely, the peddler gestured for
Cynthe to climb into the wagon. "Hurry up, now. We must
be off."

But Cynthe stepped aside for Diello to go first. Holding
her unstrung bow in both hands, standing straight and tall,
she tilted her pale head to one side like Mamee at her most
imperious, and looked up at the sergeant. "About our little
sister," she said. "Can't you please tell us . . ."

Alton stared at her blankly.

"Our sister, Amalina. Lady Bethalie kept her. Don't you
remember?"

"Remember what?"

"I told you!" Diello said in her ear. "Mention her name
and they all go very strange. They're enspelled."

Cynthe frowned. "Then why not us? Why doesn't it
affect us?"

He could only shake his head.

"Now," Alton said, "you been a right handful, both of
you. Behave, and count your blessings for not being part of
this lot."

"Thank you," Diello said, since there seemed nothing
else they could do.

Nodding to them both, Sergeant Alton walked away.

As soon as he left, the boys in the wagon began to shout: "Faelin pigs! Faelin pigs! We ain't ridin' with Faelin pigs!"

Diello backed away from the wagon steps and the boys' hostile faces. Cynthe scowled.

Muttering, the labor peddler tucked his list and travel writ into his belt purse and shoved both Cynthe and Diello aside. "Kirv!" he shouted, and his assistant came running. "Put a rag in Peck's trap and shut 'em up!"

As Kirv obeyed, the peddler climbed up and began whipping the boys. Several yelped before there was quiet in the wagon. Boys scrambled to sit meekly on the benches. But while they might be cowed at present, Diello knew they'd blame him and Cynthe for this punishment.

"Better," the peddler said, wheezing from his efforts. "Now see that you all stay quiet, or you'll have the lash again."

No one uttered so much as a squeak. The peddler gathered his whip in his hands, bunching it carelessly, and looked over his passengers. He shifted several of them about, pulling a scrawny, ugly boy to the very back and plunking him down on the seat so hard the runt gasped. Stepping down, the peddler gestured at Cynthe and Diello.

"All right, my fine pair of freeborns. You ride here at the back, and if the dust ain't to your liking, I don't care, see? I ain't obliged to carry you in my wagon, other than wanting to please his lordship. So you cause me no trouble, and I'll get you delivered like his lordship wants. But if you Faelin pigs start squealing . . ." He grabbed Cynthe by her tunic and shoved her next to the scrawny boy. There wasn't enough room for Diello, but he was pushed in anyway, and the threat left hanging.

chapter twenty-one

Wedged in tight, with Cynthe's elbow cramming his ribs and the railing pole digging into his arm, Diello squirmed to find some relief while Kirv hammered the rear panel into place. Cynthe was crowding Diello more than ever, all but sitting on top of him and pinching him for attention.

"Scoot over!" she whispered, wrinkling her nose.

Diello caught a whiff of something stinkier than pig dung. As the wagon jolted forward, he shifted to get a good look at the boy sitting on Cynthe's other side. The runt was leaning over her, much too close, and peering into her face.

Whether a simpleton or a weirdling, he was an odd-looking creature, with eyes set too close together and a pointed nose much longer than a human's. Crooked and knobby, it looked like a mummer's mask stuck on a brown and splotchy smush of a face. Worst of all, every whiff of him made Diello want to gag.

The boy had to be part goblin. Diello knew that goblin and human half-breeds existed, but he'd never seen one before. Certainly they were rare, for most were drowned at birth in Antrasia. In the past, Diello would have been curious, but now he'd had enough of goblins to last him a lifetime.

The goblin-boy tapped Cynthe's arm with a grubby finger. "We will be apprenticed together," he announced. "We will be friends."

Diello changed places with Cynthe, moving next to the smelly creature while she scooted over with a sigh of gratitude.

The goblin-boy stared at Diello. He had short, very jagged teeth and a gray tongue that was too flat and narrow.

"I'm Scree," he said happily. "You don't mind sitting next to me, do you? I don't mind sitting next to you. You're Faelin. That means no one likes you. I am not Faelin, but no one likes me, either. We are the same."

"Uh . . . I'm Diello."

Scree leaned over him to peer at Cynthe again. He emitted the ripe, pungent odor of the chronically un-washed. His tattered clothes were crusted with grime, and at this proximity Diello could see patches of bare, spotty scalp through his thin strands of dirty hair.

"I'm Scree," he said to Cynthe. "I would prefer to sit next to you."

"We're staying as we are," she said firmly.

"I like to stare at you," Scree said. "For a boy, you are pretty."

Nervously, she looked away.

Pinching a fold of dirty tunic between his fingertips,

Diello pushed Scree back. "Shut up," he said. "Don't talk like that."

The other boys sniggered.

"Lookit 'em!" a black-haired boy called out. "The piggies don't like old stinkwort. Ain't it a shame?"

Diello cringed, but at least Scree stayed quiet. The wagon rolled through the gates, crossing the drawbridge and swaying down the long ramp before turning onto King's Road. Diello could feel Cynthe relax beside him. *Soon*, he thought. They just had to be patient and wait for their chance to break away.

The morning was cloudless and bright, bidding to be a scorching summer's day. The peddler and Kirv hunched side by side on the wooden seat. The assistant did the driving, handling the reins and clucking to the old horses that never quickened their pace beyond a plodding walk. The peddler glanced over his shoulder frequently to watch his cargo. He kept his whip ready. He was smoking a clay pipe that streamed a noxious odor of burning bakky weed into the air. Now and then he bellowed out a song in a rough, untrained voice. The assistant would join in the chorus with off-key harmony.

Oh! I had me a lassie
As pretty as the day
With hair bright as pennies
And me fortune, it was made.
Hey-o! Hey-lu!
Me fortune, it was made.

The noise grated on Diello's nerves as he watched the road unwinding beneath their wheels. Dust fogged up, yet he could see the castle walls and watchtowers for a long time, looming above the thatched roofs of Wodesley, before the tall trees closed out all sight of the fortress and village.

Cynthe's hand touched his briefly. Knowing what she was thinking, he gripped her fingers hard in reassurance.

"We'll get her back," he whispered. "Remember she's safe as long as Brezog thinks we have what he wants."

His twin nodded and ran her other hand up and down her bow.

"That is a small bow," Scree said, leaning over Diello to grin at Cynthe. "Do you own it? I think you must know how to use it. You wouldn't carry it if you didn't know how to use it. Unless it is not really yours. But I think it must be yours by the way you hold it. You have a quiver of arrows, too. I watched a man making arrows once. His name was Abram Fletcher. Do you know him? He does not live in Wodesley, but he makes arrows and you have arrows so I think you must know him."

Diello pushed Scree away. But he popped right back across Diello and reached out to tug Cynthe's sleeve. He didn't have claws, but the tips of his nails were dark brown, almost black. Whether that was due to dirt or his goblin heritage, Diello didn't much care.

"I like talking to you," Scree said to her. "What is your name? Do you have a name? I think you must have a good name. I would like to know it. Names are important. Did you know that? We have names we are given, but everyone should have a name they choose for themselves. I want to choose a name for myself, but I cannot think of one I like. Do you have a chosen name? I'm sure you're very clever, clever enough to think of two names. Perhaps you would give me one of them."

Cynthe rolled her eyes at Diello. This time he shoved Scree back more roughly.

"Look," he said. "Stop asking questions. My—my brother doesn't want to talk to you. And I don't want to talk to you, either," he added hastily as Scree opened his mouth. "Just be quiet, or pester someone else. Understand?"

Scree bobbed his head, his ugly face still cheerful. "I can be quiet," he said. "Yes, I know how to be very quiet. Mouse quiet. I can think like a mouse. Can you? You close your eyes almost, and you make your thoughts whisper, 'Cheese and crumbs, cheese and crumbs.' And then you think about running down a wall and going through a hole where it is safe and dark. I like safe, dark places. Do you? What is your brother's name? I would like to know it. I can be very quiet if I know his name."

"Just shut up," Diello said.

The other boys snickered, elbowing and whispering. Someone had removed Peck's gag. He spoke up now: "Piggy don't like old stinkwort's chatter. Ain't it a shame, now? Piggy don't know that old stinkwort *never* shuts up. Stinkwort runs at the mouth unless you hit him real hard, hard enough to draw his cork." He held up his bound fists and gestured like he was going to punch Scree.

With a gasp, the goblin-boy shrank closer to Diello, who flinched away.

"Not so close!" Diello said. His new clothes were going to

stink from rubbing against this pest. They were all jammed so close together they'd be clawing one another like madmen long before the wagon reached Bannethshire. Not that Diello intended to be around to see it.

Grinning evilly, Peck leaned forward. "Scared?" he taunted Scree.

Scree cringed even closer to Diello. "I don't want to fight," he whispered. "Peck, please, please do not draw my cork. I do not like to bleed. I do not like to be hurt. I am not good at fighting."

Peck made a mocking expression of sympathy, his mouth twisting oddly because of his scar. "Aw, stinkwort don't like to hurt and bleed. Ain't that a shame?"

As he spoke, he lunged as swiftly as a snake and kicked Scree's leg very hard, almost knocking the runt off the bench. Just as quickly Peck was back in his seat, but the peddler reached down over the slats and struck the top of his head with a fist.

"OW!" Peck shouted. "What's that for?"

"Keep your place!" the peddler shouted. "If anyone's going to bruise the merchandise, it'll be me, see?"

Peck slumped on the bench, sprawling out his long legs and taking up twice the space he should have. He stared at Scree, who scrunched his eyes shut and whimpered.

With a laugh, Peck glanced around for his friends' approval and began to whistle loudly, ignoring the peddler's singing. The discordant racket was horrible, but neither Peck nor the peddler would stop. And all the while Peck was picking at the scab that had formed where the T was burned into his cheek.

Diello was glad that Peck was focusing on Scree instead of him or Cynthe. He had every intention of using that to his advantage. Strategy, Pa called it. But he could feel the goblin-boy trembling beside him.

Cynthe was also aware of the situation. She gave him a slight nod, her eyes shifting warily to Peck and his loutish friends. *We'll wait for our chance*, Diello told himself. The wagon jolted and lurched down the road, the rear axle screeching constantly as the wheels bounced over rocks and ruts.

The sun grew hotter, and the horses plodded even more slowly. Now and then, they passed beneath trees that grew over the road, casting some shade, but the choking dust worked its gritty way into every fold of Diello's clothing and down inside his tunic, where it stuck to his sweaty skin.

Cynthe tapped his knee. Twice. Sharply. Glancing around, Diello recognized the spot where they'd ventured into the woods and met the trog. Coming up was the trail that the rare visitors to their farmstead used. Diello tensed, getting ready, but Cynthe tapped his knee again and shook her head.

Her warning was clear. Diello saw that both Scree and Peck were watching them. So was the peddler. But as soon as Diello looked at the peddler, he turned around and began talking to Kirv in a loud, wheezing voice.

Diello stared so hard at the peddler's back that Cynthe whispered, "Is he Brezog in disguise?"

"No."

She let out her breath. "He's been watching us so . . . I thought he might be."

"He must know we live nearby," Diello whispered.

"We'll wait. Let him relax."

Diello wasn't sure the peddler would ever lessen his vigilance. "How long? We'll be down to Cutthroat Gully before—"

"Maybe Peck has friends planning to rescue him there," Cynthe whispered. "He's confident enough."

"I don't want to meet *them*."

She grinned. "Before we go that far . . . where the creek crosses the road . . ."

He knew the place she meant. He gave her a wink to show he understood, and let his gaze wander.

Eventually the road curved downhill, and the wagon slowed to a creaking, hesitant crawl as Kirv reined in the snorting horses. Anxiously, Diello waited for Cynthe's signal. Ahead, at the bottom of the hill, the creek trickled across the road. The fording spot was very rocky and full of holes that had washed out earlier that spring when the creek had crested. The wagon lurched into one of those holes, swaying violently. Someone whooped shrilly. Laughter rang out as the wagon lurched again. It jolted along, its wheels scraping against the stones.

Cynthe leaned over Diello to smile at Scree. "I think Peck wants to say something to you."

The goblin-boy blinked, his mouth falling open. He turned, half-standing, to face the large youth. "I will gladly talk with you if you will not hit me," he began eagerly.

As everyone stared at Scree, Cynthe jumped for the railing in one bound, scrambling over and leaping off with her short hair flying about her head. She landed in the creek with a splash, crossed it, and tore up the bank into the bushes. Shouts rang out. Kirv hauled on the reins while the peddler stood on the wagon seat and swore, shaking his whip.

By that time, Diello was already in the air, his hands scraping the splintery wagon as he jumped. He landed in the thigh-deep water, flexing his knees to keep from injuring himself and feeling his feet slip on the stones lining the creek bed. Gaining his footing, he ran behind the wagon in the opposite direction that Cynthe had taken. The peddler had climbed down, but Diello was already angling up the slippery bank, pulling himself along by grabbing bushes and saplings. At the top, he plunged into the undergrowth, letting branches whip his chest and face as he ran for all he was worth.

Behind him, the peddler was shouting and screaming curses. All the boys were yelling, some of them sounding angry but others cheering Diello and Cynthe on. Risking one glance back, Diello saw some of the boys spilling over the tall sides of the wagon and running away. He knew the more boys that joined in, the easier it would be for him and Cynthe to escape capture. The rest, however, were caught and driven back into the wagon by the peddler's skillful whip.

"Kirv!" the peddler shouted. "Go after that pair of Faelin brats!"

Diello hurried on until the noise faded in the distance. Gradually he doubled back, circling cautiously until he was headed the right way toward the farmstead.

A scrawny shape leaped from behind a bush into his path. Diello tried to dodge, tripped, and fell sprawling with a jolt that made his teeth snap together.

Panting hard, he looked up to see Scree crouched in front of him, peering at him with concern.

"I am sorry to hurt you," Scree said, his eyes nearly crossing as he looked down his long, crooked nose at Diello. "Did I hurt you? I am sorry because I do not want you to be hurt. I hurt myself, too, and I wish I had not done it." He tapped his knee, where his tattered legging had torn, revealing brown, mottled hide scraped and oozing dark blood through a layer of grime. "Do not look so frightened, Diello. I am your friend. I will help you escape."

Diello could have sworn at him, but didn't bother wasting his breath. Scrambling under cover, he listened for the sounds of approaching pursuit while Scree crept into the bush beside him.

"Look," Diello whispered. "I'm not your friend, and I don't need your help. Just go in a different direction from me, all right?"

"I will help you," Scree said.

"No." Diello pointed. "Go that way."

Scree nodded, but when Diello set off running again, Scree followed at his heels.

Diello halted. "I said to go another way."

"I will help you." Scree's eyes were bright and hopeful. "I am your friend."

"No. We're not friends. I don't need your help. Understand? Just . . . just run *that* way," Diello said, pointing again.

The eagerness faded from Scree's face.

"Go," Diello said.

Scree lowered his head and started jogging in the

direction that Diello pointed, but as soon as Diello went forward, Scree came stumbling behind him.

Exasperated, Diello ran faster to outdistance the goblin-boy. Scree fell back, unable to keep up, but continued to follow him. Diello tried dropping to his belly in a thicket and crawling a ways to throw the goblin-boy off his trail, but when he came out of the thicket, Scree was there waiting.

The shouts behind them grew closer. Trying to shake off Scree was costing Diello valuable time. Angrily he crossed the creek again, emerged dripping on the other bank, and climbed into a tree. Breathing hard, he hid among its dense, dark-green leaves. Scree stood beneath him, apparently unable to think of where to hide.

Do not climb up here, Diello thought. *Go away!*

As the peddler came huffing and puffing along the creek bank, lurching on his bandy legs, Scree plopped into the water and sank beneath the surface.

The peddler stopped under Diello's tree to pull off his broad-brimmed hat and wipe his brow. Diello held his breath, assuring himself that the peddler couldn't have tracked him. No doubt the man had just followed along the creek and by sheer bad luck they had crossed paths here. *All I have to do is stay very, very still.*

But when Diello peeked down at the creek, he nearly fell from the tree. For Scree had not swum away like anyone with sense would do. Instead, he was floating in the water, his brown, blotchy face visible beneath the rippling surface, if the peddler happened to look in his direction.

How long could a half-breed goblin hold his breath? Goblins were said to dislike water, so Diello was surprised that Scree would hide in the creek. Would the goblin-boy have to come clawing up for air right in front of the peddler? If so, he was likely to give everything away.

Hating Scree, wishing he knew a thousand Fae curses—or even just a dozen—to heap on Scree's stupid, scrawny neck, Diello held still. His nose was itching. A leaf was tickling his ear. Sweat was stinging his eyes. But he didn't move.

Kirv came stumbling into sight. "I got most everyone caught and tied to the wagon except the Faelin. No sign of either one."

"Enough!" The peddler slapped his leg with his hat before cramming it atop his greasy locks once more. "We've done our job. It's a mercy we didn't lose the rest."

Grumbling, he turned and lurched away, red-faced and wheezing with every step.

For a long time afterward, Diello remained in the tree, pressing his forehead against the trunk's rough bark in relief. Scree had disappeared, and Diello hoped the runt had finally swum downstream.

But when he climbed down from the tree and jumped lightly to the ground, Scree came popping out of a bush. Diello jumped like a frightened hare.

"Don't do that!" he said as soon as he caught his breath.

Scree grinned at him, showing those jagged teeth. "I have helped you escape," he declared. "I am a good friend to you. I hope you are glad to have me with you."

"Sure, thanks," Diello said. "Now go away."

But Scree tagged along at Diello's heels, shadowing his every step. Eventually Diello gave up trying to send Scree away. The goblin-boy simply ignored everything Diello said.

Even insults only made the runt look sad before he shook his head and said, "I do not think you wish to say such terrible things, do you? I will not say terrible things to you in return."

Ashamed, Diello fell silent.

When he met up with Cynthe in the woods just north of their home, she looked excited to see Diello until she spotted Scree dogging his heels. "What's he doing here?"

"Can't get rid of him," Diello muttered. "I tried, but short of stabbing him, nothing works."

Cynthe nocked an arrow to her bowstring and aimed it at Scree. "Do you understand *this?*" she asked sternly.

Scree backed up a step, before he grinned and came forward again. "There is much I can do to help you—"

Cynthe released the arrow, and Diello's heart jumped with it. But the arrow only struck the ground at Scree's feet. She drew her bow once more.

"The next one goes in your leg," she said. "Understand? We don't like goblins. We don't want your help."

"Get out of here, Scree," Diello said. "You're free."

"I am your friend," Scree said plaintively. "I want to—"

"No!" Diello said gruffly. "We don't want you!"

Cynthe released her arrow. Scree dodged, and the arrow whistled past his calf, barely nicking it. Sucking in a breath, Scree grabbed his leg. This time he seemed to get the message and scuttled away, looking back only once to give Diello a sad glance that almost melted his resolve.

Almost.

When Scree finally vanished into the undergrowth, Diello sighed. "What a pest. I thought he'd never go."

Cynthe jogged over to retrieve her arrows and slammed them back into her quiver. "You're too soft," she said, "and he could sense that. Now, let's see if we can find my wolf before we gather supplies."

chapter twenty-two

the farmstead was a desolate place. Someone had come by and burned the dead animal carcasses. Disappointed vultures rose, flapping and squawking, disturbed by the twins' arrival. Without the *cloigwylie*, weeds were already sprouting across the trampled fields and in the ruined garden, taking over faster than usual, especially in the places where goblin fire had burned. A green bloom of slimeweed covered the water trough's surface.

Diello tried to harden his heart against the sight. It no longer felt like home. He was an unwelcome stranger.

He kept watch while Cynthe called here and there for the wolf pup. When he checked the root cellar, he found its stone door broken in half. Vines were growing around the doorway, choking it, so he busied himself pulling them back and making sure no snakes were hiding under the leaves.

"Fuzzytop!" Cynthe called, keeping her voice low. She whistled as well, but the pup didn't show.

Diello hadn't expected the pup to be hanging around this forlorn place, but he still shared Cynthe's disappointment.

"One more pass," she said before Diello could speak. "If you'll go that way, near the edge of the field, I'll swing by the creek."

"We shouldn't stay here too long," he said. "It's not safe."

"I know. This is the last one I'll make. I promise."

"Hurry."

She strode away. Diello decided not to search the field. If the pup were here, he would have come to them by now. Instead, he climbed on top of the root cellar and surveyed the farmstead from this vantage point. There had to be a clue to Eirian, something that would solve the riddle that he had memorized by heart.

The only structure still standing was the stone cistern. Diello remembered how Brezog had been sniffing the stones the night of the attack. The goblins had dug and scratched all around it, but they hadn't actually damaged it.

Safe, where the sky's tears guard you.

"Sky's tears," he murmured. "Rain!" Storing rainwater channeled off the cottage roof was the cistern's function. He felt a spike of excitement, but held it down, trying to solve the rest of the riddle.

What was a mountain's cup?

He thought harder. The closest mountain was Egil's Point. Hadn't Pa said once that the old stones that formed the cottage foundation and the cistern had been quarried from there? Stone cut in squares to hold up the cottage and in wedge shapes to stack in a circle.

A circle closed. The cistern was round, and it had a lid. Maybe the sword was hidden inside the structure, down under the water. Frustrated, he shook his head. If that were true, the water would have rusted it to bits by now.

But if he squinted, from this angle it did look like a giant cup. . . .

The cistern had to be the hiding place! Now all he had to do was figure out where exactly in the cistern the sword could be concealed. Under the lid, perhaps, or in a wall cavity behind a loose stone . . .

"What are you doing up there?" Cynthe asked. "Trying to make sure you're seen by anyone still looking for us?"

He hadn't heard her return. *Some lookout I am.* Hastily he scrambled to the ground.

"I think the sword might be hidden in the cistern," he said.

"Diello! We agreed not to spend more time here than necessary. Food's more important than that old sword. If you aren't going to help look for Fuzzytop, at least gather supplies."

Grumbling, he climbed down the wooden ladder into the underground cellar where his family usually stored baskets of fruits and vegetables, such as apples, taties, hard marrows, turnips, and pumpkins; crocks of sour bage; and brined meat packed in barrels. The empty baskets, crocks, and barrels were stacked neatly, telling him that the goblins hadn't bothered to come down here after breaking the door. With most of the food stores gone, used up during the winter and early spring months, what had there been for them to destroy? The cellar waited for the harvest that would not come.

Just as he stepped off the last rung of the ladder onto

the packed dirt floor, Diello caught the sound of yipping above.

"Fuzzytop!" Cynthe cried in delight.

She stuck her head into the hole, grinning down at Diello. "He's all right," she said. "Just hungry."

"So am I," Diello muttered.

"Get the food!" she called to him. "Hurry."

Listening to her coo over the wolf pup, Diello reached under the lowest shelves and dug out the oldest baskets, rummaging to the bottom to scrounge three withered apples, two dirt-encrusted taties, and a small wheel of hard-rind cheese—all of which he carried up the ladder and handed over to Cynthe.

"Oh, good," she said as he brought out the cheese. "The pup can eat that."

"We'll be eating it, too, remember! Don't give him too much."

But Diello couldn't help smiling into the keen blue eyes of the little wolf. He cavorted from Cynthe to Diello and back again, sniffing their legs and feet. When he sniffed Diello's hands, however, he growled.

"Sorry," Diello said, letting himself be severely inspected. "Scree was one stinky creature."

But when he reached out, the pup licked his fingers and even permitted him to scratch his ears.

"Do you think he'll ever talk?" Cynthe asked, cutting a sliver of cheese and holding it high above the pup's upturned muzzle. "Jump for it, Fuzzytop. Jump for it!"

The wolf sat down on his haunches without taking his eyes off the cheese, making no effort to perform a trick.

Plucking the cheese from her fingers, Diello fed it to the pup.

"Hey!" she said. "He'll never learn anything if you do that."

"He's not a dog. Don't treat him like one."

The pup was watching them with his head cocked to one side. The tuft of gold fuzz between his tall ears made him look comical, but Diello was very aware of the intelligence in those blue eyes. He hadn't forgotten how the pup had kept him from being too consumed by grief the night of his parents' deaths. And he suspected that right now the pup was listening—and understanding—every word they said.

"Don't be so bossy, Diello. I know what he is," Cynthe said. She tucked a wayward strand of hair behind her ear. "I just wish he would talk."

Diello shrugged. "He will when he's ready. But in the meantime, stop calling him that stupid name."

Cynthe leaned back in the grass and smiled to herself as the pup came over to nuzzle her ears. "You're just jealous because he likes me better than you."

"I'm not jealous. It's a matter of respect."

"So what do we call him?" Cynthe asked, rolling onto her stomach. She wiggled her fingers at the pup, and he pounced on her hand, holding it in his mouth and tugging. When she laughed, the pup ran to Diello and nudged his ankle.

Just as Diello bent to pet him, he felt a sense of unease. He glanced around, but saw nothing to cause alarm.

"Well," Cynthe said, sitting up. "Do you think we're being spied on?"

"Not sure, but I think so."

"Then you'd better hurry up and make that fake sword or whatever you're planning to do. I'll hide our supplies." Cynthe rolled to her feet. "Do you really think Brezog is going to come back?"

"Set your snares, and let's get ready."

Diello poked through the barn ashes and found one of Pa's carpentry tools. Although the draw knife's handles were so charred they crumbled at his touch, Diello wrapped them with some rags to protect his hands from the steel blade. He scavenged a length of board from the wreckage, knocked off the burned parts, and whittled it crudely into the approximate length and width of a sword. Then he gathered white mud from the creek bank and smeared it over the wood.

"It doesn't look real at all," Cynthe said, coming up. "No one's going to be tricked by that."

"I'm not finished yet. Are you?"

She went away without another word, leaving him to complete his project. He hadn't attempted to tell her his full plan because he didn't want to argue with her. In this first step, Diello needed the fake sword only to tempt the gorlord from hiding. Now, while Brezog's spy was probably racing through the woods to fetch the gorlord, Diello would have to get his hands on the real weapon. He stood up cautiously, holding the fake sword close to his tunic, and fought the temptation to look around as he walked to the water cistern. He climbed the stone steps curving up one side and pushed the lid slightly ajar. He pretended to look inside and even thumped the lid with his knuckles a few times while he slid the fake sword through the metal rings underneath the lid.

After climbing down, he dusted off his hands and pulled out the deed seal, holding it across his palm. It looked as usual, with the original writing describing the property boundaries. "Eirian," he whispered.

The secret riddle did not appear, but he felt the metal turn warm. The white, shining image of the sword filled his mind, and he heard a scraping sound, like metal dragged across metal, like a weapon being drawn.

It was a real sound—not a vision. The pup yelped. Diello spun around, half-crouching in anticipation of attack.

But he was alone. There was nothing to see except the bare foundation stones and wind-swirled piles of ashes. He couldn't even locate Cynthe and the pup.

He waited, trying to slow his racing heart. What a fool he'd been to think that he and Cynthe could take on Brezog's horde by themselves. His plan to lure Brezog into the open seemed silly and childish, now that he stood here in broad daylight as bait.

What if he were completely wrong about Amalina's abduction from the castle? What if he drew the labor ped-dler here instead of Brezog?

No, it will be Brezog.

He waited a long time, but when he heard no sounds and saw no movement save the chirping of insects in the grass and rustle of wind in the trees, he turned his atten-tion back to the stone cistern. Pa had always kept it in fine repair, checking it daily for leaks or other problems. It was the perfect size for climbing on, but they'd been forbidden to do so. Mamee claimed it was too dangerous, and they might fall into the water tank and drown. That, of course, was nonsense. Diello and Cynthe had played in the creek since they were old enough to swim, and Mamee never forbade them to go *there*.

"The cistern's old," Pa always said. "It looks good and sturdy, but some of the stones are loose where the mortar has crumbled and weathered. All I need is for one of you to climb it and bring the whole thing tumbling down."

Looking at it now, Diello couldn't see any signs of it crumbling. But maybe there really was a loose stone. Maybe a loose stone that could be pulled out to reveal a wall cavity large enough for . . .

A scrawny figure with a brown blotchy face popped into sight. "Diello!"

Diello jerked around, tucking the disk beneath his tunic. "Blast you, Scree!"

"Listen. You must listen," Scree said, gesturing. "I—"

A goblin spear whistled through the air, stabbing the ground directly at Diello's feet. He jumped back against the cistern wall. Another spear struck to his left, and a third struck to his right, their wooden shafts quivering in the air.

Goblins were pouring from the woods. Diello started to run, but another spear hit the ground in front of him, driving him back. The creatures surrounded him. Tall, short, and in-between—a clash of green and brown, some mottled and some scaly, all hideous—the goblin horde hissed and growled through jagged teeth.

I'm not ready, Diello thought in despair. He tried to prepare himself for the biggest bluff of his life.

Brezog came forward, pushing his way through the

horde and striking those who did not get out of his path fast enough. His skin cloak swirled around him as sunshine gleamed on his hammered gold collar and bracelets. In one hand he carried his skull-mace. In the other, he held a spear stained with dried blood.

Diello looked around for Amalina, but didn't see her. He didn't know whether to be frightened of Brezog or furious with himself for having guessed so wrongly. Instead of catching the gorlord in a trap, he'd stepped into one. Before, Eirian had been safe because he didn't know where it was. But now . . . if Brezog reached into his mind, as he had before . . .

"And so we continue, Faelin child," the gorlord growled. "But this time there will be no one to save you."

"Where's my sister?" Diello demanded. "You'll get what you want, but I must see Amalina first!"

"Where is . . . ah! You want the little child that the baron's wife took from you."

"Yes! An even exchange. Let Amalina go, and I'll give you Eirian."

The goblins were muttering among themselves. Brezog swung his skull-mace from side to side.

"You think I have this child. You think I took her from the castle. You dare bargain with me."

Sweat trickled between Diello's shoulder blades. "Yes. We each have what the other wants."

Brezog uttered a bark of laughter. "Then give me the sword."

"First show me Amalina."

"There is no child to show you."

Diello's worst fears nearly choked him. "Liar! You have her. Give her up!"

Brezog's expression grew serious. "I do not have this child. Nor did I steal her away from that woman. But you, little Faelin morsel, will give me the sword just the same."

chapter twenty-three

Diello scrambled to understand. How could he have been so mistaken? He'd been so sure when he picked up the doll that he was seeing a vision of her abduction, and he'd assumed it was Brezog. But what he'd experienced was just the residue of Amalina's emotions as she was taken. Someone had clouded the senses of the humans into forgetting her existence. If not the gorlord, *who*?

He hoped that Cynthe—wherever she was—had the good sense to remain hidden. From the corner of his eye, Diello saw Scree trying to scuttle away. With a grunt, one of the goblins pounced on him, and he squealed shrilly. The sound reminded Diello of a rabbit's death scream.

They shoved Scree next to Diello. The scrawny half-breed stared up at him beseechingly. "I will help you. I am your—"

"Shut up," Diello muttered. "There's nothing you can do."

"But I—"

"Silence, filth!" Brezog shouted.

Scree clapped both hands over his mouth.

Brezog came close enough for Diello to see every detail of his scaled hide, to smell the sour stink of goblin musk flowing from his pores. His breath hissed through his fangs.

"Give up the sword, now!"

"I don't have any sword," Diello said sullenly.

"Lies! Lies! Lies!" Brezog jabbed his spear at the stone wall next to Diello's head, striking sparks. He gripped the front of Diello's tunic and pulled him even closer. Brezog's long pointed nose quivered with fury as he whispered, "Do you think you can play me for a fool? If you want to live, give me Eirian."

Diello could feel pressure growing in his skull, a throbbing force. He didn't know how to stop Brezog from worming into his thoughts, but he had to try.

"Look under the cistern lid!" he said.

The pressure on his head eased up. Brezog issued an order, and one of the goblins climbed the stone steps. Silence fell over the horde as the lid scraped back across the rim. The goblin pulled out the fake sword and held it aloft as he turned around.

A roar went up. But as the piece of wood came hurtling down at Diello's feet, the cheering died.

Brezog kicked the fake sword away and swung his skull-mace, ready to smash it down on Diello. "What is this?" he screamed. "Give me the real sword. Now!"

"Why don't you just take it?" Diello asked. "You know where it is. Why must I *give* it to you?"

There was a flare of respect in the gorlord's eyes before he lowered his weapon. "A Fae spell is best broken by a Fae hand. Or a Faelin. If I break it, the cistern could shatter and damage the sword. Do you want that? No. And I do not want that. Eirian is *here*." Brezog's palm brushed across the stones. He peered at the wall. "I sense it is here. Yet the cloud remains, veiling it, guarding it well. Not even when I clawed the life from Lwyneth did this magic falter."

Diello made a small, involuntary sound. Brezog's attention whipped back to him. "Yes, boy," he said. "I killed her. She was arrogant enough to defy me, but in the end she was weak, very weak for a Fae. She died like a human. You will remember Brezog as her slayer. You will fear me!"

"I'll remember it all my days," Diello said.

"And you, her spawn, will now break this spell for me."

"No."

Brezog struck him so fast Diello didn't see it coming. His head snapped around before the pain filled his mouth. He spat out blood.

"You will not defy me!" Brezog shouted. "Break the spell and give me the sword!"

"Can't," Diello replied, wincing from his split lip. He spat out more blood. "I don't know how to work magic like hers."

The pressure returned inside his skull, threatening to crack it open.

"If you kill me," he gasped, "you still won't have the sword."

"Fool!" Brezog roared. He raised his hand, flames dancing on the tips of his black talons.

Writhing, Diello staggered back against the cistern wall. The fire was consuming him from the inside, worse than any fever, its torment filling his brain and melting his bones.

"Use the key!" Brezog shouted, ripping open Diello's tunic. The deed seal hung over Diello's pounding heart, its silver surface glowing so brightly that Brezog averted his face. "Use the key, and bring out the sword."

"N-No!"

"Then I'll eat your heart!"

Diello fought savagely, well aware that his strength was no match for Brezog's. In the struggle, the deed seal brushed against Brezog's fingers. White light flashed, bringing the stink of charred flesh.

Brezog screamed, "You will pay for that, you—"

A wolf howled, loud and close. Something shimmered between Diello and the gorlord. The agonizing fire in Diello's brain cooled, and he could think again. It was almost as though the *cloigwylie* had returned, yet this was different magic than Mamee's. There was something unsettling about it, something primitive.

The goblins brandished their weapons awkwardly as they edged away from Diello, turning this way and that.

"Where is the boy?" the gorlord muttered. He pounced near Diello, and Diello jumped to one side. To his astonishment, the gorlord missed him.

Brezog growled, looking in all directions.

He can't see me! Diello realized. Glancing down, Diello couldn't see his own body. Something, or someone, had put an invisibility spell—a *cymunffyl*—on him.

Eirian? he wondered. *Could the sword do something like that?*

Brezog lunged blindly again, and Diello dodged him in time. He knew this was his best chance to get away, but while it was tempting to grab one of the spears and fight his way through, he also knew that a weapon appearing to float in mid-air would reveal his position. They'd catch him, invisible or not.

At that moment, Brezog grabbed him, shouting in triumph. Before Diello could struggle, an arrow came singing through the air and struck the gorlord's arm. There was a spurt of dark blood. Staggering back, Brezog howled a fearsome curse.

Diello twisted free. Another arrow thudded into the chest of a goblin who'd jumped to protect the gorlord. Diello pushed past the crowd rushing to their master's aid and ran.

Brezog's howl of rage filled the air. "Get him!"

But well-placed arrows were flying fast, bringing down more goblins. A green-skinned bloidy-goblin blundered into Diello's path, only to be tripped by Scree, who was darting aimlessly. The bloidy-goblin shoved Scree aside while Diello seized his chance to dive into the undergrowth.

Diello couldn't run through the bushes without giving away his position, so he skidded onto his belly and crawled beneath them. Fist-sized balls of flame flew in his direction. Some struck the trees and went out with harmless pops. Some set the brambles on fire.

Choking, Diello shot out of the blazing thicket and ran away from the fire's path. The flames, feeding on the dry vines, roared larger, leaping up for the tree limbs. The leaves blackened and curled. Diello discovered that if he ran through the smoke he became lightly visible. He stopped, anxious to flee yet driven back by the fire.

More flames burned to his right, engulfing a stand of young saplings.

Diello retreated, keeping his hands pressed over his mouth to block the smoke.

Scree appeared, jerking at the gorlord's arm before he could throw another flame ball. Brezog tried to shake off the goblin-boy, but Scree clung tightly.

Diello was surprised that Scree had turned on his own kind. He watched with reluctant admiration as Scree got in some good kicks to the gorlord's shins. Then Brezog struck with his skull-mace, knocking Scree brutally to the ground. Diello fled. He vaulted a fallen log and plunged down the bank into the creek. Knee-deep in the water, he waded upstream a short distance to mask his scent, then scrambled out and dived into another thicket.

Cynthe's arrows were still bringing down goblins while the rest scrambled for cover. A few brave ones fanned out across the farmstead, searching for her. Some of them were caught in the snares she'd set and were dragged upside down into the air to dangle by one foot, struggling and snarling. Diello knew where she was—up in the walner grove on the far side of the paddock. The three biggest trees in the grove spread entwined branches from canopy to canopy. Cynthe could move from one tree to the next, releasing her arrows from different angles to keep the goblins confused.

Some goblins, however, were still trailing Diello, for although they couldn't see him, they could follow his scent. They stopped at the creek's edge, sniffing the air like hounds and growling. Brezog was not in sight, but Diello heard his harsh orders in the distance. He only hoped that one of Cynthe's arrows would get the gorlord.

Meanwhile, he had to stay out of reach. Hurrying downstream, he chose a point where the brush grew right to the water's edge. Staying within its cover, he slipped into the water. Here, there was enough depth for swimming. Filling his lungs, he sank beneath the surface and swam across. When he came up for air, he was right where he'd intended to be, near the overhang that hid Mamee's buttery. He crawled inside the cool, dark refuge.

It was a much tighter fit for him than it had been for Amalina as he tried to curl up among the crocks and pottery jars. But much worse, the water had thwarted his invisibility spell. He could see his own form again, dimly like a tattered wraith. Fortunately, enough of the spell remained—along with the leaves and the dappled sunlight sparkling on the creek's surface—to shield him as he hid, fawn-still, with his cheek pressed against the ground. The goblins searched along both creek banks before returning to Brezog.

Listening to the guttural voices and sounds of general confusion, Diello figured that Cynthe had run out of arrows. *Now what?* he wondered.

"Where is the Faelin boy?" Brezog shouted. "Where?"

There came a cry of pain in response, and then Scree's voice, thin with terror: "I cannot tell! I do not *know*! I—"

He broke off, screaming.

Diello couldn't ignore Scree's plight, but he also didn't dare go to the goblin-boy's rescue. By now, the *cymunffyl* had faded completely, and he had no other defense except his wits.

Wringing out his wet clothes as quietly as he could, Diello circled his way cautiously through the woods to the hollow chesternut tree. Climbing it, he found Cynthe already there. The pup was not with her. When Diello wedged himself beside her, she gave him a relieved grin and went back to intently watching the goblins in the clearing.

"How—" she began.

He put his finger to her lips and pressed his other hand over hers. He touched her empty quiver and nodded his thanks.

Amalina, she mouthed.

Sadly, he shook his head and watched Cynthe's face turn grim. She gestured that they should go.

Another scream came from Scree. Diello gripped the tree as if he were back at the whipping post. He saw the semiconscious goblin-boy dragged onto his knees between two gor-goblins. They held him as Brezog struck him again and again.

"Stupid creature! Filth!" Brezog paused before he called out loudly, "Either the Faelin boy surrenders Eirian or I'll suck the marrow from your bones."

Diello and Cynthe exchanged glances. If Brezog thought they were going to fall for that one, he could think again. But they couldn't just let Scree die. . . .

Cynthe balled her fists and closed her eyes. Diello guessed that she was trying to use magic. If she could work *cymunffyls* as well as fly, then she was going to be very powerful indeed. He touched her arm in warning.

"Don't," Diello whispered. "He'll trace magic to us. Too risky."

Brezog called out again: "Do you hear me, little Faelin morsel? Come out and surrender the sword, then I might let this piece of filth live!"

Diello's shoulders twitched. Cynthe gripped his sleeve.

"He's bluffing," she whispered. "Don't listen to him."

"We have to do something," Diello whispered back. "We can't just sit here and let them—"

"No. Stay quiet. They'll hurt Scree no matter what we do. You mustn't believe Brezog."

Diello forced himself to watch and listen. Scree, now crouching at Brezog's feet, sobbed wretchedly for mercy.

Brezog struck Scree with his fist. The beating seemed to go on forever, made worse by Brezog's obvious enjoyment.

Every scream of pain drove a splinter of shame into Diello. He wanted to confront Brezog and bravely rescue Scree, yet Cynthe's cautions held him in place. *I'm not brave at all*, Diello thought miserably. *I'm scared, too scared to go out there and save Scree from dying for me or for Eirian. Pa would be ashamed of me.*

Scree's cries faded to whimpers—then silence. Diello watched to the end, punishing himself the only way he could. All his life he'd wanted to be a hero, a man who roamed the world on fabulous adventures, and yet here he was, just a frightened boy. He had never felt so small.

Finally, the beating stopped. Scree lay still on the ground.

The gorlord turned around and stared in the twins' direction.

If he catches our scent, we're finished, Diello thought. Beside him, Cynthe was motionless, except for the tears running down her face.

Oh, Guardian, let this tree shield us and protect us, Diello prayed.

The *cymunffyl* returned, sliding between them and Brezog. Cynthe vanished from Diello's sight, and he heard her gasp. So it wasn't her spell. *Whose, then?*

"There!" One of the bloidy-goblins pointed eastward, away from the tree. "I see the Faelin boy moving through the woods!"

Shouting and brandishing his skull-mace, the gorlord led the snarling horde. Their voices died away gradually as they disappeared into the woods.

chapter twenty-four

"What happened?" Diello asked. He started to climb out of the hollow tree, but Cynthe held him back with an invisible hand.

"Wait," she whispered. "What if it's a trick?"

They waited until the wolf pup trotted into view, his blue eyes focused on the chesternut tree. The pup yipped.

"It's safe," Cynthe said.

As soon as his feet hit the ground, the *cymunffyl* faded, and the twins were visible again. He hurried toward Scree.

"No!" Cynthe called after him. "Leave the dead. Let's get out of here."

Diello kept walking toward the goblin-boy. "Collect your arrows," he told her.

"Diello, don't."

He looked back. Cynthe was still standing at the base of the tree, clutching her bow, her face white. He glanced across the clearing at the dead goblins that lay scattered about. The wounded had crawled off or left with the horde. In sudden understanding, Diello returned to her.

"Cynthe," he said quietly.

"I killed six."

"And saved my life."

She rubbed her hand up and down her bow. "I should be glad," she said. "I didn't think about it. I just started releasing arrows."

"Cynthe, you did what was necessary."

"Ever since this began, I've thought about killing goblins," she whispered. "I wanted vengeance for what they did to Mamee and Pa. And now I—I don't feel the way I expected. Instead, it's like something inside me . . . is gone." She looked at him. "I don't understand. I've hunted game for years. What's different?"

"They're not animals," he said.

"They're worse than animals! They're horrible creatures, monsters! So *why*?"

"They're people."

"Never!"

"They are. They think. They have feelings like you and me."

Her expression grew stubborn. "They're evil! I don't want to be sad because I killed some of them. I want to be happy. And I'm not."

"You're supposed to feel this way. From the first time we went hunting, Pa taught us what it means to kill. Never for fun or sport, but only for need."

"That's hunting game. This is—"

"This is need, too," Diello said. "This is *war*."

Grasping her hand, Diello led her to the nearest dead goblin. He lay sprawled out, his sightless eyes open, his gray tongue hanging limply from his mouth. It was terrible to look at him, but not as bad as it had been to see their parents.

Nothing I ever face will be as bad as that, Diello told himself.

He pulled Cynthe's arrow from the body. Dipping his finger in the dark blood on the tip, he solemnly drew a mark on each of Cynthe's cheeks. A part of him envied her for having stepped across the threshold into adulthood. Another part of him mourned the loss of childhood, knowing she could not go back again.

"First blood, Cynthe," he said. "You're now a warrior."

She took her arrow from him and wiped its tip clean on the grass. "I will kill more of them someday," she said. "I will hunt them down and they'll regret coming here." Her eyes flashed. "I swear it!"

Diello started to speak, but she turned away. "I'm going to collect the rest of my arrows, as many as I can find. Then we'll go."

As she strode across the clearing, Diello went to Scree's body. Cynthe might be over her guilt, but he still had to deal with his.

The goblin-boy was lying face down. He looked like a heap of tattered rags on the trampled ground. Diello went to touch his back, but—fearing a rush of Scree's death memories—he curled his fingers into a fist.

"I'm so sorry, Scree," he said.

Scree twitched and moaned.

Diello jumped.

Cynthe came running over, carrying a handful of arrows. "What is it? What happened?"

Diello bent over Scree, rolling him onto his back. "Scree?" he asked. "Can you hear me?"

Blood poured from a gash in the goblin-boy's forehead. Vicious cuts covered his skin. His eyes were swelling shut, and his mouth looked a raw, bruised mess.

"Are you sure he's alive?" Cynthe asked.

"Scree," Diello said, touching his brown, splotchy cheek. "Wake up, please."

Scree moaned again before he managed to slit open one eye and peer blearily up at Diello. He tried pathetically to smile.

"You . . . alive," he mumbled. "'S good . . . alive."

Diello felt Scree's arms and legs for broken bones while Cynthe stayed back, her hand nervously stroking the pup. The wolf watched Scree. His tall ears were pricked forward, and a ridge of hair stood up along his spine. He growled, very softly.

"Hush," Diello said, and the growling stopped.

Scree's limbs seemed all right. But Diello had found a soft, spongy place in his side. When Diello touched the area lightly, Scree flinched and whimpered.

"Ribs," Diello said.

Nodding, Cynthe went off scrounging and returned with a dirty strip of cloth. The twins had both suffered their share of cracked and broken ribs, usually from falling out of trees. Pa had taught them how to wrap a binding tight for support, but Diello knew Scree was going to hurt like blazes for a while.

"Help me sit him up."

"Maybe he's hurt inside," Cynthe said. "We shouldn't move him."

"I can't bind him if he's lying down."

Together they pulled Scree's rags away, revealing a body

of skin and bones and the marks of older scars. With his ribs and vertebrae so prominent, it was easy to see the sunken place in his side. Diello placed his hand on the boy's thin shoulder.

Another growl came from the wolf, and Diello stepped back from Scree. "What's wrong with you?" he asked the pup.

The wolf advanced on Scree with hackles raised and tail extended. He sniffed Scree's feet and growled again.

Diello tried to use Sight, but it didn't come. All he saw was a nearly starved halfling who shouldn't be alive, but was.

More rumbles came from the wolf. Diello bent to scratch his ears. "I know he's got goblin blood," he said. "And goblins are as much your enemies as ours. But he's not one of Brezog's horde. He did me a good turn today, and I owe him."

The pup gave Diello's hand a lick before lying down and resting his muzzle on his paws.

Diello put a stick between Scree's jaws to give him something to bite on and went to work cleaning his wounds and binding his broken ribs. By the time Diello finished, he was sweating nearly as much as Scree. The goblin-boy had not whimpered, but everything he was feeling could be seen in that one slitted eye, focused on Diello.

"Rest," Diello murmured.

Cynthe gathered their food and other meager supplies before washing her arrows in the creek. When she came back, she plunked the arrows one by one into her quiver and then sat cross-legged as she scratched six marks on her quiver strap.

The wolf pup wandered off, only to return, carrying something in his jaws that he laid at Diello's feet. Recognizing the horn box, Diello grabbed it and pulled it open. The pungent herbal aroma was unmistakable. There was magic in it, too. It tingled in his nostrils.

"Mamee's healing salve," he said. "Good boy! Where did you find it?"

Laughing, Cynthe pulled the pup into her lap. He wriggled and licked her chin. "What a smart, good boy you are."

"Let's put some on your arm," Diello said to her. "The sooner that gash heals, the better."

She gestured at Scree. "Finish with him first, but don't use too much. We have to make it last."

Both of them were well aware that Mamee would never concoct another batch.

Diello tried to apply salve to the worst of Scree's wounds, especially the gash over his eye, but Scree kept flinching away.

"Hold still!" Diello said. "I'm trying to help you."

Scree didn't move after that, although his bruised mouth drew tight. "This burns me," he muttered. "I do not want it on my skin. I do not like it. I do not like to burn and itch. You like it, and you should use it, but I wish you would not put it on me."

"Fine," Diello said. He turned to his sister.

She'd unwound the bandage on her arm. The wound was starting to close, but in a puckered, jagged way.

"Yes, you're definitely going to have a fearsome scar," Diello said. "Better than any of mine."

Grinning, Cynthe nodded. "Like I said, don't use too much salve."

Diello coated her wound with the ointment and rebandaged her arm.

"You need anything?" she asked. "Do you want me to put ointment on some of your welts?"

"Better not waste it. I'm all right." Since his pockets were full, Diello gave the salve to his sister for safekeeping.

There was one more thing he had to do. Pa had taught him that an apology should be made promptly and fully, with no excuses.

"Thank you, Scree," Diello said. "You were very brave, and I'm grateful. I shouldn't have been so rude to you, and I should have come to your aid when Brezog was beating you."

Scree stared at Diello through his one good eye.

Diello held out his hand. "I hope you'll accept my apology and grant me your pardon before you go on your way."

"Pardon," Scree muttered, rocking back and forth. "My pardon!" As he looked up, two tears streaked down his grubby face. He sniffed. "I am—I do not—no one has ever asked my pardon. I am dung. I am a—a bad thing."

"That isn't true," Cynthe said. She knelt by Scree, only to wrinkle her nose and move hastily back. "You're not bad. You—you just need washing."

"Cynthe," Diello said, trying not to laugh.

"Well, it's true!" she said. "Even the Ferrins' pigs aren't as dirty."

"Then I will wash." Scree began to get up, but Diello stopped him.

"You need to rest."

"Kindness to me," Scree whispered. "Asking pardon of me. Am I not hated?"

"No," Diello said. "We don't hate you."

Scree shifted his gaze away as if he could bear no more. "Was this your home?"

"Yes."

"Bad things happened here. Brezog burned your home, yes, and worse. I can see. You are angry, you and Cynthe, very angry with the one called Brezog." Scree was staring at the blood painted on Cynthe's cheeks. "You hate him because he is goblin. You will kill him if you can. Will you not kill me because I have goblin blood?"

Cynthe made a face at him. "Don't be daft. You're not the enemy. They are."

"Goblin is goblin," Scree said.

"We don't believe that way," Diello told him. "We were raised to judge by what someone does, not by what they are." He cleared his throat. "Most of the time."

The wolf growled, then walked away.

Diello smiled. "Well, that's his opinion. Now, Scree, we'll share some of our food, and then you can go."

"I want to stay," the goblin-boy said eagerly. "I want to be friend. Here is a home. I want to be here."

"Now wait just a moment—"

"I want to be your friend. You do not like me because I need washing but I will wash. I will not eat all the food. I can eat almost no food. I like you, and Cynthe is not a boy. She is pretty."

Rolling her eyes, Cynthe made a worse face than before.

Diello sighed, regretting his kindness. "We aren't staying here," he said. "We no longer have a home, and we've got to search for our sister. If we find her—"

"When," Cynthe insisted.

"*When* we find her, we'll be going on a long journey."

Scree got to his feet stiffly, keeping his arm pressed against his side. "If you go on a journey," he declared, "then I will go, too."

The twins looked at each other in dismay. "No," they said together.

"I will go, too," Scree repeated stubbornly.

Cynthe pulled Diello aside. "You shouldn't have patched him up. It's like feeding a stray cat. He'll never leave. Now we're going to be stuck with him forever."

"He's like a wheldie burr. The more you try to get rid of him, the harder he sticks."

"You made a mistake by apologizing to him. He's not used to it. Now he thinks you're his hero. Do something!"

"What do you want me to do?" Diello asked. "You put an arrow in him before to run him off, and it didn't work, did it?"

"We could tie him up."

"And leave him to starve?"

"Then you think of something."

Scree joined them, looking anxious. "I want to be Diello's friend. I want to be Cynthe's friend. No one was kind until *you* were kind. There are not many such as me, mixed blood, unwanted. I want to stay with you—my friends—and if you must go, then I will go with you. That's what friends do."

What could Diello say to convince Scree to leave on his

own? Before he could think of anything, the wolf pup walked between them and put his paw on Diello's foot.

"Don't argue," the wolf said. "Take Eirian now. The spell on Brezog, the spell that drove him from here, it is ending." He looked at each of them, his blue eyes intense. "Hurry!"

chapter twenty-five

"You *can* speak," Cynthe said, crouching beside him. "What a smart boy you are indeed. Tell us your name."

"Vassou." The pup looked at Cynthe. "*Not* Fuzzytop."

Her face turned red. "Sorry," she muttered. "You just look cute with that tuft between your ears."

"Not Fuzzytop," the pup said firmly. "Vassou."

"Thank you, Vassou, for sharing your name—and trust—with us," Diello said. "Was it you that cast the *cymunffyl*?"

"I thought *you* were working that magic," Cynthe said to Diello.

"No. Was it you, Vassou?"

The wolf pup flattened his ears briefly in acknowledgment. "What I did to send the goblins away is done," he said. "I am young. It is hard to trick the gorlord long."

"So why haven't you been talking to us before?" Cynthe asked.

"Talking is for what is most important. I have been listening, learning your tongue. I am not yet strong enough to do many things at once. Hurry."

Diello needed no more urging. Yanking the deed seal

over his head, he clutched the cord and ran to the cistern. Cynthe was right on his heels.

"Stop!" she said, flinging herself between him and the structure. "We shouldn't do this now. Didn't you hear Vassou? The goblins are coming back."

Ignoring her, Diello held up the deed seal. "Eirian," he said.

As before, his voice seemed to have no effect on the engraved Antrasin words.

Scree hobbled up to join them. "What is this you are doing? How may I help you? What is it that you are holding?"

"You can help," Diello said, "by going to the creek. There's a hole cut into the bank. That way." He pointed. "If you find any crocks with milk or butter, empty them and wash them. Then stack them neatly and come back."

Scree bobbed his head several times and scurried off.

"That's got him out of the way for a while." Diello snapped his fingers at Cynthe. "Say the name of the sword."

"Why should I? The only reason to seek it was so we could bargain with Brezog for Amie. What good will it do us now?"

Diello closed his eyes, concentrating. The sword's image shimmered into his mind. When he opened his eyes, Sight filled him.

He could see the spell of concealment that Mamee had woven. It covered the stone cistern like a web, glowing in a rainbow of colors that hurt his eyes if he stared at them too long.

"Diello," Cynthe said, pulling at his wrist. "Forget the sword. It's safe where it is. We've got to go while we can."

His concentration broken, Diello turned to her. "We're not leaving it behind for Brezog."

She locked eyes with him. "I know you promised Pa, but if we take it, Brezog will come after us. The same way that gold draws trogs. He's obsessed. Without the sword, we'll have a better chance of getting away. And later, Uncle Owain will help us."

"Brezog's *not* an ordinary goblin after plunder," Diello argued. "He's the gorlord—their supreme leader. What's so special about this sword that Mamee and Pa died for it? We can't leave it behind, Cynthe. It's too important."

"I heard him tell you that he can't break the spell without damaging the sword. So it's safe."

But Diello was remembering the anxiety in his father's voice. "I'm not going to fail Pa. Vassou, how do I open it?"

Vassou flattened his ears and said nothing. Diello felt his resolve hardening. *I will figure it out*, he vowed.

"Diello, *don't!*" Cynthe said.

"Say the word," he ordered. "Do it!"

"Eirian," she mumbled reluctantly.

As the Antrasin engraving faded on the seal, the words of the Fae riddle appeared in the air as before. At the same time, a course of stones near the top of the cistern glowed a brighter blue than all the other colors in the spell. Holding his breath, Diello touched the blue band.

Tingling fire shot up his arm and into his chest. But it was too late to stop now. Diello kept his right hand on the stone. His whole body shuddered. His hair was standing on end. His mouth opened, but if he was screaming he couldn't hear it as the inner roar engulfed his senses.

The spell seemed to flow from the stone through his right arm into the disk, which grew so hot it was scorching his skin. He tried to hang on, but couldn't. With a cry, he dropped the seal on the ground and felt the connection break inside him.

He sank to his knees. He had failed. He was too weak, too human to handle the full power of Fae magic. Gazing down at his left hand, he saw that his flesh was healthy and unharmed. The illusion had tricked him into giving up too soon. *Cynthe was right.* He should have left it alone.

"Diello, look!" Cynthe pointed.

One of the stones in the wall was now jutting out away from the others.

"You did it!" she shouted and tugged at the stone.

He sprang to his feet. "Let me help."

They managed to lift the stone and drop it on the ground next to the seal. The silver disk was no longer glowing. Diello started to pick it up, but Vassou placed his paw on it.

"Here!" Cynthe said, pulling something from the cavity.

Why couldn't she wait? Diello thought. He'd done the magic. He should be the one taking out the sword.

She handed him an irregular-shaped lump wrapped in soft, supple leather. *This is it?* It was too small to be any kind of weapon. But when he unrolled it, he saw that it was a sword hilt.

And no ordinary one. Decorative tracings of silver adorned the guard, and the pommel jewel was a huge, multi-faceted diamond that glittered in the late-afternoon sunlight.

"There's something else," Cynthe said. She held up a

star-shaped object affixed to a faded bit of ribbon. "What is this?"

Still fascinated by the gorgeous diamond in the hilt, Diello looked up with scant interest until he caught sight of the metal star dangling from Cynthe's fingers.

He grabbed the star and peered at the tarnished metal, rubbing away the black to reveal the raised lettering on its surface. He gasped.

"What is it?" Cynthe asked, trying to take it back. "Let me see!"

Diello held it out of reach, then uncurled his fist to stare at the star once again. "Carnethie," he whispered. "It's a Carnethie Star!"

"So what Lord Malques said is true?" Cynthe snatched it away from him. She rubbed her fingertips across its surface. "Pa's name is engraved on the back of it. Why didn't he ever tell us?"

"I wonder what really happened," Diello said. "The baron said he was disgraced and stripped of his honors."

"Maybe," Cynthe snapped. "And maybe Lord Malques is wrong. If Pa fell in battle, terribly wounded, he would have had to leave the knighthood."

"They wouldn't have driven him out of the order for that."

Cynthe tucked the star into her belt purse. "If he couldn't fight anymore, he might have wanted to come home to the farm. Or maybe he left the order to marry Mamee."

It made sense. Almost.

A cold nose nudged his ankle. It was Vassou, who gave an impatient yip.

"The blade," Diello said. "Where's the sword blade?"

Again Cynthe reached into the cavity. She stood on tiptoe to reach farther. "I don't think it's . . . Wait a moment! Yes, I feel something."

Diello grabbed at her shoulder. "Hurry. Hurry!"

"I can't quite reach . . . Got it!"

She pulled out a long, narrow bundle wrapped in leather and unrolled it on the ground. There it was—a blade of what appeared to be tempered glass covered with intricate designs down its length. Diello laid the hilt next to it and crouched there, lost in admiration. His fingers traced over the word *Eirian* etched in Fae script on the blade.

"It's beautiful," Cynthe said. "But who can use a glass sword?"

"Magnificent," he breathed. He'd never seen anything more beautiful. The Fae artistry was unmistakable. It made the steel swords carried by Lord Malques and his men look like crude bludgeons. "I see why Brezog wants it."

"Pity it's broken," Cynthe said.

Diello thought of the last bit of the Fae riddle. "Apart, yet together," he quoted. "Separate, yet unbroken."

"It looks broken to me," Cynthe insisted.

Diello inspected the pieces. The top of the blade narrowed to a finger-sized rod, clearly designed to be fitted into the hilt.

Make me whole, whispered a voice in his mind.

It was not a human voice. Not a Fae voice. It rushed like the wind. There was music to this voice, and cold, compelling purpose. *Make me whole*, it whispered again.

His hands reached out and took up the hilt. It seemed to weigh nothing, and although it was too large for him, his fingers wrapped around the grip perfectly. Just below the guard, he could see the rectangular hole where the blade was supposed to snap into place. Eirian was designed to be taken apart. It wasn't broken at all!

Make me whole, the voice commanded.

Diello picked up the blade, taking care not to cut himself, and began to fit the pieces together.

"Diello!" It was Vassou, jumping and nipping at his hands, pawing his leg. "Do not unite Eirian. Leave it be!"

Diello stared at the pup. "But it should be—"

"No!" Vassou said. "It has too much power! Eirian is not made for mortal hand."

"What is it?" Cynthe asked.

"Shalla, my mother, could have explained this better than I. For many generations Eirian has been closely guarded inside the first of three Silver Wheels, with all protected by the Twelve Watchers of Afon Heyrn."

"The Twelve what?" Cynthe asked.

"Legends," Diello mumbled. The pieces seemed to hum in his hands.

"The Watchers are not myth," Vassou said. "They are potent forces pulled from nature, appearing in this world as pillars of light."

"Like that face you saw," Cynthe said to Diello. "In the lightning."

"Clevn," Diello said.

Vassou whined. "You have seen the mage-chancellor? You know him?"

"Sort of," Diello said. "Is he a Watcher?"

"No," Vassou said. "He is the second-most powerful Fae

in all of Embarthi, after the queen. He controls the Watchers and much more."

Diello believed that. He'd witnessed Clevn stopping the Death Wind, after all.

"Why did you and your mother come to warn us?" Diello asked. "Aren't you afraid of Clevn smiting you dead or something?"

Vassou hesitated slightly. "Our pack was allied to Lwyneth. She and Shalla were sworn pack-sisters. Friends, you would say. Allies. When Shalla learned that Lwyneth's whereabouts had been discovered, she had to bring the warning. She did not trust messages sent by the Talking Wind. They can be listened to, and sometimes altered. I am sorry we were too late."

"But why would anyone hate Mamee so?" Cynthe asked.

"Because of Eirian," Vassou replied. "It was guarded by the Watchers, secure inside Embarthi. This made all Fae territory safe from attack. Then great evil was done. There was a traitor in the Liedhe Court. The sword was stolen and brought here."

"Not by—no, they wouldn't!" Cynthe shouted. "Pa and Mamee weren't thieves! They weren't!"

"This is not the time to discuss blame," the pup replied. "Since losing Eirian, Embarthi has fought the goblins many times. There have been many battles. No decided victories. There is danger—always danger now—for the Fae."

Diello still had so many questions, some he wasn't sure he wanted to ask. "Who is the rightful owner of Eirian?"

Vassou lowered his head. "If you hold Eirian, you are its master."

Diello stood straight, grasping a piece of the sword in each hand. "Then I have all the power, and I can—"

"Wait," Cynthe broke in. "Vassou said it isn't for mortals."

"Just because I'm not Fae doesn't mean I can't have it."

"But I'm a better fighter than you," she argued. "You aren't—"

"Wait and see," Diello snapped. "Pa was a knight, as I shall be. He had this sword, and now it's mine. It's not made of steel, so I can use it."

"There is more to hear," Vassou said before they could go on arguing. "The sword's power is not complete without its scabbard."

"Brezog has it," Diello said. "He was bragging about it."

"If he obtains the sword," Vassou said, "then he will lead all creatures. That is the power of Eirian. He will destroy all Fae and all friends of Fae."

Diello thought about what he could do with Eirian. Be the leader of all men. Even if he didn't have the scabbard, he could keep Brezog from ever getting his claws on the sword, and when he was grown he could—

"Diello," Cynthe said loudly, "drop the pieces now!"

He realized that while he was dreaming of future glory his hands were fumbling with the hilt and blade, trying to snap them together.

"Stop it!" Cynthe cried, tugging at his arm. "Didn't you hear Vassou? It's too dangerous!"

"If Brezog comes back, I'll fight him."

"He'll take the sword from you. Since he already has the scabbard, he'll be invincible. Drop them!" Cynthe yelled.

But Diello couldn't obey her. His fingers remained locked around the pieces. Something in the sword had taken possession of him and was trying to force him to assemble it.

"I can't let go! I'm trying, but my hands won't—"

Cynthe folded the leather wrapping around the sword tip and yanked the blade from his hand. The edge sliced his palm, and the sharp sting of pain cleared his mind. He forced open his fingers, and the hilt tumbled to the ground. Diello staggered back, cradling his bleeding hand. He was frightened and ashamed by how strongly the sword had taken control of him.

Cynthe rolled up both pieces in their wrappings. She looked frightened, too, as she cleaned the cut on Diello's hand, binding it with a scrap of cloth taken from her rucksack.

"Now," Vassou said, nudging Diello with his muzzle, "you know its danger."

"Yes," Diello said, subdued. "I understand."

"Eirian has torn packs apart. Divided friends. Destroyed families." Vassou's ears flicked back. "Among wolves, sometimes one goes strange. It slobbers and shivers and howls its torment. Such a one must be killed for the good of the pack. Eirian has driven many to torment, and some cannot recover."

Diello nodded slowly.

"It has made those with good hearts greedy and turned those who are already wicked into monsters. The sword withered your sire's hand when he struck down one of the Twelve Watchers and carried it from Afon Heyrn. It drove your dam from her pack and brought the full wrath of the queen upon her. For this sword, Lwyneth surrendered her magic and lived as one broken, lost from all that she loved. And now, Eirian has brought death to them both." Vassou's blue gaze held Diello's. "Fear it, Diello. Fear what it can do."

Despite everything, a part of Diello still craved the sword. *Why had Pa taken it?*

"Now," Cynthe asked, "what do we do with it?"

"Pa said it must return," Diello announced with fresh resolve. "So that's what we'll do. We'll restore Pa's honor."

"Are you daft?" Cynthe cried. "We've no business messing with something this powerful."

"You heard Vassou. It doesn't belong here. It never has. It's up to us to correct the wrong that Pa and Mamee did and take it back to Embarthi."

Cynthe nervously tucked her hair behind her ears. "I don't like it. If you could have seen the strange look in your eyes when you held it . . ."

"We'll carry the pieces separately. You take the blade. I'll carry the hilt."

"This is for grownups, not us," she said. "We can't deal with something like this. We—we shouldn't have to."

"There aren't any grownups here," Diello said. "Like it or not, we're in charge. We have to decide. We—"

A gust of wind buffeted him, nearly knocking him over, and lightning cracked from the sunny, cloudless sky. Instead of fading, the light remained, brighter than sunshine, blazing all around Diello. The air smelled stormy and hot.

Diello braced his feet against the gusting wind and squinted, shielding his eyes with his hand. At first, he couldn't see anything except glaring whiteness.

"Diello, son of Lwyneth!" boomed a voice.

He spun about. White eyes glared at him from a countenance as unyielding as marble. *Clevn.*

"What do you want?" Diello shouted.

Clevn's disembodied face increased in size until it loomed over Diello. "What have you done? Who has unlocked the *amddif* here?"

Diello held aloft the leather-wrapped pieces of the sword. "Is this what you want? Is this why you punished my mother?"

"Eirian is in danger. It must return to Embarthi."

Diello believed that, too, but the cold command sparked his defiance. "Why? So you can have it?"

"Ignorant child! You toy with things you do not understand."

"Then explain."

Lightning flashed across the blue sky. Thunder shook the ground. Diello clutched the pieces of Eirian tightly. "I don't care, Clevn!" he yelled. "Mamee called to you for forgiveness and mercy, but you refused her. You condemned her to eternal exile. Why should I do anything you say?"

The stony face vanished, and in its place Diello saw a vision of Amalina. The child was standing in a room lined with stone, bare of any furnishings. She was clad in a pretty dress of celestial blue, with a matching ribbon tying back her ringlets. Tears streaked her face, and her eyes held bewilderment. A man stood behind her, in a long dark robe, his face hidden by a cowl. The robe was made of heavy cloth, not skins, as Diello had assumed earlier. It was an understandable mistake, but Diello told himself to be less hasty the next time he interpreted Sight.

"Amalina," he whispered. He reached out, but he could not touch the vision. "Amie! Amie!"

Desperately he looked around. "Where is she, Clevn?" he shouted. "Is that what you want? A trade? I'll give you the sword for her! I'll give you anything you ask for if only she stays safe!"

"That is precisely what I expected," Clevn's voice boomed. His face did not reappear. "You are a bigger fool than Lwyneth."

The image of Amalina was fading.

"No, please!" Diello cried out. He dropped the sword pieces and lifted both hands, pleading. "Please give her back."

"Bring the sword to me," Clevn said.

"Why don't you just take it, the way you took my little sister?"

"An ignorant fool is the worst kind. Lose Eirian, and you will never see your sister again."

"I said I'll trade!" Diello shouted again. "Why don't you help me? You have all the magic. You found us. You took Amie away. Why make us—"

"Bring Eirian to *me* and me alone."

The sultry wind spun Diello around, knocking him this way and that. His bones were itching and tingling. He stumbled, trying to keep his balance, and picked up the deed seal off the ground. He'd never heard of an *amddif* before, but the spell that had been drawn away from the cistern was thrumming harder than ever through the metal. It pulsed against Diello's palm, as hot as when he'd first unlocked the spell.

"Mamee!" he cried to the heavens. "What do I *do*? How do I help her?"

The wind knocked him off his feet, tumbling him over the ground before he managed to grab the cistern's base. He had no idea what had happened to Cynthe, Vassou, or Scree. He could see almost nothing except the white light swirling around him and the arch of sky overhead. *Why the secrets and riddles?* he wondered. *Why can't Clevn just be honest with me?*

For an instant, beneath the roar of the wind, he heard the faintest of cries.

"Del!"

He scrambled up, his arms and legs throbbing from all the magic around him. "Amie!" he shouted back.

He could see the vision of his sister floating above him.

And then he was rising, as light and free as a bubble. Higher and higher he went, leaving the buffeting wind and blinding light below him. Up here, between ground and clouds, he felt suddenly safe. An invisible hand clasped his, slowing his ascent.

"Give her the key," murmured a lilting voice in his ear, a voice he thought he would never hear again.

"Mamee!" he gasped.

He did not see her. Instead, the vision of Amalina appeared right in front of him. She'd stopped crying and was gazing upward as if listening to something. The robed figure no longer stood next to her.

"Mamee?" Amalina called out. "Del?"

"The *amddif* is all that remains of me," said Mamee. "Give it to her now, as protection, until you find her."

Diello tipped his body forward. He held out the deed seal, and tossed it toward the vision of Amalina. His aim could not have been more true.

The disk spun through the air, its cord streaming out behind it, straight to Amalina. The loop of the cord fell around her tiny wrist. Her fingers closed on the metal.

"I will find you, Amie!" Diello called to her. "I promise I will find you!"

She smiled at him.

A shriek below distracted him. Diello glanced down, and the image of Amalina vanished.

"No!" he shouted, lunging through the air for her.

But she was gone.

Below him, he saw that the goblins had returned—brandishing spears and cudgels. They surrounded the cistern, where Cynthe stood, holding the pieces of Eirian.

"Cynthe!" Diello yelled.

She looked up.

Without warning, he found himself plummeting toward the ground.

There was no time to be afraid. Diello fell into the storm cloud Clevn had created. Inside the foggy mass, he was buffeted by wind with lightning sizzling around him. It was all magic, the power crisscrossing through him until his body began to vibrate. He could feel the power channeling through his bones, focusing and growing stronger. But it was too potent. Diello instinctively gathered what he could and flung the force at the goblins.

He missed them, and hit the cistern instead. The very sky and ground seemed to blast apart. There was only wind and flames and screaming.

Then he hit the ground so hard his bones rattled together. And all went dark.

chapter twenty-six

iello swam through layers of darkness and sound and found himself lying on rubble-strewn ground. Goblin bodies lay sprawled on all sides, many of them crushed by stones and other debris.

Diello struggled to sit up. The world tilted around him, and he closed his eyes, holding his head to keep it from tumbling off.

"There he is!" Cynthe yelled.

Kneeling beside him, she gripped his shoulders and rubbed his cheek with her fingers, brushing his hair back from his brow. "You're alive," she said. "Guardian be thanked, you're *alive!*"

His memory seemed to be in pieces, but as he blinked at the faces surrounding him—Cynthe's, Scree's, and Vassou's—he remembered Amalina's vision, and Mamee's help, and the goblins surrounding his twin.

He clutched Cynthe's sleeve. "Are you hurt? The sword, is it—"

"I'm fine," she said. "And the sword is here."

"But the goblins! They—"

"The ones that weren't crushed were blown away by the wind."

Diello blinked. *Did I do this, or was it Clevn?*

"What about Brezog?" he asked.

"Swept away." Cynthe blew a strand of hair from her eyes. "I should have been struck by lightning, since I was the closest to the cistern when it hit, but nothing touched me. And the wind left me behind. So where were you? One moment you were arguing about Eirian and the next you were gone. You just vanished. What happened?"

A slow smile spread across Diello's face. "I can fly, too," he whispered. "I went up into the sky. It's like you said, free and wonderful."

Cynthe hugged him. "I'm so glad. I didn't want to be the only one. When you have visions and see things I can't, I hate it. I didn't want to fly and leave you behind."

Diello nodded. "And, Cynthe, I saw Amalina."

"You did? Where is she? Is she all right? What is—"

"*Listen!* Mamee helped me. She's not lost, like we thought. Not entirely."

Cynthe's eyes grew huge. "You saw her?"

"No, but I heard her voice. Just for a few moments."

"So some part of her transformed before her Death Wind stopped?"

"More like a piece of her lingered in the *amddif*." Diello thought of the mage-chancellor who was his mother's enemy, and now his. "Clevn's got Amalina and he wants the sword in exchange. At least I think so. He kept jeering at me when I tried to offer it to him as if he couldn't take it on his own."

Cynthe pulled Diello to his feet and supported him with

her shoulder. "We'll sort it out later. Come. Vassou says we shouldn't stay here."

The little band made its way through the woods, with Diello and Cynthe each carrying a piece of the sword. Scree hobbled along painfully with the rucksack of food slung over his shoulder, and Vassou sniffed busily as he shepherded them along.

Twilight was falling by the time they climbed to the top of Egil's Point. The air smelled fresh and clean, scented by the pines. There was a stream trickling nearby. A rocky ledge jutting over a precipitous drop gave them a wide view of the shire below.

Diello sat down to rest, still not entirely sure why he hadn't broken every bone in his body. Cynthe took charge, bustling about and giving orders. While she used a stick to rake fallen pine needles into bedding, she sent Scree to wash in the stream; although he'd cleaned the crocks for Diello, he'd managed to avoid getting wet and was as smelly as ever.

Diello stared out over the open fields to the east beyond Wodesley. He saw the castle with Lord Malques's banner flying from its watchtower, King's Road winding toward neighboring hills, and a finger of smoke rising from the site of their farmstead.

First goblin fire, then Fae fire. Would he ever see their home again? Diello would never forgive the baron for stealing the land, but everything that mattered there was already gone. *Someday I'll get it back*, he vowed.

Scree, having washed up with mixed results, ventured near the cliff edge only to retreat. "Is this a ravine?" he asked. "It looks very deep. I would smash my skull if I fell into it.

May I go and look for grubs to eat? I am hungry, and I do not like marrows."

Diello gestured at the woods. "All the grubs are yours for the taking."

Ducking his head with a shy smile, Scree went off scavenging, talking to himself as he went. Cynthe settled herself beside Diello. Vassou sat between them, calmly gazing out over the vista. His dark nose twitched now and then, catching some scent they could not.

"So are we going to Embarthi?" Cynthe asked. "Are you really sure Amalina's been taken there? You thought Brezog stole her the last time."

Diello frowned but realized that his twin was just trying to understand. "No, I'm not sure," he admitted. "I'm only telling you what I saw and heard. Returning the sword is our best hope of getting Amie back."

"I don't care what anyone says. Mamee wasn't a thief. She and Pa would *never* steal!"

Vassou lay down and rested his muzzle on his paws.

"I know they wouldn't," Diello said. "But how else did they get possession of Eirian?"

Cynthe's eyes were filling with tears. "Maybe Mamee found it. Maybe she and Pa rescued it from the real thief and tried to hide it for safekeeping. I don't know!"

"But Vassou told us—"

"So?" she cried. "We're talking about our parents, Diello! I'm sorry, Vassou. I don't mean to call you a liar, but something's missing from your story. Pa and Mamee just wouldn't—"

"But they did," Vassou said, sitting up again. "Even if this grieves you, you must learn to accept it."

"We don't know anything for certain," Diello said, "except that our parents had secrets, secrets we don't understand yet." He rubbed his knee with his palm. "I hate Clevn and what he's done, but Pa always said two wrongs don't make a right. If Eirian belongs in Embarthi, then it does."

"Once we have Amalina safe, we're going to live with Uncle Owain and be happy again," Cynthe added. "We'll learn how to fly properly. We'll have a home among the Fae. We'll regain the farm somehow, and no one will ever take advantage of us again."

Diello turned his head to follow an eagle spiraling on a wind current. There were several more eagles of different sizes. He realized the fledglings had left the nest and were spreading their wings.

At his back, the sun was sinking on the horizon in a blazing ball of orange splendor. He hoped that Cynthe's optimism would be justified, but he was no longer willing to put all his trust in big dreams.

"We must make a pact, all of us," Diello said.

Scree—munching on something white and crawly he'd found—had returned to the camp. The four of them gathered in a circle. Diello looked earnestly at each of their faces. They could hardly be called friends, and yet fate had brought them together.

"Cynthe and I are going to Embarthi," he said. "We ask you, Vassou, to be our guide."

"I am honored," Vassou replied solemnly.

Diello turned to Scree. "We also hope that you will come with us."

Scree's swollen eyes blinked rapidly. "You ask me? You think I can be useful?"

"We do," Cynthe said while the goblin-boy grinned. "The more of us, the safer we are. We'll all need to work together and help each other survive."

"Are we agreed?" Diello said. "For Embarthi?"

"Embarthi!" they echoed.

Cynthe opened the rucksack and pulled out the battered wheel of cheese to share. "Do we dare make a fire for the night?"

With the sun going down, the mountain air was already cool. Licking his finger, Diello tested the breeze. It was very light, coming from the east. He didn't think the goblins were still pursuing them, not after Clevn's attack, but he wasn't taking any chances.

"If we build a small fire under the outcropping over there," he said, "it should be hidden. It's dark enough now to conceal our smoke."

Cynthe knelt and made a ring of stones on a patch of bare rock. Scree, happy to be useful, brought her sticks and bark strips for kindling.

But when she started to snap her fingers to make the fire, Diello nudged her aside and pulled out his tinderbox. The tinderbox he hadn't wanted for his birthday because Pa valued hard work over magic.

Diello had used more magic in the past few days than he'd ever dreamed possible, but he knew he would never again ignore what his father had tried to teach him. No one ignored a Carnethie Knight. And he understood now why his parents had always been so cautious, why Mamee had parceled out her magic in bits under the shield of a *cloigwylie*. Clevn, Brezog—and maybe others—all wanted the power of Eirian.

From now on, smart and careful—that's what we have to be, Diello thought.

His eyes met Cynthe's.

"A tinderbox is sure," Diello quoted their father and struck a spark.

Coming in Spring 2012

the faelin chronicles

Book Two